'Allow me!' Owain said quietly.

'Sir, I can manage.' There was a tremor in her voice.

'It's no trouble.' He brought her against him and, taking a handful of her hair, began to drag the comb through her curls.

He was much too close for Kate's peace of mind, and she shivered as his fingers brushed her neck, sending pleasing ripples through her.

'Please, don't do that!'

'Don't do what, my lady? Some of your curls are in such a tangle they need teasing out.'

His fingers brushed her ear and the nape of her neck. She could bear it no longer and forced herself to step away from him. The skirts fluttered about her bare ankles in a manner that felt very sensuous.

'Sir, this has gone far enough. I cannot permit such intimacies,' she said, trying to sound firm.

D0348080

June Francis's interest in old wives' tales and folk customs led her into a writing career. History has always fascinated her, and her first five novels were set in Medieval times. She has also written fourteen sagas based in Liverpool and Chester. Married with three grown-up sons, she lives on Merseyside. On a clear day she can see the sea and the distant Welsh hills from her house. She enjoys swimming, fell walking, music, lunching with friends and smoochie dancing with her husband. More information about June can be found at her website: www.junefrancis.co.uk

ROWAN'S REVENGE

Chapter One

Thunder clapped over the straw roof of the *palloza* at El Cebrero, making Kate Fletcher flinch and draw further into the folds of her tunic. Dirty and exhausted, she was partaking of the meagre rations served to the pilgrims, but the soup and bread was doing little to comfort her. For weeks she had been living in this youth's disguise, determined to carry out her duty to her Lady, but terrified that her true identity would be revealed. Each new face posed a potential threat, and the man who had arrived shortly after her that evening was no different. Now sitting just a few feet away, she had been aware of the stranger's gaze upon her ever since he'd entered the *palloza*. At first she had taken him for a Spaniard, with his olive skin and curling jet-black hair, but then their eyes had met and she experienced a vague sense of recognition. Those orbs were the deep dark blue of the Irish Sea on a sunny day and, when he stood to speak to a monk, she realised he was head and shoulders above many of the local men, giving her cause to revise her opinion.

For a moment, she watched the two men conversing

in Spanish and then dragged her gaze away, unwilling to draw more attention to herself than was necessary. Lowering her eyes to her bowl, she focused on her soup, trying to draw nourishment from the watery fluid, willing herself to be invisible.

Suddenly she was aware of a figure at her shoulder. She glanced round, her heart missing a beat as she saw the stranger beside her. He spoke to her in Spanish, but she remained silent. He tried questioning her in French, his tone urgent, his eyes searching her face intently, but still she gave no reply. He repeated his question, this time in English, and her blood ran cold.

With no immediate means of escape, Kate raised a finger and pointed to her open mouth. He stared at her, frowning for a moment, before understanding that she was mute. With a defeated air he passed on to interrogate other pilgrims, but his gaze returned to her every so often, curiosity burning in his eyes.

Who was he? He had the appearance of a pilgrim, wearing the familiar homespun brown tunic and displaying the scallop badge of one having accomplished the journey to St James's shrine at Compostela in the north-west of Spain. Yet there was nothing humble about him. Pride was written in the manner in which he had walked into the hostel. His tread had been firm, his head held high and over one broad shoulder he had carried a pair of saddlebags.

Instantly she had found it difficult to believe his aim was to gain indulgences. The saddlebags declared that he had made the journey on horseback. As a true pilgrim, he would have hobbled through the doorway, his feet blistered and bleeding, his face scorched by the

Castilian sun. As soon as he'd eaten his frugal meal, he would have sought his pallet and fallen asleep from exhaustion. Instead, he continued to navigate the room, addressing others with the same urgency he had questioned Kate. She knew she needed to make her escape, but, lacking the energy to do so, she sought her pallet and, curling into a ball, sleep claimed her. Her final prayer was that she might remain undetected through this long night.

But her prayers were not to be answered, the nightmare returned to haunt her, and she clawed her way out of the terrifying darkness to lie panting and rubbing at the scars on her wrists, trying to calm herself, hoping that she had uttered no sound. As her breathing steadied she took in her surroundings. The grey light indicated dawn was not far off, the snores and grunts of her fellow travellers calmed her, and she turned over in an attempt to get more comfortable. It was then she realised that she was being watched.

Despite not being able to see his profile clearly, its strength was already engraved on her memory. He was the pursuer whom she had feared would hound her and her mistress to their deaths. She had lived in trepidation of such a thing happening ever since she and Lady Catherine had left the manor in Lancashire towards the end of July 1453, almost a year ago. Was he Stanley's man? It could explain why he appeared familiar…and yet she was convinced he had not recognised her.

Perhaps that was not so strange. She would have been surprised if her mother, Beth Fletcher, and brother, Diccon, would have recognised her now. Kate had al-

most lost count of the months since she and the Lady
Catherine had left England. During that time, her soft
pale skin had been weathered by the sun and the wind
and her flaxen hair had been shorn. Whilst crossing the
Aubrac Mountains in the south-east of France, they
had been attacked by brigands. A great number of their
group had been killed and her Lady had been raped.
Kate had only escaped such a fate by the timely arrival
of an armed group of pilgrim knights. Her Lady's pack-
horse had been stolen, leaving them with only the
clothes they stood up in and what they had in their
scrip.

Afterwards Kate's poor Lady, still suffering from
the effects of being ravished, had taken a knife from the
next hostel on the pilgrims' way and insisted on hack-
ing off Kate's waist-length flaxen hair—inherited, so
her mother had told her, from a Saxon princess. The
Lady Catherine was convinced that by cutting Kate's
hair to just below her ears, her virtue could be saved—
but a week later worse was to come.

Suddenly Kate heard movement. *He was coming
over! Had she cried out during her nightmare and betrayed herself?* She could make out the man's tall figure as he approached, stepping carefully between the
slumbering bodies on their pallets. Her heart thudded
in her breast and her hand reached out and gripped her
pilgrim's staff. He knelt down beside her and she forced
herself not to shrink from him, extremely conscious of
his strength and musky male scent.

He spoke softly; it was as she had feared, she had cried
out in her sleep. Fortunately he had been unable to make
out her words, but his suspicions were obviously aroused.

She decided to pretend to be French, Lady Catherine had long prepared her to accompany her on a pilgrimage to St James's shrine if the opportunity should arise, and the journey through that war-torn country had increased Kate's grasp of the language, although, she was far from word perfect. *'Je ne comprends pas!'* she said in a shaky whisper. *'Allez-vous, s'il vous plâit!'* She made a shooing motion with her staff.

He frowned. *'Non, s'il vous plâit! Vous avez parlé?'*

'Une miracle!' she exclaimed in a joy-filled voice.

He muttered something under his breath, that she did not catch, before raising his voice and saying, *'Entendez-moi! Je cherche trois femmes et un garçon. Anglais! Une vieille femme et deux jeunes femmes!'*

Her heart leapt into her throat. She had not been mistaken earlier. He was searching for three English women, one old, two young, as well as a boy. Obviously he had no idea that she and Lady Catherine had parted from Kate's mother and brother in England and that was to the good. It meant that they must still be safe.

'Pardon, m'sieur? J'ai vu beaucoup de femmes anglaises, mais pas garçons,' said Kate with an expressive shrug.

He responded in urgent tones, *'Le cheval de la dame est noir et blanc.'*

Kate stiffened. The lady had a black and white horse? How could he know such a thing unless he had visited her Lady's manor and had watched her out riding? She must act stupidly, pretend to believe he had muddled up the French words for horse and hair as she had done when learning the language. *'Pardon? La dame a les cheveux noirs et blancs?'*

'Non! Le cheval!' He reached out and grasped her arm. *'Noir et blanc…une pie.'*

A horse that was black and white like a magpie. His mention of the bird caused Kate's mouth to go dry as she remembered a number of the birds clacking in the grave-yard outside Walton-on-the-Hill church. There the four of them had received a blessing for their pilgrimage, but all the time Kate had been thinking that magpies were an ill omen—*seven for a secret never to be told*. Lady Catherine had no such qualms and made no secret of her plan to visit the shrine of St James to the rector. He in turn showed no surprise at the recently widowed Lady Catherine's desire to undertake such a dangerous jour-ney. Kate gave silent thanks to the Holy Trinity that her Lady had made no mention of their intention to part from Kate's mother and brother at Chester.

Nervously, Kate's tongue darted out and moistened her lips. She needed information from him and for that she was going to chance speaking in English because her grasp of French was not sufficient for what she needed to ask. 'You are not French, I see,' she said in gruff and heavily accented English.

She heard the hiss of his indrawn breath. 'I thought you did not speak English, lad. You would make a fool of me?' His suspicion was there in his whispering tone and he grabbed her by the shoulder.

'Non, m'sieur! But these women and the boy…they were afeared. I would not betray them if you are an en-emy,' she babbled.

'You have seen them?' His grip tightened.

She winced. 'I travelled from Le Puy in their com-pany,' she said sullenly, not forgetting to speak with a thick accent. 'They had been on the road many months, visiting Canterbury before making the crossing to Calais. They encountered many dangers as they journeyed through France. I suspect, *m'sieur*, that your own journey has not been so…' she hesitated as if searching for a word '…arduous?'

'I took a pilgrim ship from England to La Coruña and from there I rode to Santiago de Compostela. I am no true pilgrim such as yourself. I had need of haste and I deem you would have done better travelling on horseback, lad.' He reached out and, to her amazement and sweet torture, grasped her bare foot. The skin on the sole and heel had blistered and bled, but then hardened. Even so, his touch sent sensations along her nerve ends and she rattled off a rebuke in French.

He dropped her foot and said emphatically, 'I must find these women and the lad. You will tell me whence and where did you last see them.'

Kate considered telling him that they had been killed in the ambush crossing the mountains, but that might not necessarily get rid of him so she decided on a distortion of the truth. 'I left them at a Cluniac hospice. The old woman was sick unto death, and her companions would not leave her.'

'Do you remember the name of the place?' he rasped, leaning closer to her so that their faces almost touched.

She shrugged expressively. 'So many holy places along the way where we had our pilgrim passports signed. I cannot remember all of them.'

'Think!'

Kate decided she must send him on a wild goose chase. Clearing her throat, she said, 'Perhaps it was at

Conques, on the high hills where we saw the relics of St Foy!' Her lips formed a moue. 'A Romanesque church and so cool inside out of the baking sun. The saint was said to care for prisoners taken in the Spanish Wars and held captive by the Moors. When they were released, they made an altar chain of their fetters in the saint's honour.' There was a tremor in her voice, remembering a time when she herself had been captive and the terrible fate planned for her. 'Is that not *merveilleux, m'sieur*?'

'Conques is in the domain of your king,' he retorted in a grim voice. 'You are certain it was there you left them?'

'*Oui!*'

He was silent for what seemed such a long time that she felt the need to add hastily, 'But perhaps the old woman recovered and you will not need to go all the way to Conques. They could be just a day behind me. Their aim will be the same as mine: to reach Santiago de Compostela in time for the saint's feast day on the twenty-fifth of July.'

She was relieved when he thanked her and wished her Godspeed. She watched him go, wishing him far away. He had roused memories that she wanted to forget. She lay down and closed her eyes, wondering what the day ahead would bring. She did not rest long. Within a short time, the other pilgrims began to stir and she sat up and slipped on her sandals and went outside.

During the night, the storm had blown itself out and Kate feasted her eyes on a glorious dawn, watching the sun striking great banks of snowy white clouds that filled the valley below. The air was chill and she hugged herself. Then she caught sight of the man who had questioned her and a nervous excitement snaked down her spine. He was already astride a great chestnut stallion. The beast reminded her of those she had seen being led down the gangplanks of ships on to the quayside at Liverpool.

As if sensing her eyes on him, he turned his head. For a moment his blue gaze seemed to bore into hers and then he raised a hand in farewell. She raised her own and, with a fast beating heart, watched him set out on the road that would lead him eventually to Burgos to the east. She prayed that she would reach Santiago de Compostela before he realised she had tricked him. With so many pilgrims crowding the city, surely he would not be able to find her there if he were to attempt to hunt her down.

Master Owain ap Rowan passed beneath the gateway of Burgos. He had been all day in the saddle and was angry. The scar of the wound in his thigh throbbed, despite it being four years since the Battle of Formigny, which had resulted in England's loss of Normandy. He was also hot in the linen shirt, padded leather japon and linen breeches beneath the homespun tunic. Until yesterday there had still been pilgrims on the road, and he had asked after the three women and boy, but had met with no luck. Today he had not seen a single pilgrim, so had enquired of the monks at Santo Domingo of the Lady Catherine Miles and the Fletchers, only to be informed that they had seen no one of their description. It had been suggested that they had either been killed by brigands crossing the mountains into Spain or had taken another route.

Owain had no choice but to accept what the monks had said. Besides, the conviction that he had been duped had been growing on him for some time. Since he had left the *palloza* at El Cebrero there had come into his mind every now and again a sunburnt, delicately shaped face with blue-green eyes, framed by curling wisps of flaxen hair. It had appeared almost like a ghostly vision, and a question had framed itself in his thoughts concerning the identity of its owner. He knew he had to find the lad again, but not today. He swayed wearily in the saddle, desperate to be rid of his garments, to bathe, eat, drink and find a woman to soothe away his aches and frustrations.

Then, amazingly, a voice called his name. 'Owain! By all that's holy, what are you doing here…and in that garb? Since when have you given up horse-dealing to turn pilgrim?'

Owain could scarcely believe his ears and looked about him for the owner of the voice. Then he caught sight of a tawny-haired giant of a man, dressed as fine as a jay in a deep blue doublet and russet hose. The curve of Owain's mouth widened into a smile. Last time he and widower Nat Milburn had met had been in Calais, which Owain had managed to reach in a mad, pain-filled ride after the defeat at Formigny. Nat had provided him with a roof over his head and paid for a physician to tend his wounds. They had first become acquainted in Liverpool where Nat had kin. Owain had been with his elder brother, Martin, delivering horses to the stables of the Stanleys.

'What are you doing here, Nat? I thought you'd be visiting the fairs at Bruges and Venice. I never knew your business had spread to Castile.'

'I have been to those fair cities and even had several gowns made for my sister in the latest fashion…a reward for her taking care of my offspring. There I renewed another old acquaintance who dwells here in Burgos. But you have not answered my question. What are you doing here?' The older man's grey eyes were deeply curious.

Owain barely hesitated before saying, 'I am here on Sir Thomas Stanley's business. I seek the Lady Catherine Miles and a family called Fletcher.'

Nat's expression altered. 'I pity that lady being married to Sir Roger Miles. My aunt in Liverpool whispered rumours about his dark dealings in my ear eighteen months ago when I visited the port. But why do you seek the Lady here?'

'Sir Roger is dead.'

Nat sucked in his cheeks and then exhaled. 'By the Holy Trinity, that's the best news I've heard for some time. Could not bear to be in the man's company, but heard he managed to worm his way into the King's good graces.'

'Don't I know it,' said Owain with a grim smile. 'I'll tell you all once you've led me to a decent tavern.'

Nat grinned. 'I can do better than a tavern, friend. That acquaintance I mentioned invited me to stay in his most splendid house, so cool and spacious...built in the Moorish design, I may add.' He patted the stallion's neck, glancing up at Owain. 'I see you still have Merlin. You might be able to do some horse-dealing with them. They have a stable of fine Castilian and Andalusian horses at their estate in the country. Although, you'd have to stay a while if you wish to meet them. A kinsman of theirs has died in Salamanca, so they have gone to give comfort and support to his wife and children. I'm certain the fact that your great-grandmother was Castilian will not go amiss in your dealings with them.'

Owain's expression was regretful. 'Alas! I can stay only the one night.'

Nat's ruddy face showed disappointment. 'Another time perhaps. This way.' He led Owain through the bustling streets, regaling him with the legends of Burgos, the city of El Cid, whose favourite warhorse had borne the hero's dead body, strapped in the saddle, on one last charge against the Moors.

'I've heard the tales,' murmured Owain. 'I especially like the one of how he fell in love with the beautiful Ximena and made her his wife.'

Nat sighed expressively. 'What wouldn't we both give for wives with money, beauty and love for only us, eh? Alas, I always knew my wife was happiest when I was away on my travels.' He came to a halt in front of a door in a whitewashed wall, turned the handle and led the horse into a courtyard. He cocked a quizzical eye up at his young friend. 'When are you going to settle down, Owain? Now my kinswoman, Marguerite, is widowed—have you any plans to visit her in Caen? God willing, I will be at her house, myself, in a couple of weeks or so.'

'Such a visit has no part in my plans,' said Owain in clipped tones.

'Lady Catherine then?' persisted Nat. 'Any chance of a marriage there?'

'Patience, friend,' drawled Owain, glancing about him as he dismounted.

Water tinkled from a fountain and the sweet smell of

roses and gillyflowers scented the air. Colonnaded terraces occupied two sides of the courtyard and, on the third, was stabling. 'You do fall on your feet, Nat. What are your dealings with this business acquaintance?'

'What do you think? The finest woollen cloth on my side, and wine and almonds and the occasional horse for my father to improve his stud on theirs.' Nat winked. 'See to Merlin while I have a tub prepared for you and afterwards you can taste the wine.'

Two hours later, the two men were seated on a marble bench on one of the terraces, drinking a Rioja wine and sharing a dish of salted almonds while the servants prepared their evening meal.

'A fine wine, is it not?' said Nat, holding the goblet aloft and peering into its glowing ruby depths.

Owain agreed that it was indeed extremely palatable. 'I'll put in an order once I'm settled in Lancashire.' His tone was light.

Nat started and wine spilt like drops of blood onto the marble bench. 'You jest!'

'I'm not wanted at home, so I have to make my own way,' rasped Owain. Nat opened his mouth to protest, but Owain added swiftly, 'Forget my family. How long since you were last in England?'

Nat hesitated and then his ruddy face screwed up in thought. 'Eight or nine months. I visited my father's manor in Yorkshire. We discussed the flocks and cloth and the unrest in the north.'

There was a brooding expression on Owain's face. 'Have you heard that the King has lost his wits?'

Nat frowned. 'I hoped it was but a rumour.'

'Nay! It is true. If he had been a stronger king, then the disasters in France would not have happened. His father would never have allowed Dunois, Bastard of Orleans, to take Bordeaux in '51, and the King knew that. Hence his determination to try to retake territory that had been part of the kingdom of England these last three hundred years.'

'I heard the French were not too considerate of the local sensibilities when they took Bordeaux.'

Owain smiled grimly. 'Reason enough why the gates were opened to our army under the command of Sir John Talbot in the autumn of '52. I organised the supply of horses so I saw it happen. Naturally Charles of France was not going to allow things to rest there and spent the following months raising an army with a plentiful supply of field guns and men with the military knowledge to use them. Fortunately I had returned to England before battle commenced.'

Nat shuddered.

'In July 1453,' murmured Owain, his eyes bright with unshed tears, 'a force of eight thousand men under the command of Talbot and his son, Lord of Lisle, marched out to meet Charles VII's army, still expecting their English archers to gain them victory…but the French had learnt much about warfare since Agincourt. Their guns decimated the front lines of our army and more were killed in cavalry charges. The remnants were driven back and either surrounded or drowned in the river. Talbot and his son were killed and the French entered Bordeaux in October. Of all the wide Plantagenet lands only Calais remains.' He sighed heavily. 'I had many comrades in arms who met their deaths…and no wonder Henry has gone a little mad. The Duke of York is Protectorate of England now.'

Nat sighed. 'Terrible. What else do you know? If you are in Sir Thomas Stanley's employ, then you must know more, since he's in control of the King's troops in Lancashire.'

Owain nodded his dark head. 'The King is living quietly at Windsor, taking no interest in matters of state and showing no feelings towards his heir, *this son* for which the country waited seven years!' He clenched his fist. 'Sir Thomas says King Henry is incapable of making a decision about anything these days…which is not good news for me.'

Nat swore, reached for an almond and popped it into his mouth. 'It's terrible news, but why is it particularly bad for you?'

Owain tossed off the rest of his wine and reached for the pewter jug and refilled his goblet. 'Some of this you might know, but let me tell it in my own way. It is rather complicated, so you'll have to listen carefully.' He took a gulp of the wine and swallowed. 'Five years ago in '49, the Lady Catherine's father died and she inherited the manor of Merebury, which is near the Stanleys' manor in Lathom. She was only fourteen, so immediately became a ward of the King. It was in his power to give the Lady and her land to a man of his choosing.'

'Hoping to get something else in return from the man, I presume?'

Owain nodded. 'He had heard that Sir Roger dabbled in alchemy and that he was close to finding the means to turn base metal into gold.' Nat snorted and Owain smiled grimly. 'The King is a man of faith and not always wise in distributing his favours. Sir Roger assured him that with a little investment, he would never be short of money again…but that he needed a quiet place to carry out his experiments.'

Nat groaned and shook his head as if in disbelief. 'The poor lass. Hadn't the king heard that Sir Roger was involved in the black arts?'

'He must have heard rumours. As a youth Sir Roger accompanied his father to France and fought under the banner of the King's uncle, Duke of Bedford and Regent of France. He was present at the burning of the Maid of Orleans, whom they swore was a witch. Perhaps that was when his interest in witchcraft and the devil began.'

'Sounds feasible to me.'

'Sir Roger was also a murderer and that's what I was trying to prove when he died unexpectedly,' said Owain, his blue eyes glinting with cold fire. 'Died, I might add, in suspicious circumstances.'

'A dagger in the back one dark night, was it?'

Owain shook his head. 'The day after his death, Lady Catherine disappeared from her manor, along with the Fletcher family.'

'So the poor lass is suspected of his murder?'

'Some definitely consider her leaving so soon as an admission of guilt.'

Nat frowned again. 'The Fletcher family? What have they to do with it?'

Owain drank some more wine. 'The mother was Lady Catherine's wet nurse. She had a daughter of her own that she was also giving suck to at the time, so she and Lady Catherine are of an age. Mother and daughter are naturally close to the Lady and were of great support to her during her marriage, despite all that Sir Roger tried to do to break the bond.'

'What about the Fletcher father?'

'Richard Fletcher was an archer and fought at Agincourt, as did his Lord, Lady Catherine's father. As a reward for his services, he was given a field to farm at an extremely low rent.'

'Sir Roger did not care for that?'

Owain shrugged expressively. 'There was naught he could do. It was perfectly legal. Then Master Fletcher died in a fall a year ago. Sir Roger immediately demanded the heriot due to him as lord of the manor from the family, thinking to get rid of them.'

'And did he?'

Owain shook his head. 'He died that day.'

'What happened next?'

Owain smiled sombrely. 'I am still searching for answers. The Lady and the Fletchers seemingly disappeared. The King appointed Sir Thomas Stanley to oversee the running of the manor in the Lady's absence. He also promised the Lady's manor to the man who could find his missing money and solve the mystery of Sir Roger's death.'

'God's blood! You, I presume, consider it a prize worth risking your life for? You consider the Lady and the Fletcher family responsible for his murder?'

Owain twisted the goblet between his long, strong fingers. 'I believe they can help me in my search for the truth and for that reason I need to find them. I have plans to breed horses in Lancashire and, if the Lady is innocent, I am prepared to wed her.'

Nat stared at him, agog. 'So what is this mystery surrounding Sir Roger's death?'

Owain leaned forward. 'He was found in a room locked from the inside with not a mark on him to show how he died. According to the steward there was such a look of terror in his eyes, it was "*as if he had seen Old Nick himself*"!' he quoted softly.

Nat grunted. 'I don't like this talk of the devil. Superstitious lot in that part of the world. Besides, if the King's run mad, who is to say you'll get your reward?'

Owain's blue eyes clouded. 'It is a gamble I have to take. He could recover. Besides, Sir Thomas is in charge of all and I have his support. When I find the Lady…if she is innocent, then I will woo her and ask for her hand. Hopefully she will look with favour on my suit.'

'So why do you think the Lady is in Spain?'

'I discovered that she took herself off on pilgrimage with the Fletchers to the shrine of St James. I'm presuming her plan was to take her time calling at different religious houses and shrines on the way so as to reach the city for the celebrations of the saint's day this month. No doubt they also had to take into consideration the weather and the fighting in France.

Nat grimaced. 'I don't like the sound of any of this. I'd return to Cheshire if I was you and forget her. You're your father's heir. He'll be glad to have you home.'

Owain's face darkened. 'I'll be damned if I'll cut and run. You're the eldest in your family, Nat. You will never understand what it was like being a second son. I loved Martin, but when he was killed in France in '48, Father held me responsible. Me! He said I wanted him dead, that I was jealous of him.' Owain's voice cracked. 'I would have given my life for my brother.'

'I didn't know,' said Nat, looking concerned.

'It was not something I shouted abroad. I blame my stepmother. She seduced Father and now he believes everything she says against me.' Owain made no mention of finding his father's naked wife in his bed last time he was home, and how he'd barely escaped with his life.

Nat said gloomily, 'I never met her. It seems a great pity to me. Still, you know more than I do so I will not persist. Only be careful what you are about. Sir Thomas is a true Stanley and I doubt not that he would like more power and more land to add to that which the family already owns. You could solve this mystery and still end up dead.'

Owain smiled faintly. 'That's a chance I'll have to take. Besides, my life will be at no more risk than it has been these last few years. Thanks to my grandmother I have some money put aside and Sir Thomas is paying my expenses.'

Nat stared at him and said slowly, 'What if you find the Lady and discover she is guilty of her husband's death? What then?'

Owain sighed. 'It's an interesting question. Her reeve and tenants say she is very religious and good— a saint for putting up with Sir Roger's behaviour.'

Nat looked uneasy. 'I like the sound of this less and less. When folk start talking about saintly women and Old Nick himself being involved in a death, it stinks. If she's so religious, the Lady could betray you. Don't let that chivalrous streak of yours get you into deep water.'

Owain's mouth set stubbornly and he slammed the pitcher down on the bench. 'Sir Thomas is behind me in this. He is connected to many of the landed gentry, so that I could outdo my father in supplying all the great families of England with the finest breeding horses in Europe.' His blue eyes sparkled. 'Life is for living, Nat, not cowering in corners for fear of death.'

Nat did not speak for several minutes; then, when he did, it was to demand what luck Owain had had in his search for the Lady so far.

Owain stretched out his long muscular legs, and his face was empty of all expression. 'I believe I might have met the Fletcher lad and so I will return to Santiago de Compostela. He tricked me, but I will find him again and he will lead me to the Lady. Why they have separated I do not know. I did hear that a number of pilgrims were killed and some robbed of all they had when crossing the mountains into Spain. Even so, he will have some information. Might I ask of you a favour?'

'Certainly,' said Nat, as a serving wench appeared to tell them their supper was ready. 'Name it.'

Owain smiled. 'If the Lady looks anything like Master Fletcher, then she will appreciate a change of raiment. A new gown in the latest fashion! What say you, Nat, to parting with one of those you purchased for your sister? I will pay you well for it.'

Nat groaned, but Owain knew that he would not refuse him this boon, and surely it would work in his favour if he was able to present the Lady with such a gift. For what woman could not resist a new gown?

Chapter Two

Kate stood ankle deep in the stream and laved her face and hands in the cool, sparkling water of the spring at Lavacolla. She would have enjoyed stripping off the hated homespun tunic and linen shift and bathing naked in the stream, but not only modesty forbade such an act. She had to keep reminding herself that she was supposed to be a youth. Instead, she washed as much of her body as she could reach beneath her shift with a scrap of linen taken from her scrip. After stepping out of the stream, she wiped her feet on the grass, before fastening on her sandals and hurrying after the other pilgrims up Monte del Gozo in the region of Galicia.

From its summit, she gazed down at the spires of the Cathedral of Santiago de Compostela gleaming in the sun. Suddenly, her eyes filled with tears and she grieved for her Lady who, exhausted and emaciated with fasting, had eventually succumbed to a fever. There had been few moments of lucidity during her last days but, in one of them, she had begged Kate to complete the pilgrimage and pray for her soul at the shrine of Saint

James. Kate had vowed that she would do so. Her Lady had, also, touched on other matters, but Kate knew she must not put too much reliance on what the dying woman had told her whilst her mind was in confusion.

Since her Lady's death, Kate's concern as to how she would get back to England had increased tenfold. With no money in her scrip, it seemed impossible that she would ever be reunited with her mother and Diccon. Yet she must not give up hope. She thought of the man who had questioned her and, for a moment, misgivings seized her. What if she had been mistaken and he could have been a friend? Was she a fool to see enemies at every turn? Yet she was reluctant to trust anyone when her life was not the only one at stake.

A tug on her sleeve and the voices of other pilgrims singing a psalm reminded her that she had yet to fulfil the vow she had made to her Lady, and the next moment she plunged down the hill towards the city.

Once there the first task Kate performed was to go to the cathedral and touch the Pilgrim Pillar, made smooth with the hands of thousands of other travellers of the Way of St James. Then she paid her respects at the saint's shrine and prayed for her Lady's soul. She realised that to have her pilgrim passport inspected and stamped to obtain her *compostelle* she would have to visit the Cathedral secretariat as herself. If only she had thought of bringing Diccon's passport with her. But the tunics worn by both male and female pilgrims were almost identical—it was her shorn hair that was the problem. If she concealed every curl beneath her hat, then perhaps she would pass muster. She had to have the *compostelle* because it entitled her to three nights' board at the pilgrims' hostel in the city and free bed and food at hostels on the return journey. Her heart plummeted at the thought of traversing that difficult road again— but at least she would not starve and would have a roof over her head once she had the *compostelle* in her possession.

Fortunately, due to the press of pilgrims waiting to have their passports inspected and stamped, the secretariat scarcely looked at her as he did all that was necessary and provided her with a *compostelle* with no questions asked. Relieved, Kate went in search of a bed for the next three nights.

Built by the Knights of Santiago, Kate found the hostel a depressing-looking building and in need of renovation. Yet it was conveniently situated, overlooking the vast expanse of the Plaza de Obradoiro where the festivities would take place on the morrow. That night she slept fitfully on her pallet, plagued by fleas and dreams that caused her to drag herself awake and to sit, hugging her knees, as she tried to drive the dark memories away.

She was glad when morning came and she heard the sound of bagpipes and drums. Other pilgrims were stirring, so she rose and padded over to the window to gaze with pleasure at the people of Galicia, dancing down the Rua del Villar in the sunshine. She was surprised to see how fair skinned so many of them were. The men wore doublets of black and brilliant red sashes and the women were clad in the same colours; both displayed the white scallop of Saint James on their shoulder. Soon they would be joined by the dignitaries of the city and the hundreds of pilgrims who had come to celebrate this

day. She would have to stir herself if she was to get a
decent view of the festivities.

She was just about to turn from the window when a
rider on a chestnut horse came cantering into the square
from the direction of the Monte del Gozo. For a moment she was reminded of the story of St James and
how he had miraculously appeared on a great charger
at the battle of Clavijo, carrying a red cross and intent
on slaying the Moorish enemy. Then the rider lifted his
face to the sun and her heart seemed to somersault inside her chest and hot blood stained her cheeks.

She drew back into the shadows and remained there
for several minutes, remembering how the man had
questioned her and the fool's errand she had sent him
on. After a few minutes, she could bear the suspense no
longer and, peeping out of the window, was relieved to
see no sign of him. Perhaps in her weary and heightened
state of excitement, she had truly imagined a vision of
the saint. She shook herself and, without more ado, left
the sleeping quarters.

Kate joined those crowding into the cathedral for the
service and then afterwards became part of the massed
throng singing and dancing in the square. There was
wine and food to be bought from stalls in the streets:
fish cooked on charcoal braziers, octopus stew, and
scallops braised in their shells, as well as the most de-
licious-looking honey and almond tarts. She could only
drool over the food, knowing she would have to make
do with a simple supper at the hostel that evening.

Then, some time during the afternoon, Kate lost
touch with her companions and the weather changed;

thunder rumbled in the distance and lightning flashed across the sky. A westerly wind rose, sweeping in the rain from the distant sea, taking the hat from Kate's head and carrying it over the roof tops. The crowds dispersed and headed for shelter.

Lamenting the loss of her hat, Kate entered the hostel in a rush. Her flaxen hair was plastered to her head and her sodden tunic heavy and cold against her skin. She started when she saw the man sitting on a bench in the hall. He had a cloak slung over his shoulders and his strong body was clad in a coney-trimmed black cotehardie; his long legs encased in red hose were stretched out before him. His nostrils flared and his finely drawn mouth lifted at the corners in a sardonic smile as his eyes lighted on her.

'Master Fletcher, I presume?' His voice was silky soft.

Kate was already feeling light-headed with hunger, but as he rose to his feet, apprehension caused her head to spin. She tried to speak, but no words came and the next moment it was as if a dark pit opened up and swallowed her.

Owain uttered an oath and caught her before she reached the ground. He swung her up into his arms and was instantly aware of soft breasts squashed against his chest. The realisation that he held a woman in his arms hit him like a blow to the stomach and, ignoring the clamour about them, he carried her out of the hostel and across the Plaza. Already the rain was easing off, but he was barely conscious of it as he hurried between porticoed buildings of golden granite, along the deserted *ruas*. She shifted in his grasp and he felt a stirring in his loins. 'Keep still,' he ordered, his voice rough.

'Where are you taking me?' Kate sat up in his arms. The action brought his shaven chin and his lips but a few inches from her mouth. Incredulously she found herself wondering what it would feel like to be kissed by him. Immediately on the heels of that thought came the words, *This man could be set on my destruction*. Instantly she began to struggle.

'I will drop you if you don't keep still. You lied to me and sent me on a fruitless journey.' His words lashed her. 'For that I should beat you.'

'I feared you. Let me down,' she gasped.

'That would serve no purpose in the circumstances. Lady or maid, I'm taking you to my lodgings and there we will talk.'

His words caused her heart to somersault. 'I do not have anything to say. I don't know how Sir Roger died and nor do I wish to know.'

Owain gazed into the tawny fringed blue-green eyes, wide with fear, and pity smote him to the heart. 'Then you have nothing to be frightened of. Trust me,' he said gently, still unsure who it was that he held in his arms. He knew both, the Lady Catherine and the younger Mistress Fletcher, to be fair haired. This woman's voice was well modulated, but then he had been informed by Sir Thomas that young Mistress Fletcher was no common maid. 'Tell me who are you?' he asked.

Looking up into his strongly jawed face Kate estimated him to have lived twenty-five summers. She decided that it might be best to keep silence for the moment, so she pressed her lips tightly together and shook her head.

He scowled. 'You will tell me, but I'll be patient until we reach shelter,' he said under his breath.

Kate did not like the sound of that, but could see no way of escaping him. Perhaps once they reached his lodging there might be a chance. They came to an inn and he carried her through an arched opening into a paved courtyard, where a flight of steps, edged with potted plants, led to a door in an upper storey of the building. She protested when he set foot on the bottom step. 'This is a foolishness! You can't carry me up there.' How could she possibly escape if he did not put her down?

He smiled tightly and proceeded up the steps, still carrying her. On reaching the top, he fumbled in the pouch attached to his belt. She struggled to get down, but he clutched her against his chest and somehow managed to open the door. He carried her inside and set her on her feet. She swayed and grasped the back of a nearby chair to steady herself. She refused to meet his eyes, fearing what she might see in them and instead gazed about her, taking in the bed first, which seemed to occupy most of the space.

Her heart pounded. If she confessed to being Kate Fletcher, then perhaps he would bed her. There were so many men who thought little of deflowering one such as herself. She glanced about her for a weapon. At the bed's foot was a clothing chest and on the whitewashed wall behind the bed hung a crucifix. She decided it would not be right to hit him with that holy object. Her gaze slid to the opposite wall where two hanging poles protruded. She watched him hang his damp cloak on one of the poles before unfastening the leather belt from his waist. From it dangled a sword, which he dropped on the table. He must have seen the expression in her eyes because he said, 'I wouldn't if I were you.'

She flushed and took note of the rest of the table's contents: a book, an earthenware cup, a candlestick and a jug of wine. His saddlebags were on the floor. There was no fire in the chamber and she was damp and cold. As if from a distance came the noise of what sounded like a swarm of bees, but almost immediately she realised it was the hum of conversation coming through the floor of the taproom below. She guessed it would be full of men and was not tempted to bang on the floor. Shivering in her sodden garment, she watched as her abductor reached for the jug and poured wine into the cup.

'Here, drink this,' he said.

She made no move to take the cup. 'How do I know you haven't drugged it?'

'Perhaps you betray yourself by asking that. Maybe Sir Roger was poisoned.'

She made no response to his words.

Owain raised dark eyebrows and, lifting the cup to his lips, drank deeply. Then he refilled the vessel and held it out to her. Still she hesitated and he looked amused. 'Come. Do I look like a man who needs to drug a woman to bend her to my will? Besides, how would I know you might be here in this bedchamber with me? I can assure you that my intentions are honourable.'

She thought he might not be making such assurances if he knew for sure that she was no lady. Taking the cup, she sipped the wine, whilst watching him over the rim.

'You have asked who I am, but I would know the name of the man who pursues me,' she demanded.

'Pursues?' He appeared to savour the word and she could not take her eyes from his lips. The nether one was full and beautifully curved, the upper long and clearly defined. 'I would not use that word. This is not a chase, although your eyes are as beautiful as those of any deer,' he said softly.

She straightened her drooping shoulders and tilted her chin. 'You have a silver tongue, sir, but there is no need to flatter me,' she said with a touch of hauteur. 'I ask why you seek me?'

Owain smiled. 'I want answers, as you already know.'

'Why—why do you—you not answer mi-mine first?' she asked through teeth that suddenly began to chatter, and she wrapped her arms round herself as if to control her body's actions. 'It—it is pr-probably true that I have mor-more to lose if I speak honestly. Are you St-Stanley's man or have—have you been se-sent by Friar Stephen? Perhaps you are related to the C-Comte d'Azay? If that is his real name.'

'D'Azay?' His dark brows furrowed and then he shrugged. 'You give me a choice. A foolishness because I could so easily lie to you and how would you know it? I suggest you get out of your wet garments before you catch a chill. Your pilgrimage is at an end and I am taking you to England once you tell me where the rest of your companions are.'

Kate gasped. It would be a relief to be rid of the hated tunic—but to undress here in this chamber with him present? Never. Besides, what could she wear in its stead?

'I know what you are thinking,' he murmured. 'Your eyes betray you. I will provide you with a change of raiment, which will suit you better than that tunic you are wearing.' He made a move towards her and she would have taken a step back if the wall had not been behind her. He reached out with a single finger to caress her cheek and neck and to touch the pulse that beat at the base of her throat. She jumped as the back of his fingers brushed the upper curve of her breast as he tugged on the drawstring of her tunic.

For a moment she felt as if without breath and had to inhale deeply. Then, thinking if she could convince him that she was the Lady Catherine he was more likely to treat her with respect, she reached up and knocked his hand aside. 'You forget yourself, sir!' she said angrily.

He stepped back and bowed slightly. 'I beg pardon…my lady? Just for a moment I fell under the spell of your…beauty.'

Her eyes glinted. 'You mock me. With my hair hacked so cruelly I am no beauty. Nor am I an enchantress that I would cast spells. Show me the raiment you speak of and then I demand that you remove yourself from this chamber.'

'I would hear the tale of how your hair was hacked off,' he mused, 'but for now I will humour you.'

Owain went over to the chest and flung back its lid. From its depths he took a black lace mantilla and a linen kirtle with long tight sleeves. Placing both on the bed, he returned to the chest and this time he lifted out a green gown and laid that carefully beside them. Kate stepped forward and fingered the fabric of the gown. The act gave her pleasure, for she was certain it was Venetian cotton. Hadn't she helped her Lady sew such material on several occasions? Where did he have it from?

She held the gown against her. Its style was like nothing she had seen before. The skirt fell in loose flowing lines from a high waist and tiny black bows fastened up the bodice, which had a plunging V neckline with lace reveres and a collar that curved low round the neck.

'Where did you get this gown?' she asked in wonder and delight, lifting her gaze to his face.

Her delight obviously pleased him. 'I have a friend who is a merchant. He attends all the great fairs. Bruges, Lyon, Venice. By the greatest good fortune I met him in Burgos and by even greater good fortune he'd had several gowns made up for his sister in the latest fashion. I am glad it pleases you.'

'You bought it from him for me? You were so sure you would find me and yet before you said…' Her voice was husky with emotion for she had never worn such a gown in her life.

His eyes mocked her. 'Although I believed you to be Master Fletcher, I hoped he would lead me to the Lady Catherine, his sister and mother. I was vexed with *him*. Yet I knew his destination and deemed that the reason why he had spoken falsely was most likely due to his protecting someone. I would serve and protect the Lady Catherine, not betray.'

So he wished to serve her Lady, thought Kate. For a moment her grief for her dead mistress was like a weight in her chest. If only the King had wed Catherine to someone other than Sir Roger…a man prepared to protect and not betray…how different both their lives would have been. And yet what was she thinking? She had only this man's word that he spoke honestly. Was she to trust him just because he had produced a gown and spoke fine words? What should she say? What was she to do? Quickly! She must make up her mind because he was waiting.

'I thank you, sir, that my behaviour did not give you a distaste for me.' Her voice was stilted. 'If you would be so kind as to leave me, I will get out of this damp garment.' She added, 'I much appreciate your gift.'

His eyes searched her face, then he bowed slightly and left her alone.

Kate sighed and further loosened the drawstring at the neck of her tunic before unfastening the belt about her waist, from which hung her scrip and water bottle. She pulled the tunic from her shoulders and allowed it to fall to the floor. Then she removed the plain linen shift. She looked down at herself, noticing several red marks where the fleas had bit into her flesh last night and her eyes darkened with distaste. Then she ran her hands over her naked body, frowning as she considered the weight she had lost. Her breasts were not as full as when she had left England and her hips and stomach showed no spare flesh. She wondered what he would think of her if he saw her so and grew hot at such an immodest and sinful thought.

Hastily she reached for the cream linen kirtle and dragged it over her head, concerned in case he re-entered the room before she was ready for him. Then her hand closed on the green gown. For a moment she pressed a fold of it against her cheek, savouring the fresh smell of the fabric and the faint fragrance of lavender that clung to it. She undid the fastenings of the long sleeves and finished dressing.

Unfortunately, there was no mirror in the bedchamber to inspect her appearance. She grimaced, but then told herself that was to the good because vanity was a sin. Even so she needed to do something with her hair, which was surely in even more of a mess than it had been earlier. From her scrip she took a bone comb that had been the Lady Catherine's, but before she could set about tidying her hair there came the rap of knuckles on the outer door and it opened a fraction.

'May I come in? It's raining again,' said her captor. She hesitated only a second before bidding him enter.

Owain stared at her, stunned by the difference the gown made to her appearance. It was true that the looseness of the skirts concealed the narrowness of her waist and curves of her hips, but the plunging V of the bodice revealed her cleavage and he could not take his eyes from the sweet shape of her breasts. Desire warmed his body and he was aware that she was staring at him with a flush on her cheeks and a question in her eyes.

'It fits as if it had been made for you,' he said slowly.

She would have had to be blind not to notice the admiration in his eyes and shyness caused her to turn from him with the comb in her hand. 'I thank you, sir. It is a long time since I have worn such a gown.' Kate smiled to herself at the thought that never had she worn such a gown.

'It is my pleasure.' He watched her struggle to tug the comb through her short, unruly curls; before she realised what he was about, he had taken it from her fingers. 'Allow me!' he said quietly.

'Sir, I can manage.' There was a tremor in her voice.

'It's no trouble.' He brought her against him and, taking a handful of her hair, began to drag the comb through her curls.

He was much too close for Kate's peace of mind and she shivered as his fingers brushed her neck, sending pleasing ripples through her. 'Please, don't do that!' she blurted out.

'Don't do what, my lady? Some of your curls are in such a tangle they need teasing out.'

His fingers brushed her ear and the nape of her neck. She could bear it no longer and forced herself to step away from him. The skirts fluttered about her bare ankles in a manner that felt very sensuous. 'Sir, this has gone far enough. I cannot permit such intimacies,' she said, trying to sound firm. 'You will desist. I much appreciate your—your kindness in providing me with a new gown and will recompense you as soon as I am able.'

He smiled. 'You have money? I deemed that your scrip was empty.'

She tilted her dimpled chin. 'I have lived the life of a pilgrim for what seems an age. Of course I have no money. But you know who I am…so you also know that I am a widow with a manor in Lancashire. I will see that you get your money when I return home. Now I wish to go back to the hostel.'

He frowned. 'Are you sure about that? The rain might have stopped, but the hostel is such a dismal place.'

She made no answer but lowered her eyes. 'I have companions there.'

'The Fletchers? Did they not have just cause for wishing Sir Roger dead?'

Kate paled and knew that she had to come up with an answer that would destroy any desire in him to seek them out. 'They were killed when we passed over the mountains…that was when I hacked off my hair and prayed I would be mistaken for a lad. The companions I talk of are those of the Way. Other pilgrims like myself.'

He was taken aback, thinking that Sir Thomas would not be pleased with this news. Seeing his reaction, Kate decided she had made the right decision. 'I must return to the hostel. I cannot stay here with you. It is not seemly.'

He did not deny it but said, 'Neither is travelling without a chaperon in a group of strangers, but I will humour you and accompany you to the hostel. Although, whether they will accept you in such a gown…' His words trailed off.

She was dismayed. Was he suggesting that she had to remove the new gown and undergarment and dress in the tunic again? She knew that most of those she had seen on the pilgrims' way were simply clad. She sighed. 'Then I will have to return the gown to you.'

His blue eyes were speculative. 'It suits you well. Are you certain you want to do this?'

She tilted her chin. 'If you would turn your back, sir?' This time he did not try to persuade her, but did as she asked.

Kate could have wept as she removed the gown and donned the hated tunic again. 'I am ready,' she said.

He faced her with a frown. 'This is a foolishness. There are still questions I have to ask you. I will see you on the morrow and escort you back to England.'

Here was the answer to her prayer, yet how could she trust him? They would be thrown into each other's company far too much—and who was to say that she might not betray herself and her mother and brother by a slip of the tongue? 'I have no more to say to you on the matter of Sir Roger's death. I will return home the way I came,' she assured him, her voice shaking slightly.

His eyes narrowed, became blue slits. 'If that is your decision I cannot force you into accepting my help. I can only say that you have a long and dangerous road ahead of you. Sleep with that thought in your mind, Lady Catherine.'

She was surprised by his acquiescence, having expected him to try and bend her to his will. Had he done so she would have been happier with the decision she had made because it would have proved her right not to trust him. She pinned a bright smile on her lips. 'You tell me what I already know. I bid thee farewell, sir.'

For some reason her words caused him to smile. A smile of such singular charm that, for a moment, the breath caught in her throat and her chest felt tight. 'I said I will escort you back to the hostel,' he said, picking up the mantilla from the bed and placing it over her shorn hair before she could prevent him. 'Keep this. There are those who might think your hair has been shorn because of some great sin now you seem to have lost your hat. You're far too pretty for a youth.'

Tears pricked her eyes at the compliment and the gesture. Clearing her throat, she suggested that they set out immediately.

With a shrug, he placed the mantilla on the bed and opened the door. He escorted her down the steps and along the quickly drying streets at such a pace that she decided she had been wrong about his intentions and that he could not be rid of her quickly enough. When they reached the hostel he lifted her hand to his lips and placed a kiss in its palm before bidding her *adieu*.

Kate watched him go, aware that the palm of her hand tingled where his lips had touched it. She dismissed the sensation as of no consequence and went indoors. She had missed the evening meal and hunger gnawed at her innards. She did not expect to rest that night, but, as she relived the events of the day, she drifted into sleep.

She woke as the fingers of dawn filled the sky. Her mood was melancholy, almost fey, her head filled with the remembrance of dreams of knights who slew dragons, beautiful maidens and evil men, of prehistoric stones, flint knives, blood and incantations.

Kate shivered. Would she ever forget the events that had led to the death of her father? He had been a secret follower of the old religion, believing trees, rocks and rivers contained spirits that spoke to him. If only he had not got involved in Sir Roger's frightening mixture of nature worship and a dual god and devil, who demanded a blood sacrifice. She must not think about it; less chance, then, of the truth accidentally tumbling from her lips.

Her stomach rumbled and she told herself to forget the past for now. She needed fresh air and food. Rising from her pallet, she put on her sandals and left the sleeping quarters and hurried downstairs. The front doors were already open and a monk was brushing the steps. She walked outside and took a deep breath, flinging her arms wide as if to embrace the morning.

She almost jumped out of her skin when a male voice said, 'Good morn to you, my Lady. My path lies in the direction of La Coruña, where we can take a ship to England. I have an early start in mind and it would be a delight to take you up with me…that is, if you've had second thoughts about traversing the hot plains of Castile and risking the mountain passes into France again?'

Kate's eyes darted towards the man sitting on the steps of the cathedral. 'How long have you been there?' she demanded hotly.

Owain rose to his feet and approached her with an easy grace. 'Long enough to make sure you would not leave before I could speak to you again. It is a foolishness for you not to accept my escort. I understand your reluctance to place your trust in me and return home.'

A bitter laugh escaped Kate as she stepped into her dead mistress's shoes. 'It was once a happy house, but after my marriage it was as if a dark shadow crept over it.'

'A house can be exorcised. Running away doesn't solve anything, my Lady.' His gaze held hers. 'Trust me with the truth and I will do my uttermost to help you.'

Her eyes flashed blue-green fire. 'You don't understand. I might have died had I stayed there.'

'Why would you have died?'

She wrapped her arms about her and stared into his strong-boned face. 'I cannot tell you. I would like to trust you, but…'

Owain said seriously, 'I would like to trust you, too, and I will if you show some trust in me.'

Her heart beat fast as she continued to stare at him, considering her options. Suddenly a thought occurred to her and she frowned. 'Why should you not trust me? Did they say I killed him by magic?'

'Your reeve and those who work on your manor spoke only good of you, but much that was bad about your husband.'

The muscles of her face relaxed. 'Did what they say give you a picture of the kind of man he was?'

'I know the kind of man he was. I met him several years ago when in France with one of my brothers.' His expression was suddenly bleak.

She was curious. 'You have brothers?'

'Two alive…one dead.' He forced a smile. 'You will come with me?'

She did not return his smile, telling herself she must try to behave distantly towards him. 'I am hungry. Do you have any food, sir?'

His smile deepened, causing tiny creases to fan out at the side of his eyes. 'I will purchase some whilst you change your garments.'

They returned to his lodgings where he left her alone. It was obvious that he at least trusted her not to run away.

Chapter Three

Owain returned to the bedchamber, bearing several small loaves, slices of smoked pork, cheese, oranges, all wrapped in a napkin, as well as carrying a jug of wine mixed with water. Kate was wearing the green gown and, once again, he was struck by the difference it made to her appearance. He placed the food and jug on the table.

Immediately Kate settled herself on an upright chair, arranging her skirts carefully, and reached for one of the loaves and tore a piece from it. She placed a slice of smoked pork and cheese on the bread and bit in to it with her small teeth.

'You are hungry,' he said drily.

She slanted him an amused look but did not speak until she had swallowed. 'Before I answer any more of your questions…who are you, sir? I must know your name if I am to travel to La Coruña with you.'

Owain dug a leather travelling cup from one of his saddlebags and filled that and the earthenware cup on the table with wine and water. He nudged one of the cups towards Kate. 'My name is Master Owain ap Rowan. My family breeds horses in the Palatine of Chester. I have travelled Europe, buying and selling horses. I have also fought in the French wars and served as a supplier of horses for the King's master of horse whilst abroad. At this moment I serve Sir Thomas Stanley, who was in attendance on the King before he lost his wits. It was his initial suggestion to the King that I look into the matter of your husband's death and your disappearance along with that of the Fletcher family.'

Kate had stiffened at his mention of Sir Thomas Stanley. 'Who has lost his wits? Sir Thomas or the King? I tell you now, Master ap Rowan, your words alarm me. Sir Thomas is a powerful man and his manor at Lathom lies too close to Merebury.' She bit savagely into the food.

Owain frowned and a lock of curling black hair fell on his forehead. 'It is the King who has lost his wits, but what I've told you was decided before that happened. I understand your concern about Sir Thomas, but he is sympathetic towards you.'

Her expression hardened. 'I do not want the sympathy of any Stanley. I see Sir Thomas's concern only as a way of taking Merebury from me.'

Owain was not surprised by her reaction and pondered on how to reassure her whilst he broke his fast. 'The King has already granted him the authority to oversee your manor. He had no choice after your disappearance. You are now the ward of the King and your manor is in his gift. Once your innocence is proved, then he will find you a husband and he will take care of you.'

Kate's fingers toyed with her cup and she was stony-faced. 'I want no husband.'

Owain frowned. 'I understand your feelings, my lady, but these are uncertain and dangerous times in England. You will need the protection of a husband. I assure you not all men are as Sir Roger.'

'And what if the King does not regain his wits, will it be Sir Thomas who will decide my fate?' she demanded.

'It could be the Duke of York, but he might leave the task to Sir Thomas, who, I assure you, really does want what is best for you.' He scraped the back of his hand on his unshaven chin. 'Be reasonable, my lady. You have no one else to look to with the Fletcher family dead. You have no kin and, from what I've discovered, your husband positively discouraged you from having visitors or your visiting outside your manor.'

Kate said heavily, 'It is true what you say. The Fletchers were the only true friends I had. They cared much for me, as I did them.'

'Then your grief for them must go deep. It is a terrible thing to lose those we care for. I still grieve for my grandmother.' He reached out a hand and covered hers.

Her fingers tingled at his touch and her heart raced. 'I appreciate your sympathy,' she said, a mite breathlessly, 'but I wish fervently that you were not in the pay of Sir Thomas. Power and pride in rank and possessions are all the Stanleys care about.' She was remembering all that her mother had told her about them.

'That power can work in your favour,' insisted Owain, freeing her hand. 'If you would trust me to do what I believe is best for both of us, you will return to live on your manor in safety.'

'You talk of trust. Tell me, Master ap Rowan, what have you to gain from finding the person responsible for Sir Roger's death? What has Sir Thomas promised you?' She bit into the last morsel of food and reached for more bread.

'My father has banned me from returning home. I must support myself as best I can. The King has promised to reward the man who solves the mystery of your husband's death.'

A surprised laugh escaped her. 'An honest answer at last. I knew the King had given money to fund Sir Roger's experiments with alchemy, but I never thought that he cared so much for the man. Yet if the King has lost his wits, how will you gain your reward?'

'Hopefully he will recover and I will not be out of pocket for my efforts as Sir Thomas is funding my search.'

'No doubt he is spending the income from Merebury,' murmured Kate. He gave her a hard look and she flushed. 'No doubt you would deny that, yet if I were in his shoes it would make perfect sense. Tell me, Master ap Rowan, why has your father banned you from your home?'

He stiffened. 'That is none of your concern, my lady. You have my assurance that it has nothing to do with the matter under discussion. But perhaps I should tell you what I have done so far in my search.'

'Speak on.'

'I have met with your reeve. He is of the opinion that there was some devilry afoot at your manor that led to your husband's death.'

Kate stared at him and said lightly, 'When people

dwell on such then they will conjure up Ol' Nick and his demons.'

'So you do not deny it. Tell me more.'

She shook her head. 'I will only repeat what I have just said.'

Owain's blue eyes met hers and she felt he was trying to burrow into her very soul—it was a struggle to meet his gaze and refuse to look away or allow him in. Suddenly he reached for his cup and rasped, 'I need to hear your version of events leading up to his death if I am to help you. You say you left Merebury because you feared for your life. Which either means that despite any denial you might make you killed Sir Roger or you fear those who did kill him.'

'I do not know who killed Sir Roger,' said Kate in a low voice. 'The Fletchers might have known, but I told them that I did not want to know…so after leaving Merebury we did not discuss the matter.'

'I find that difficult to believe.'

She shrugged, knowing she must be careful. 'What do you know of any of us? Since being forced into a marriage that proved distasteful to me, all I ever wanted was to leave that life behind and go on pilgrimage.'

'And the Fletchers?'

She blinked at him. 'They loved me and would have given their lives for me.'

'So they never spoke to you about the human bones your reeve found…the lights he swears he saw out near the old stones, the men in robes and a devilish figure?'

Kate half-opened her mouth and then shut it again and reached for her cup. The tips of her fingers were trembling and she prayed he would not notice. She drank deeply, her thoughts darting hither and thither beneath his intent blue gaze. She put down the cup and wiped her mouth with the back of her hand. 'Did he tell you about the mummers who came to Merebury the Christmas before last? How one was dressed in horns and tail and caused much merriment amongst the revellers. Even Sir Roger enjoyed the jape until the figure turned his attention on him…then he appeared not to be so amused.'

Owain said, 'He did, indeed, tell me of the mummery that took place and how that devilish figure warned Sir Roger to have care or his life would be forfeit. But he did not believe that parody of Ol' Nick had aught to do with the lights and figure at the old stones.'

She said firmly, 'But was Ol' Nick really there? It's easy to see a sheep or a goat in the mist and imagine things when rumours are flying round that the lord of the manor is having truck with the devil to produce gold for the King.' A smile lighted her face and she leaned towards him across the table. 'There. I have said more than I intended. But I ask you, Master ap Rowan, is this really the right time for such a conversation? You said you wanted an early start. Perhaps we should pack the rest of the food to eat later. If you continue with this any further, it could be noon before we are on our way.'

He hesitated and then nodded. 'Of course. If you would of your courtesy wrap the food in the napkin whilst I fill our water bottles and saddle up Merlin, I will meet you in the courtyard.'

She started. 'Merlin! Why do you call your horse…?'

'He is a wonder of a horse even if he is of mixed

parentage,' said Owain, opening the door. 'Part Welsh, part Germanic and with a strain of illicit Berber. I saw him born.'

'I remember horses being led off the ships in Liverpool when I was there with my brother,' she said softly.

He started. 'Brother?'

Kate's heart leapt with fear and for a moment she felt as if suffocating, then she drew a breath and swallowed. 'What am I thinking of?' she said, laughing. 'I speak of my father's godson. His parents were dead and he lived at Merebury for a while. Having no brothers or sisters, we played at being such to the other.'

'What happened to him?'

She lied smoothly. 'A mist came down and he wandered into the great mere and was never seen again.' She gazed at Owain from soulful eyes. 'It's a sad tale. I was heartbroken.'

He made a noise in his throat and left the bedchamber without further comment.

Kate sat down, feeling weak at the knees and a need to draw several deep breaths. Was he suspicious? She must not rush into speech, but pause for thought. It had always been a fault with her and had got her into trouble more times than she could remember.

She rose to her feet and wrapped the food in the napkin and placed it in one of the saddlebags. Then she picked up her pilgrim's garb and looked at it with distaste. She would like to be rid of it, but, having been reared in habits of thrift, it would be a sin to throw it away. She folded it up and found a place for it in the saddlebags. She prayed that God would forgive her for her deception.

Merlin was a magnificent beast, strong in the shoulders and deep in the chest. Built for endurance not speed, thought Kate, watching his master climb nimbly into the saddle. She stood on a mounting block and he held down a hand to her. She grasped it above the elbow and he swung her up behind him. She bundled up her skirts for comfort's sake. The ground appeared a long way down and it was a relief to take a firm grip on the back of Master ap Rowan's belt. His closeness was enough to set her pulses racing and she told herself that she must stay calm. There were many miles ahead before they reached England and it would not do to lose her head or her heart to this man.

They made their way through the bustling streets in a westerly direction and had soon left the city behind. Merchants and pilgrims, monks and clerics, citizens and country folk, alike, wended their way on foot, horseback, mule or by wagon. For a while Kate forgot her troubles, gazing with interest at the scene about her. After months of walking it was a pleasure to be carried to her destination and on such a horse. She knew enough to realise that this one had been put through its paces and trained so its gait was comfortable even at a walk. She had once ridden an animal that had made her feel seasick when it slowed its gait.

The road was slippery in places, due to tiny streams, which cascaded from the wooded, rocky hillsides, to wend their way through lush meadowland. Those that did not peter out trickled across the road of beaten earth to be absorbed by the undergrowth on the other side bordering the forest. She thought how different the landscape was from the burning plains of Castile; for, although the sun shone from a cloudless sky, there was a cool westerly breeze that tempered the heat.

'This land reminds me of Wales.' Owain flung the words over his shoulder at her.

'I have never been to Wales but I would say it is also akin to parts of Lancashire. I notice that many of the Galicians are fair skinned.'

'That is because they are descended from the same race as those that crossed the ocean to Briton, driven out of the eastern lands by the barbarians in the dark times,' replied Owain.

'Would you say that would be after St James landed on the coast here near a place called Finisterre?'

'Nay! This would be before then. They believed they had reached the end of the world, but the great ocean they found is the same as that which washes the shores of western Ireland. Men have left that land to sail for days on end in the search for the Land of the Ever Young.'

Kate was enchanted, sensing a tale that would take his mind off Sir Roger's murder and while away the hours. 'What is this land you speak of? Does it belong to those who found the elixir of youth, which the alchemists speak of?' Fie! She had not meant to say that.

'Who knows? All I can tell you is that it is spoken of in the tales passed down by the old ones. There is a story that one of them reached that land and fell in love with a beautiful lady there. She loved him, also, and for years they lived together, but he pined for his own country and decided to return there…both knew that if she went with him she would die.'

'What happened?'

'It is a sad tale. Both died. Their hearts broken.'

Kate said softly, 'To be loved in such a way is surely rare.'

'Yet it happens. The King's mother fell in love with one of her son's squires. A Welsh yeoman called Owain ap Twydr. He and my father fought side by side at Agincourt. I am named after him. Owain and that Catherine wed secretly. But it was not until after she died that it became known that they had wed and she had borne him three sons. He was imprisoned for a while, but later released. Two of his sons were given the titles of Earl of Richmond and Pembroke. They have gained by being half-brothers to the King and this has caused much jealousy.' Owain hesitated before saying, 'You mentioned earlier a man you called the Comte d'Azay.'

Kate said tersely, 'He visited Merebury during the spring of last year, showing great interest in Sir Roger's experiments in alchemy. Once he let slip the Comte was connected with a Welsh magnate further south.' She fell silent, not wanting to talk of the Frenchman, thinking he was another who shared Sir Roger's dark heart. She changed the subject swiftly, 'When I first set eyes on you, Master ap Rowan, I considered you a Spaniard because of the colour of your skin and hair.' She clutched his shoulder as the horse jerked a little to the left as if avoiding a rut in the road.

She heard him sigh, but he answered speedily enough, 'You detect another strand of my ancestry, Lady Catherine, and it will reveal to you why I have a fondness for Lancashire. My great-grandmother was from Castile and was a maid-in-waiting to the second

wife of John of Gaunt, the King's great-grandfather—
she married one of his knights.'

She was about to ask him how his mother had come
to marry a Welshman and whether he had a wife or betrothed waiting for him in England when there came a
sound like that of distant thunder. She looked to her left
and drew in her breath with a hiss as she saw a herd of
horses pouring like spilt honey down the hillside. Never
had she seen so many horses in one place together and
the sight filled her with awe and not a little fear, for, as
she watched, she realised they were heading towards the
road.

'Hold tight, my Lady!' yelled Owain and he urged
Merlin into a gallop.

Apprehension tightened Kate's throat, aware that
there was no escape into the dense forest of oak and
chestnut on their right. She slid her arms about Owain's
waist and laced her fingers together, pressing her cheek
against his back. As they increased speed, she was uncertain whether the thudding she could hear was her heart
beating or his. Perhaps it was that both were beating to
the drumming of Merlin's hooves on the hard earth.

The leading horses were now close enough for her
to see their manes, flying like banners. For a moment
she was terrified that they would be caught up in the
herd, knocked to the ground and trampled on. But at
what felt the last moment, the leaders swerved and
began to gallop alongside the road before swerving
again and sweeping round in a great curve and heading
back across the meadowlands.

Owain let out a whoop and shouted something in
what she presumed was Welsh. She felt the same ex-

hilaration and gladness to be alive. Merlin began to slow down, snorting and tossing his mane. Eventually he was trotting, then walking. Kate still clung to Owain, conscious of the heat and strength emanating from his body. It had a strange effect on her, making her reluctant to separate herself from him. Together, they had survived a brush with death and she knew she would never forget it.

He leaned forward to stroke Merlin's sweating neck and Kate loosened her grip on him, listening as he whispered to the horse. They came to a halt and he turned his head, gazing at her from eyes that sparkled with excitement. 'That was a near-run thing! Dangerous, but you did not panic and that says something to me about you.'

Kate was pleased by his words. She straightened up and asked him where the horses had come from and who owned them.

He dismounted. 'They belong to St James. A gift from the people of this region in the last century when the plague was rife. Apparently no one ever reclaimed them and they have bred and multiplied.' His expression sharpened as his gaze rested on her face, flushed and damp with perspiration. 'We'll pause for a while and rest. We can finish the food and Merlin can find his second wind.' He held up his arms to her.

For an instant Kate hesitated, then, resting her hands on his shoulders, allowed herself to fall towards him. He caught her and, for a moment, she was pressed against the length of him. Their faces were but inches apart and there was an awareness in his eyes that caused the breath to catch in her throat. She had a crazy urge to run a finger over his lips and then kiss him. But then Merlin tossed his head and shifted restlessly, causing Owain to take several paces back. The spell was broken and she slid between his hands until her feet touched the ground. Shaken, she turned her back on him and, despite her legs feeling as if they had turned to water, she made for the trees.

'There could be wild boar in the forest. Do not wander far,' shouted Owain.

What was wrong with her? Why did his touch have such an effect on her? He was Stanley's man and for that reason alone she should keep her distance. She relieved herself and then leaned against a tree, fanning her face with a leaf, wanting time to calm her agitated nerves.

When she left the forest it was to find Owain leaning against a boulder, the food on a napkin spread out on a flat rock. He had removed his cotehardie and unfastened the neck of his shirt, baring his olive-skinned throat. He was drinking from the leather cup, which he wiped with the edge of the napkin and held out to her. She thanked him and drank deeply. He had placed cheese and salted pork between bread and now he gave that to her. She returned the cup to him and ate standing, aching in places she would rather not think about.

'I notice you do not wear a wedding ring, Lady Catherine.'

His words took her unawares and her head shot up. His eyes narrowed as she fought to keep down her colour and thought swiftly. 'I did not regard it as so precious that I should keep it. My marriage was not a normal one. I sold it to buy food and salves,' she retorted.

Whatever he saw in her face must have satisfied him because he nodded and wiped his brow. She was just allowing herself to relax when he said, 'Tell me more about the Fletcher family?'

She visibly jumped, but almost instantly recovered herself. 'W-what good is it to t-talk of them when they are dead?' she stuttered.

He frowned. 'You will not like what I am about to say, but I will say it nevertheless… If we can prove them guilty, it means you will stand innocent.'

'But—but they would not have killed him,' she cried, furious with him for scaring her so. 'How could they? You know as much as I do that he was found dead in a room locked from the inside.'

'I did hear that Mistress Fletcher knew much about herb lore,' he said, watching her like a hawk. 'That she was often called upon to help the sick, women in child-birth and the dying. She was training her daughter to follow in her footsteps. They would know of poisons.'

'I tell you they did not kill him,' she yelled.

He stared at her, suspicion in his face. 'There is no need to shout, Lady Catherine.'

She bit her nether lip, groaning inwardly, knowing she must not allow him to rile her into acting unwisely. 'I beg pardon. But such a notion is abhorrent to me. You did not know them. I knew them better than anyone else at Merebury.'

'We can never know all there is to know about another person. Mistress Fletcher had acted nurse to you when you were a babe. You and her daughter suckled from the same breast. Of a surety that created a strong bond between the three of you. A bond strong enough for mother and daughter to kill for you, knowing how unhappy you were with Sir Roger.'

She stared at him with stricken eyes and yet still she answered him. 'If every woman were to rid herself of a loathed husband, then England would be half-empty of its men, Master ap Rowan.' She forced a smile. 'Believe me—neither the Fletchers nor myself killed him. You must work harder for your reward and seek your murderer elsewhere instead of slandering the dead.'

His dark brows drew together and his fingers curled into the palm of his hand. 'I repeat, Lady Catherine, that if the blame for your husband's death can be laid at the Fletchers' door, then the matter will be dropped and people will accept that you are innocent. What harm will it do them? They are dead and beyond human punishment.'

'You would have me countenance something that I know is not true?' Her voice rose and she unfolded her arms and poked him in the chest. 'Does truth not matter to you, Master ap Rowan? You say Sir Thomas Stanley and the King want you to discover the person responsible for Sir Roger's death. I suggest you abide by the orders meted out to you. Now, let's be on our way. The sooner I am in England and rid of your company, the safer I will feel.'

Owain half-opened his mouth and then clamped it shut, breathing deeply before striding off into the forest. Trembling, Kate leaned against the rock and closed her eyes. The man was impossibly stubborn and she must not allow him to rile her and in so doing give herself away. She opened her eyes and, picking up the empty cup, packed it away in one of the saddlebags with the water bottle and reached for an orange and began to peel it. Losing one's temper was always a mistake. Master ap Rowan was no fool and, depending on the tenacity of his nature, he might decide to give chase when she escaped him once back in England. He had managed to seek her out twice in Spain and he might do the same again once they were across the channel. Then he would also find her mother and brother, and that would never do if he was so determined on laying the blame on them for Sir Roger's murder.

'Come, Lady Catherine. Do not stand there daydreaming.' She started and lifted her eyes. He was grim-faced—who could blame him after what she had said to him—but she would not retract her words.

'I am eating.'

'You can finish the orange on horseback. Place your foot in my hands, Lady Catherine, if you please.'

He bent over and laced his hands together. With only the barest of hesitation she did as ordered and he lifted her high into the air, enabling her to scramble on to the back of the horse. For a moment she swayed perilously, losing her grip because of the orange in her hand. He shot out an arm and held her in place until she regained her balance. Their eyes met and she knew that she had to make peace between them. 'I should not have spoken to you so rudely.' Her voice was stiff. 'I am certain you were thinking only of what is best for me. I beg your pardon, Master ap Rowan.'

For a moment he just stared at her and then slowly the anger faded from his eyes and he said thoughtfully, 'I wonder how much you mean that, my Lady. I sense you fear me and that is a grief to me. I really do want only what is best for you.' Before she could respond he hauled himself up behind her.

He took the reins and clicked his tongue against his teeth. The horse moved forward, jerking Kate against his chest. She felt that she had been put firmly in her place. For the rest of the journey she did not speak.

By the time they reached their destination Kate was hot and sticky with sweat. She ached all over and longed for nothing more than to wash, lie down and not move for several hours. But that was not to be.

La Coruña was a town cut off from the mainland by a neck of sand. Its narrow streets were bustling with people and its waterfront was just as busy. Kate gazed at the ships in the harbour, wondering which one would take them to England. She watched from beneath drooping eyelids as Owain dismounted and left her high and dry on Merlin's back, whilst he wandered the waterfront, inspecting the vessels moored at the quayside. She thought he must trust her, leaving her alone on his horse. She supposed that she could ride off and leave him. But where would she go? Much better to allow him to find a ship that would take her to England and escape him once there. She saw him speak to a mariner fishing over the side of one of the ships. The next moment Owain had gone below, to eventually reappear in the company of a bearded man. They spoke animatedly and then she saw Owain pointing in her direction. She was aware of being stared at with open curiosity. Then the two men parted and Owain came striding towards her.

'Well, Master ap Rowan, have you bespoke berths for us on that ship?' she asked politely.

'The master of the *Philippa* does have the King's licence to ferry pilgrims, but normally, that's a one-way trade with him. He has a shipment of wine, brandy, fruit and salted almonds to take to England…but for a price he's prepared to take us and Merlin aboard.'

Kate's weary face lit up. 'When do we sail?'

'On the morning tide, although he wants us aboard tonight.'

'How long will it take to reach England?' Her tone was eager.

'That depends on whether we have fair winds.' His expression was serious. 'There is only one cabin available, so I had to tell him that you're my wife.'

Kate could only stare at him as differing emotions tore through her. She would have had difficulty deciding which was the strongest: anger, suspicion or, to her shame, excitement. She reined them all in and said in a soft voice, 'You take much upon yourself, Master ap Rowan. Surely, you should have asked me first.'

He nodded. 'Aye. But the outcome would have been the same. You will be safer playing the role of my wife. Now I must arrange for bedding and fodder to be delivered to the ship.' His tone had changed and was now brisk. 'If there is aught in the way of food and drink you wish to purchase to supplement the meals aboard, then we will buy it. Afterwards we will visit an inn, refresh ourselves and have a meal.'

She was relieved to hear that they would wash and eat before going aboard and thanked him for his thoughtfulness. He smiled briefly and asked her would she rather walk than ride. She nodded and he lifted her down in one swift movement, releasing her instantly. He led the way with Merlin. Kate followed in their wake, feeling stiff and sore, and yet soon she was taking an interest in her surroundings. She could see a tall narrow building that soared into the air. 'What is that?' she asked curiously.

He glanced over his shoulder. 'A lighthouse. It was built by the Romans and still serves to warn ships of the dangerous waters that lie along this coast.'

She asked no more questions, telling herself she must not dwell on storms at sea, shipwrecks, pirates or sharing a cabin with Owain ap Rowan. Instead she concentrated on considering what to buy to eat aboard ship.

They wended their way through the narrow streets, pausing to purchase oranges, apricots, cheese, and salted almonds. Kate was grateful for his willingness to buy whatever she suggested, but she had difficulty saying so, only promising to recompense him when they returned to her manor. He assured her that was not necessary, and she reminded herself that the money they were spending had most likely come from Merebury and not the Stanley estates.

Their evening meal was taken at an inn, not far from the Romanesque church of Santa Maria, and consisted of bean soup with bread, mussels in garlic sauce, and almond tartlets, washed down with rough red wine and finished off with the speciality of the region, Queimada. The liquor burned her throat, causing her to gasp and demand to know its ingredients.

There had been little conversation between them during the meal, but now Owain smiled at her across the table. 'I suspect the Galicians would rather keep that secret. A mariner told me the last time I was here that it was first brewed by witches under a magical oak to the accompaniment of Celtic chants. It has a slightly burnt flavour, don't you think?' He sipped the liquor and held it in his mouth for a moment, savouring it and then swallowed. 'Of a surety there is brandy there.'

More cautiously this time, Kate took a sip and held it in her mouth before swallowing. 'It isn't sweetened with honey.'

'I'd hazard sugar…and there's some kind of fruit.' He drank the rest of the liquor down and beckoned a serving wench. 'Time we were going. Drink up, Lady Catherine.'

Once outside Kate felt light-headed, but it was a pleasant feeling and she burst into a ditty about a cheating pardoner getting his toes toasted in hell. Owain gazed at her from thoughtful eyes. 'You are feeling well, Lady Catherine?'

She broke off in mid-note. 'Never better.' She placed both her hands on his chest. 'Call me Kate. You would be a friend to me, am I not right?' Her words were slurred.

'A friend such as the substitute brother, who disappeared in the great mere never to be seen again?' There was a note of mockery in his voice.

His mention of a brother caused a warning bell to ring on the edge of her consciousness. She squinted ferociously as she tried to focus on Owain's face. 'Have you seen the great mere? If you had, then you would not mock,' she enunciated slowly.

'I have seen the great mere, but would have thought someone familiar with the area would know their way about,' said Owain.

'It was misty,' she said, swaying towards him. Her

head drooped against his chest and she felt as if about to float away. She heard his muffled oath and was aware of being lifted and slung over a strong shoulder. She sighed, thinking that she should never have let slip those words about her brother. At least she had not named him, but maybe her inquisitor would put two and two together and come up with the right answer and what would happen to her then? She blinked up at the starlit sky as it whizzed about her and then she lost consciousness.

Chapter Four

Water splashed onto Kate's face, causing her to gasp and strike out blindly. Her wrist was seized in a strong grasp. 'Good morn to you, Lady Kate. I thought you were never going to wake.'

Recognising Master ap Owain's voice, she groaned and forced her eyes open to see her persecutor looming over her with a dripping cloth in his hand. He was fully dressed. His dark hair was damp and curling and his eyes were watchful. She wrenched her wrist from his grasp and even as he voiced a warning, pushed herself up. Her head hit the underside of the bunk above. She winced, rubbed her head and said through gritted teeth, 'Don't laugh.'

'I wouldn't dare. I wager that hurt, though, Lady Kate.'

She started. Not only had he called her Kate but she could feel water running down her neck and soaking into the material of her kirtle so that it clung to her breast. She was aware of the direction of his eyes and felt the colour rise in her cheeks as he handed her a dry cloth. Immediately she held it against her bosom. 'Will you please remove yourself from this cabin so I may dress, Master ap Rowan?' she said with as much dignity as she could muster.

He raised his eyebrows. 'You may call me Owain, seeing as how you have given me permission to address you as Kate.'

Her stomach flipped over. 'I—I did?'

His blue eyes were guileless. 'Aye! Surely you can't have forgotten what a merry time we had last even?' He sounded amused.

His tone of voice made her believe she must have behaved like a wanton and her cheeks burned. 'I—I don't remember.'

'Oh, Lady Kate! How could you forget? To be sure and didn't I believe you meant it when you said you wished for us to become lov—better acquainted?' Now his tone was mournful.

She swallowed. Surely even under the influence of strong drink she would not have suggested they become lovers, but why should he tease her? What did he expect to gain? She groaned inwardly, wishing she could remember what had happened last night. 'I think you are not behaving like a gentleman,' she muttered. 'I can't even remember how I got here.'

'I carried you aboard and put you to bed.'

She was aghast, thinking Lady Catherine would never have been the worse for strong drink. 'I—I am ashamed,' she said in a low voice. 'What must you think of me? Have I not just completed my pilgrimage and I have behaved like a—a...?'

He ran a finger down a cheek. 'Like a woman who

needed to take her ease and enjoy herself for once. Why berate yourself? You have suffered in body and mind and our Lord supped with publicans and sinners. Are we to set ourselves up as better than He?'

'Nay! But…I have never done such a thing before.'

'I believe it. Poor lady!' He ran a finger up the other side of her face. 'And now you have to do your best to contend with such as I. Surely, something you must hate.'

Her spirits lifted. Due not only to his gentle touch but, also, because he had called her *poor lady*, which meant he had no suspicion of her real identity so she had not betrayed herself. 'I appreciate your taking care of me.'

'That is part of my task. A pleasant part, I might add.' His voice was soft as he took her hand and toyed with her fingers.

She was aware of pleasurable tremors shooting up her arm and thanked him for his words. He smiled and she returned his smile. In the sudden silence she caught the sound of waves slapping against the hull of the ship and was aware of restless movement, whilst at the same time she was conscious that his fingers were moving over her wrist. Suddenly his grip slackened and he gazed down at the scars that marred her flesh. 'What caused these?' His voice was sharp.

The remembrance caused the breath to catch in her throat and she looked away. 'I would rather not talk about it,' she whispered. 'Would you be so kind, Ma…Owain, as to fetch me a drink of water?'

He gazed at her intently and laid her hand down gently before abruptly leaving the cabin.

Kate's heart was racing and she pressed a hand against her ribs as if to slow it down, wishing that she could trust him enough to tell him about the scars. She remembered that night when Sir Roger and Friar Stephen had chained her by her wrists to the stone slab after placing her blindfolded in what had felt like a stone coffin during the day. She had been utterly confused as to why they had taken her prisoner. She had been naked. Her only protection from their eyes had been her long flaxen hair, so like her Lady's. At first she had wondered if somehow they had mistaken her for Lady Catherine but then the friar had whispered foul things in her ear and nicked her lobe with a thin blade so the blood ran down her neck. Then both men had questioned her about the whereabouts of a small chest bound with a leather strap. Of course, she had denied knowing anything about it; this had been after she had discovered her elderly father's involvement with Sir Roger. The knight and the friar had begun to discuss alchemy and their lack of success in changing base metal into gold. When they started to talk of black magic, calling up the devil and providing him with a sacrifice of an unblemished virgin in exchange for his help, her blood had run cold.

She could still remember the pain as the chains bit into her flesh in her struggle to escape, her terror at hearing the flint blade being sharpened on the stone. Then, praise God and all the saints, there had come a mist that had blinded and confounded her enemies. Its freezing dampness would have seeped into her very bones and killed her if she had not been freed by a man wearing a devilish mask. He had wrapped her in a cloak and carried her away. She had fainted with pain and fear, only to wake in her mother's house.

When she asked Beth how she had come there, her mother told her that she had been wakened by a knock on the door and found Kate on the step. During the days that followed she had hovered between life and death, muttering in her fever. Of her mother's husband there had been no sign but she remembered her Lady sitting by her side, holding her hand and praying for her recovery. When at last Kate began to recover she had wondered if she had imagined that figure in the devilish mask. Whether he had been real or not she had decided not to speak of him to anyone. After all he had saved her life. But she did tell her mother what had happened before her rescue and Beth had spoken of her husband's foolishness in being drawn into Sir Roger's devilish schemes; his once having believed him a true seeker of the old ways. The next day Lady Catherine had called, informing Kate that Sir Roger and Friar Stephen had departed to stay in the Palatine of Chester for a short time. Kate never discovered why she had been allowed to live. Because she had feared for her mother's and brother's lives, the only other person Kate had spoken to about what had happened was her Lady. For whatever reason she had thanked God and prayed for judgement to fall on those who had acted so cruelly.

She pushed down the blankets and swung her feet over the side of the bunk and stood up. She almost fell as the floor tilted and so she sat down again. Her mind straying to her conversation with Owain. She must be on her guard against that charm of his, for he would beguile her into telling him her secrets if she was not careful. She must dress. Her gaze took in the cramped cabin in one swift glance. There was nowhere to hang clothes, but she felt under the bunk and discovered there were drawers with brass handles.

She knelt on the floor, balancing herself by gripping the edge of the bunk with one hand. She managed to pull out a drawer. Inside were her mantilla, gown, pilgrim's tunic, sandals and scrip, as well as some male garments, a belt and sword, and a vellum-backed book, which she handled with reverence before returning it to its place next to a wooden box.

She donned her gown and tidied her hair. Once that was done, she sat, twiddling her thumbs, before curiosity took hold of her and, opening the drawer again, she removed the wooden box. It had a key in its lock and, turning it, she discovered a small chessboard with figures. She was delighted, thinking here was a way to pass the time on the voyage. She turned to the other drawer and found the food they had bought in La Coruña. Her eyes brightened and she took out an orange.

By the time Owain returned, bearing a tray, she was seated on her bunk, eating the last slice of fruit. 'I see you found your gown and sandals,' he said, placing the tray beside her.

'I see you play chess, Owain,' she responded.

He fixed her with a stare. 'I see you've been rummaging amongst my possessions.'

Her lips twitched. 'We both see a lot. But I take umbrage at your use of words. The box was clearly in sight and you had left the key in the lock. If you had minded my seeing its contents, you would have removed the key.'

Owain agreed, adding, 'And that reminds me that if

you are to pass as my wife then you had best wear my signet ring.'

She flushed and stared at him. 'I have not forgotten that I had taken on that role. I presume you do not already have a wife, Owain?'

'You presume rightly. I am a second son and, although I am my father's heir since my elder brother's death, I have two younger brothers so there was no haste for me to wed.' He sat the other side of the tray and eased the ring from the little finger of his right hand.

Kate could not help but be glad that he was not bound by the ties of matrimony. 'Surely you will want to marry someday, though?'

'Aye! Preferably a woman with the spirited yet loving nature of my grandmother. This ring belonged to my grandfather, but she had it melted down and made smaller to fit her. In old age her fingers shrunk and it kept slipping off so she gave it to me.' He took Kate's hand and slipped the ring on to the third finger of her left hand. It was heavy and a little loose, but some thread wrapped round the back of it would keep it in place. Its presence gave her a strange feeling. As if he had set his seal on her. 'You must remember to answer to Mistress ap Rowan whilst aboard ship,' he added.

'I will not forget, but you, too, must remember that us being man and wife is only a pretence and keep your distance, Master ap Rowan.' Nervously her tongue flicked over lips wet from eating the orange.

A muscle in Owain's throat moved and he wanted to catch her tongue between his teeth and then plunder her mouth. When he had held her last night and removed her gown he had wanted to continue cradling her delightfully soft body against his own and wished that she had not felt the need to remind him to behave honourably towards her now. 'There is no need to fear I will take advantage of you. Now I will leave you to eat whilst I reassure myself of Merlin's comfort. Sea travel does not agree with him and he is restless.'

Kate nodded in understanding, but, once the door closed behind him, her shoulders drooped and she sighed, realising she might enjoy his taking advantage of her, but, if she was not to be unmasked, she must ape Lady Catherine and behave as a lady aught.

Her eyes fell on the platter of food and the cup and she picked up the tray and placed it on her knee. She might as well make the most of the coddled eggs because unless they had hens aboard there would definitely be none tomorrow. The cup contained not water but what tasted like small-ale. It was not as good as that which the ale wife at Merebury brewed, but it quenched her thirst. She began to eat, wondering what lay ahead and hoping she could cope with the difficulties of forgetting she had once simply been Kate Fletcher and was now not only the Lady Catherine but also Mistress ap Rowan, wife of Master Owain ap Rowan.

Later she draped the mantilla over her hair and went up on deck. She leaned over the side of the ship, watching the cook haul up a barrel hung over the side and take out some salted beef. Oblivious to the stares of the mariners, she chose to ignore Owain's presence; he was standing on the poop deck, talking to the ship's master. She shifted her attention from the cook and, with a hand shading her eyes from the sun, gazed over the sea, wondering where they would make landfall after they crossed the Channel. If it was in the south—and in the light of the unrest in England—then it could be a mistake to quit his company too soon as she would need the protection of a man. In the meantime she would try to enjoy the voyage, praying that the winds would be fair and no sea monsters, enemy ships or pirates would impede their progress.

That evening Kate and Owain supped with the master and his mate on a salted beef, onion and bean stew seasoned with garlic and herbs. She drank little of the red wine that accompanied it and spoke even less. Afterwards she stayed on deck for a while watching the sun go down before making her way to the cabin whilst there was still some light in the sky. She said her prayers and then removed her gown before sliding beneath the blankets. Closing her eyes, she willed sleep to come quickly, but her mind was too active with all the happenings of the last two days. It hardly seemed possible that she had known Owain such a short time.

She was still awake when he entered the cabin a little later with a rush light in a pot; she feigned sleep, expecting him to make as little noise as possible, but he whistled between his teeth and when he spoke she jumped. 'It won't do, Lady Kate.'

She could make a pretence of sleep no longer, so asked him what wouldn't do.

'The master thinks you are dissatisfied with your quarters. Even that we have quarrelled about my arrangements. I had to make excuses for your behaviour.'

She was indignant. 'I have behaved with propriety.

What would you have me do, sir? Dog your footsteps and hang on to your arm and every word?'

'It would be a beginning. You are supposed to be my lady wife.'

'Most marriages are made for convenience, Master Owain. But perhaps you wish for a love match like Owain Twydr?' she mocked.

'You must call me Owain. I am surprised that you can jest about love, Kate. I am no dreamer and know there are plenty of marriages made in hell rather than in heaven...but outside this cabin I would that you would behave at least as if you had a fondness for my company. You play chess?'

'Aye,' she murmured. It was one of the pastimes she and her Lady had played to while away the winter evenings when confined to the house. Lady Catherine's father had taught them both.

'Then on the morrow, if the weather is fair, we will play on deck.' He blew out the light and the cabin was immediately pitched into darkness so that she could only hear him as he climbed into the upper bunk. She was aware of movement overhead and thought how he would have difficulty stretching out his long legs, poor man. She closed her eyes and found herself visualising him lying beside her on a bed of a size in which a marriage could comfortably be consummated. This will not do, she admonished herself, but still she could not help but imagine the feel of his lips against hers. Of course, there could never be anything between them once he discovered she had deceived him, but even so she could not prevent herself from dreaming that she was being rocked in his arms and he was calling her his sweeting, his fair Kate, his dearest, as she tumbled into a deep sleep.

Kate and Owain sat under an awning on the deck with the chessboard on a barrel between them. It was almost a week since they had left La Coruña and this was their tenth match. Perhaps if he had truly been her husband then she might not have been so determined to level the score, which stood at six-three. Also, she might have lightened the mood with chatter and so distracted him. She had tried that just the once and he had asked in that musical voice of his, *Is it that you'd like me to muffle you, sweet Kate?*

You wouldn't dare, dearest Owain! she'd retorted. He had given her such a sparkling look out of those blue eyes of his that she had wanted to laugh out loud. She really did enjoy playing games with him. She had not put it past him to gag her if she had provoked him further and make a merry game of it in front of the mariners. But after getting drunk that first night she was careful not to make the same mistake and was inclined to let him do most of the talking in company and that he did, speaking of his travels, of places, people and horses.

Sometimes, when they were alone, she would question him about different customs he had seen, of food, drink and clothing. One time she surprised him looking at her with a baffled expression in his eyes, but when he noticed her staring at him, he smiled and asked her whether she had done much riding on her manor? She had responded to his question by reminding him that Sir Roger had allowed her scarcely any freedom to wander outside the house so she had done very little.

Surprisingly he refrained from quizzing her about her whereabouts the day of Sir Roger's death. Even when they retired to the cabin for the night he did not touch on the subject and she was relieved by that.

She would have liked to ask him why his father had banned him from his home but, remembering his reaction the last time, she resisted. Instead she enquired after his mother, only to be told that she was dead.

'Are either of your younger brothers married?'

He shook his head. 'Father is in no rush for them to wed.'

'Then who orders the household for him?'

'My stepmother, Gwendolyn,' he said shortly. A shadow seemed to darken his eyes and he changed the subject by asking about her substitute brother.

Her heart sank. She was lost for words. He raised his eyebrows and his beautifully shaped mouth twisted in a wry smile. 'Surely you can't have forgotten him?'

She found her voice. 'Of course not. But it hurts me to talk about him. Do you not feel a similar reluctance when it comes to questions about your family?'

'Touché!' said Owain in a dry voice and fell silent.

The following morning they sat beside each other on the lower bunk as a sudden squall had sprung up and it was wet on deck. He offered to read to her from his English translation of the New Testament. An opportunity not to be missed, so she agreed eagerly. He read from St Paul's First Letter to the Corinthians, chapter thirteen, verse one, beginning with the words: *Though I speak with the tongues of men and of angels and hath not charity, I am become as a sounding brass or a tin-*

kling cymbal. It was a long piece, but Kate listened eagerly, soothed by his voice and the beautiful words. He ended by saying, *And now abideth faith, hope and charity; these three; but the greatest of these is charity.*

A hush fell over the cabin and then after a few minutes he said, 'What do you think St Paul is saying, Kate?'

She thought for a moment. 'He says much that I can't comprehend fully without giving it more thought, but I think he is saying that a person can do all kinds of good works and even give their body up to be burnt for the faith, but if they do not feel true charity…real love, that is…towards others, then their works are not acceptable to God,' she said softly. 'But feeling charitable towards certain folk is sometimes nigh impossible, which is why we need the Holy Ghost. Even then…' A frown puckered her brow. 'Do you not agree, Owain?'

He sighed heavily, closing the New Testament. 'Aye, I do. It is not easy to dig out the seed of hate once it is embedded in one's heart.'

They both fell silent.

Then Kate said tentatively, 'Surely the same could be said for love? Once it takes root…'

He stared at her and she felt her heart hammering in her breast, but then he turned away and replaced the New Testament in the drawer. He left the cabin and she wondered if she had annoyed him by talking of love in such a way. Yet he had spoken of love favourably on a couple of occasions. Was there a woman in his past whom he loved still? Perhaps her father had forced her to wed another because Owain had only been a second son and he had never been able to forget her. That thought caused Kate pain and she knew then that she was coming to care for him far more than was sensible.

She sighed, thinking that perhaps, when they reached England, she should definitely leave him and find other company in which to make her way north. She still had her pilgrim's garb and it should not be too difficult to find others to walk the way of the pilgrim with her.

She left the cabin and went up on deck. The weather had improved and she went over to Owain, who was gazing out over the sea, and suggested they play chess. He nodded and soon they were seated on deck with the board on a barrel between them.

Initially, Kate had made the mistake of expecting him to play with the same caution as Lady Catherine, but while he was a careful player, he did have flashes of recklessness, which had taken her by surprise and caused her to respond likewise. Then she began to realise that some of his moves were inspired to make her react without thinking.

He made his move and she viewed the board.

Owain watched her, his eyes warm with desire as they rested on the sweet swell of her breasts as she bent over the board. He could feel the sun's heat on the back of his neck and was glad when the sun went behind the clouds being tumbled across the sky by the strong breeze filling the large square sail at the centre of the ship. He knew he must control the strong urges inside him, but it was getting more difficult the more time he spent in her company. He must look away and did so, noting the second mast with its billowing sail set forward to the fo'c's'le was being whipped by the wind.

A much smaller sail was attached to the yards at the stern. Last even, according to the master, they had been making good time and if the wind stayed with them then they should reach the English Channel within the next few days. Suddenly he sniffed the air. 'The wind's changing,' he said.

'If you are trying to distract me, Owain, dearest, then it won't work,' said Kate sweetly, not looking up from the board.

He smiled and glanced towards the master standing on the poop deck, calling orders to his mariners. Owain decided he seemed to have everything under control and turned his attention back to Kate.

She smiled at him, believing she had him trapped. He returned her smile and then lowered his eyes to the board. For several minutes she watched him, taking in every nuance of his expression; her eyes lingered on his lips. He continued to stare at the board, and, with the slightest of sighs, she rolled her neck und shoulders and let her gaze wander. Eventually it came to rest on the horizon to starboard. After gazing over the open sea for so long, at first she thought her eyes were playing tricks on her. Yet surely that slight hump in the distance was land? She glanced towards the sun and realised that what Owain had said was true. The wind had veered and they were no longer travelling north-west, but north-east towards the coast of France.

'Owain,' she whispered.

'I know,' he said, sweeping the figures into the box before folding the board and placing it on top of them. He rose and headed across the deck in the direction of their cabin. She went after him, aware that the mariners were shouting to one another and pulling on ropes. 'Do you think the master will need to bring down the sails?' she panted, catching him up outside their cabin.

'Perhaps. But wind and tide could still sweep us towards France and in that case he might decide to make for the nearest port. Which means…' Owain's voice trailed off as he lifted down his saddle bags, which he kept at the foot of his bed.

She sat on hers. 'What are you doing?'

'What does it look like I'm doing?' He moved her feet and pulled out a drawer.

'You're packing.'

'Aye.' It did not take him long and then he fastened on his sword.

Her mouth went suddenly dry. 'You think there'll be a fight if we are blown towards France?'

He smiled grimly. 'I hope not. Much depends on how far north we are. If we can make Brittany that will suit me. The Duke of Brittany's alliance with the King of France is an uneasy one. The Bretons have always been an independent race and have traded with England for hundreds of years.'

'You believe they won't harm us?'

'I hope not. It depends.'

She thought about that *depends* and murmured, 'There are always those who will see easy pickings if a ship ends up in distress.'

He did not deny it, but threw his saddlebags over his shoulder and opened the cabin door, ushering her out. She followed him across the deck to where Merlin was tethered. He asked her to stay with the horse whilst he spoke to the master. She rested a hand on the animal's neck, willing herself to hold in check her dismay and the fear that she might never see her mother and Diccon again.

Owain was away only a short time; when he returned, he suggested she accompany him to the starboard side of the ship. 'What did the master have to say?' she asked.

'He hopes to maintain this distance and sail along the coast.'

'Whether he can do so depends on the wind, tide and currents here, I suppose,' she murmured, recalling a conversation between two mariners in Liverpool when she was a girl.

'Do you recall my telling you of the Celts who left their lands in the east?' said Owain in conversational tones.

'Aye.' She glanced into his strong, determined features and wondered why he spoke of that now.

'Some settled in Brittany. It, too, has its land of Finisterre.'

Her smile faded as she remembered the soaring cliffs and rocky coastline of Finisterre in Spain, and in her imagination she could picture the ship being smashed to pieces on rocks. 'Why do you say that?'

He hastened into speech. 'I thought it would be of interest to you. Do not fear. Brittany has many safe harbours and long stretches of beach, even small low-lying islands.'

His words achieved their aim, reassuring her. She remained at the side of the ship, gazing across the choppy surface of the water towards the coast. It was much closer now and she could make out the white spume being thrown into the air as waves crashed against rocks behind which cliffs soared to a hundred feet or more.

She had no idea how long they stood there in silence,

keeping an eye on the distance between the ship and the shore as they sailed north. Only once did they move away to sit on a barrel apiece when the cook brought them some onion soup and tankards of small ale. Then suddenly the sun disappeared and Kate shivered, looking up to see muddy-looking clouds gathering. Owain rose and, taking her hand, lifted her to her feet. He put both arms round her from behind and she leaned against him, grateful for his warmth, but did not allow herself to read what she wanted in his action, telling herself he was just playing a part. He suggested that she might like to go to the cabin, but she shook her head.

'I'll fetch you if the weather gets worse,' he assured her.

'Even so I'd rather stay here,' she said firmly.

Owain did not insist, but moved away to stand at the ship's side. 'I think the tide has turned. I can smell the land,' he said.

She followed him over. 'The landscape is changing. I can see sand hills and fields instead of cliffs. I think all will be well after all.'

Kate spoke too soon. Within the hour the sky darkened and the rain came sheeting down. Owain hurried her beneath the awning, but the deluge of water was too much for the canvas to contain and came cascading onto the deck. The master was shouting to his men. It was almost impossible to see ahead; everywhere was grey. Suddenly there was a sound that reminded Kate of waves crashing onto a shore. The next moment the ship shuddered and lurched to starboard. The sea came pouring in and within minutes Kate was up to her thighs in water. Filled with trepidation, she clung to Owain.

One of the mariners clawed his way up the sloping deck. He gazed over the side and then looked in the master's direction. 'We've hit a sandbank,' he shouted.

Kate glanced up at Owain and said in a trembling voice, 'I imagined us founding on rocks, but not a sandbank. Yet I've heard of more ships doing so whilst trying to navigate the channels in the Mersey estuary than have hit rocks.'

'Then you'll know this ship is doomed. It will not be able to right itself now the sea is flooding in,' he rasped. 'No doubt there'll be those ashore who will soon spot her and row out to see what they can salvage. My duty is to keep you safe. The crew must take care of themselves.'

'What do you suggest?' asked Kate.

'Will you trust me?' queried Owain.

She did not hesitate. 'Aye.'

He seized her hand and, by dint of clinging to various items, they managed to make their way over to Merlin, who was frantically trying to keep his footing on the sloping deck. Owain caught hold of his tossing head and whispered soothing words of comfort and encouragement as he saddled up. To Kate's relief the rain began to slacken and she watched the grey pall that hung over the sea start to lift as he helped her climb on to the horse and got up behind her.

She did not need telling to hold tightly, but clung to Merlin's mane as Owain bent, untied the reins looped about a beam of wood, and wrapped them around his wrist. Then he dug in his heels. The horse needed no further encouragement, but plunged into the sea.

Kate surfaced, choking on water and gasping for breath. She still clutched Merlin's mane and was aware of one of Owain's arms about her waist. She could only pray that the horse could carry them both to land. What with the swell it was extremely difficult to see in which direction the coast lay, but the horse was now swimming strongly. She wondered if he could smell the sweet scent of grass and whether that was acting like a lodestone, drawing him to shore.

She could feel Owain's chest against her back and was grateful for a share of his warmth. Already she could barely feel her toes, but his whispered words, 'Courage, my heart!' meant she was able to keep her fear of drowning under control. Whether the words were meant for her or the horse did not matter, she took them to her heart, knowing that endurance was what mattered at such a time. Every now and again she caught a glimpse of sand hills as the horse ploughed through the waves. Then she began to realise that Merlin was making heavy weather of swimming against the tide—and her nether regions were drenched. Would they be able to reach the shore before the horse's strength gave out?

Then Owain spoke against her ear. 'I'm going to swim the rest of the way. You stay with Merlin.'

He slipped into the sea and she felt bereft and colder, much colder. It could be that she would be warmer in the water out of the wind—and it would be better for the horse. Watching Owain swimming a short distance alongside Merlin gave her courage. Somehow she managed to release her hold on the horse's mane and she slipped into the sea beside him. There was a swoosh and water went up her nose and into her mouth. She forced her head up, coughing and spluttering, and then she was striking out towards the shore. She turned her face towards Owain, determined not to take her eyes from him, praying fervently that they would both manage to reach the shore. He shouted something to her, but she did not catch the words for the sound of the sea. Every now and again his head would disappear, but then she caught sight of his dark curls plastered against the side of his face and the sight gave her strength.

The horse was swimming strongly now and she kept her eye on him as much as she could, as well. By the time Merlin was scrabbling for a footing on the sandy bottom Kate was exhausted, and struggling to stay afloat. Yet she was aware that Owain was only a few feet away.

Forcing her eyes wide open, she saw the horse now on the shore. The next moment she was aware that Owain was upright in the water which reached his chest. With sluggish movements she forced herself to stretch out a hand to him. He seized it and drew her towards him. Her feet touched bottom and then, hand in hand, they waded out of the sea. In a tangle of arms and legs she and Owain collapsed on the sandy shore.

Chapter Five

Neither Owain nor Kate moved for a long time. Then she became aware of the beating of his heart against her ear and of the evening sun warming her back through her sodden clothing. She lifted her head and looked into his face. His eyes were closed and thick dark eyelashes fanned his olive skin. She was filled with such a sense of warmth and gratitude towards him that she could not resist stroking his lean cheek with the back of her hand.

Owain's eyelids lifted and he gazed at her. The expression in his eyes set her nerves tingling as she stared at him in frozen awareness. She wondered if he could feel the shudder of the heavy strokes of her heartbeat through their clothing.

His mouth eased into a smile and he reached up and cupped her face between his hands. 'What is it?' he asked, stroking her cheeks gently. There was such tenderness in that gesture that a lump rose in her throat and tears filled her eyes. 'My poor Kate, what a time of it you're having. I never thought you would be able to swim. Brave girl. Thank God, that in His mercy He has decreed that our lives on this earth are still of some use to Him, so there is no need to weep.'

So intense were her emotions she could only nod. But there were other ways of showing how she felt than speaking and, before she could have second thoughts, she pressed her lips against his. She never expected such an explosive reaction. Both his arms went round her and he brought her hard against him without breaking off the kiss. His mouth appeared to be about to devour hers as he forced her lips apart and his tongue licked rapidly along the rim of her inner lip before dallying with the tip of her tongue.

Her initial sense of shock quickly turned to pleasure and she dared to allow her tongue to return his salute. The low groan he gave echoed down her throat and roused a trembling response. Then he rolled her over in the sand so that he was on top of her. A wave lapped against her feet and vaguely she thought that perhaps they should move further up the beach. Then sensible thought fled as she experienced another of those devouring kisses. She surrendered herself utterly to the pleasure of being in his arms, giving no thought to discomfort or danger. Never had she experienced such feelings. Their kisses seemed to go on forever, deepening and slackening, so that every now and again she thought they were going to come to an end, but it was only so they could catch their breath.

Dear God in Heaven, how he wanted her, thought Owain, rolling over in the sand with her again. Maid or mistress?—echoed and re-echoed inside his head. His erection was such that she must be conscious of it. Yet as he gazed up into her face he saw no sign of revulsion; her lips were swollen from his kisses and her face was soft with desire. He dared to caress the outline of a nipple through the damp, ruined fabric of her gown.

A sigh escaped her and she caught his hand and pressed it over her breast. He marvelled that, without a word, she had given him permission to go a little further. He could not deny himself so began to undo the fastenings of her gown with hasty fingers, then unlaced the bodice of her kirtle until her breasts fell into his hands like ripe apples. He brought one rosy peak to his lips and caressed it lightly with his tongue.

A low moan of pleasure issued between her lips, which caused him to pause for thought. Would a lady, married to Sir Roger, known for her piety, express such delight in the sins of the flesh? His other hand wandered down her back before lifting her skirts, He stroked the soft rounded curves of her buttocks. She pressed down hard against him and he groaned inwardly, wondering if she knew what she was doing to him as they rolled over in the sand again. She tempted him and he longed to see her body revealed in all its glorious nakedness.

Kate looked up at him and knew from the smouldering desire on his face that he wanted to couple with her. How did one think sensibly at such a time? The fact that she could rouse such longing within him made her feel more alive than she had ever done before and power swelled inside her—despite knowing that, if she surrendered to him then, it could be her downfall. When she had first bled from her secret place, her mother had explained that she would be cursed in such a way every month—unless a man got her with child. She had explained how that happened and it came as little surprise to Kate—for hadn't she seen animals mating in the fields and noticed that young resulted from such an act? Yet never had she believed that coupling could be preceded by such urges and pleasure that bowled one along so there seemed to be no stopping until they were satisfied.

Owain lowered his head and caressed one rosy peak of her breast with his tongue before suckling, and setting her afire again. She was lost. Her body cried out for him. A tiny part of her mind was aware of the waves on the shore washing over their feet, the cry of the seabirds, the rattle of tiny pebbles and rocks shifting underfoot, of Merlin cropping the grass somewhere behind them, but she no longer felt part of that world. With Owain she was creating a different one that belonged solely to them.

Owain moved her slightly further up the beach away from the water's edge. With her compliance he eased her gown and kirtle down over her hips until she lay without even a kerchief for modesty's sake. For several seconds he hesitated, recalling the moment she had let slip the word *brother* and he had begun to suspect she was not the Lady Catherine. Her reluctance to lay the blame for Sir Roger's death on the Fletchers had, also, deepened his suspicion. Then she had drunk too much and asked him to call her Kate. Also, there were those scars on her wrists. She was a puzzle to him because most of the time she played the lady extremely well. He hated to think that she might be a woman of Gwendolyn's ilk. Whatever the truth about Kate, he was in something of a quandary because he desperately wanted her.

'Why do you hesitate?' she whispered, breaking into his thoughts, and, reaching up a hand, she brought his face down to hers. He tossed caution to the winds, despite knowing that Sir Thomas might give him cause to regret his actions one day, and removed his wet clothing.

Kate devoured him with her eyes, feeling no shame as she took in every aspect of his manhood. It was obvious to her that God had made male and female to fit neatly together. He dropped beside her on the sand, his gaze washing over her comely figure before coming to rest on her face. 'You are lovely. Are you willing that this happen, Lady Catherine?' His voice was deep and husky.

She wished he had not addressed her so. Instantly guilt surged hot and strong inside her, forcing the truth past her dry throat to emerge as a whisper. 'I'm not the Lady Catherine.'

His blue eyes darkened and a muscle tightened about his jaw. He half opened his mouth, only to close it again as there came the clamour of voices. He acted swiftly, reaching for her gown and throwing it to her. Then he lunged for his sword, only to have second thoughts when a woman shrieked. Instead, he picked up his breeches and covered his manhood. *'Pardonez-moi, madame!'* he said easily, sweeping her a bow as if it was nothing to him to have been caught in a state of undress.

Kate knew she could not carry off the situation with such aplomb. Her blush reached from her scalp to her toes and she could do no more than kneel on the sand, shielding her nakedness from the eyes of the men. Owain was responding to whatever they were saying with such *savoir-faire* that she was spellbound. What had passed before was thrust aside as she tried to make sense of what he was saying. She could understand little and wondered if he was speaking in the local *patois* of the Bretons. He was interrupted several times and obviously had to repeat himself. At last he turned to Kate and said, 'They're fisher farmers. They're offering us shelter for the night and the chance to dry our garments.'

'Can we trust them?'

'I deem we have no choice as we're outnumbered,' he said grimly. 'They know about the ship founding. I told them we are only recently wed, so naturally, I was concerned you would catch a fever after being in the sea…and that is why we removed our wet clothing.'

How quick-witted he is, she thought in admiration and told him so. He scowled and told her to get some clothes on.

Kate felt the blood rush to her cheeks. 'Can you order the men to look away?'

But there was no need for him to do so because they were already making their way back to their village through the low-lying sand hills. The old woman, though, stood, watching them, a simpering expression on her face. Kate turned her back and, not bothering with her kirtle, dragged on her damp gown with some difficulty. It was ruined and she could have wept. But uppermost in her thoughts was what Owain had made of her confession. Perhaps the sound of the men coming had drowned out her words. The expression on his face might have been caused by frustration. He had been so close to making her his. Her heart was heavy with trepidation, concerning what he might do next. How could they ever resume the relationship they had shared before they had reached these shores?

She could not tell from his behaviour what he was thinking. He helped her up on to Merlin's back, but did not himself bother mounting. Instead, he led the horse in the wake of the old woman shuffling on ahead. They came to a huddle of buildings that clustered about a small inlet, both noticing that several boats were putting out to sea. Watched by a number of younger women, they were welcomed inside the largest of the wood, stone and earth-built houses by the old woman.

Downstairs consisted of a large space divided by a couple of steps. The upper part was obviously the living area for the human inhabitants, whilst the lower was for the animals when the weather was bad. Kate presumed the ladder in a corner led to a sleeping loft. A fire burned on a stone hearth, over which a blackened pot simmered. The pungent smell of fish and seaweed permeated the air.

Owain was taking no chances of having Merlin stolen by leaving him outside to crop the grass, but unsaddled and settled him in the far end of the room. He reached into the saddlebags and dragged out Kate's pilgrim garb. The tunic was damp, but not so badly affected by the sea as the gown she wore. His change of clothing was in a similar condition and he pulled that forth, too. He was trying to put off the moment when he would have to decide what to do about Kate's confession. She had wanted him as much as he had wanted her, so why had she chosen that moment to tell him the truth? Was it that at heart she was an honest maid?

What had she thought to gain by playing him false in the first place? She must have known as soon as they reached Merebury that she would be recognized, so was she planning to escape from him before they arrived at the manor? Did that mean she was guilty of the murder of Sir Roger? The answer to that and other questions must wait. He made the decision to behave as if he had not heard those few whispered words until he could give it more thought.

He handed the homespun tunic to Kate. 'It's somewhat damp, but no doubt it will be more comfortable than that which you wear now.'

In a stiff voice she thanked him, appeared about to say something more, but then changed her mind and looked about her for a place to remove her sodden garment and put on the tunic. The woman met her gaze and, nodding her head and giggling, she took Kate's arm and dragged her to the ladder in the corner of the room and pointed upwards.

Kate climbed into the loft, dimly lit by the rays of the dying sun that shone through the open shutters. The space was sparsely furnished with just a large bed and a roughly hewn chest on bare boards. She felt the mattress and it rustled. Straw! There were no sheets, just a couple of homespun blankets.

She changed quickly, aware of the scrabble of mice in the rafters. The woollen material itched, but at least she felt warmer. She climbed down the ladder, her ruined gown over one arm, to find Owain standing in front of the fire wearing hose and doublet. The latter was short, whilst the former fitted so snugly that, remembering how he had looked naked, her body felt hot. She wondered if he would broach the subject of her confession. He motioned her over and she joined him by the fire, where a cat sat cleaning itself. Only then did she notice his sodden garments spread over a bench in front of the blaze. Without speaking, he made room for her gown next to his clothing.

The woman signalled Kate to sit at the table. She ladled soup into a bowl and set it in front of her. Owain sat opposite her and helped himself to bread. Kate dipped her spoon into the creamy fish soup and forced herself to make conversation. 'Is it Breton you spoke to her?'

'Aye! An Irish friend taught me some of the language. It's a mixture of French and Gaelic.'

'It's good to understand other tongues.'

'I learnt because of necessity.' He smiled.

Relieved by that smile, she said, 'Have you found out where we are?'

He poured cider into cups. 'If we head north-east, we'll eventually reach the English Channel.' He handed a cup to her and drank deeply from his own.

She gulped down the cider, glad to slake her thirst. Only when the cup was empty did she say, 'By boat or by land?'

'By land.'

'How long will that take?'

He shrugged broad shoulders and topped up their drinking vessels. 'I can't say for sure.'

She moistened her lips, still slightly swollen from his kisses. 'Will it be dangerous?'

The muscular fingers holding the spoon halfway to his mouth stilled as his blue eyes fastened on her lips.

He cleared his throat before saying, 'Are you afeared, my Lady? You, who travelled with but an old woman, a maid and a lad hundreds of miles to Spain across land and water?'

Kate flushed a fiery red. Was he mocking her or was he sincere? Did his words mean that he had not heard her confession and truly believed her the Lady Catherine? She could only pray it was so and answered his question. 'When I set out I prayed to our Lord, the Holy Mother and the saints that they would protect us.'

He smiled grimly. 'And now there is but you alone of your group left alive, do you doubt that protection?'

She lowered her eyes to her food. 'I sinned and had no sense of shame today.' Her voice quivered.

'Were you not a sinner before, hence your reason for going on pilgrimage? Or is it that you regard our actions as more sinful than the murder of Sir Roger?'

The spoon slipped through her fingers into the remains of the soup, causing liquid to splatter over her hand. To her amazement he reached out and brought her fingers to his mouth and sucked them clean.

She wrenched her hand out of his grasp. 'I have told you that I did not kill him,' she said vehemently.

'Aye, but you do not always speak the truth.'

She whispered in a stricken voice, 'What do you mean?'

'You did not repulse my advances and that causes me to wonder whether you had a lover, who was prepared to rid you of your husband?' Kate thought of her Lady, who would have taken the veil rather than have a lover. 'You have no answer for me?' asked Owain.

'I am innocent of your accusations. Sir Roger preferred other beds to mine,' she retorted, unable to conceal her distaste. 'I am still a maid.'

Owain's hand curled into a fist. 'I have heard such about him and I crave your pardon for upsetting you.' His tone was gentle. 'We will drop the matter of his murder until we reach England. I would ask you one more question…did you make a will before leaving England?'

She stiffened. 'A will?'

A sharp laugh escaped him. 'You sound surprised. Yet surely making your wishes known as to how you want your property disposed of after your death is a wise thing to do when setting out on such a perilous journey?'

He must have visited the rector of Walton and discovered Lady Catherine had deposited her will with him, thought Kate, feeling on dangerous ground. If that was so, then he would know that the Lady had left her manor to her, and, in the event of Kate's death, her mother, Beth. Although little good it would do either of them with Sir Thomas Stanley in charge of Merebury.

Kate sighed, 'I see no point in this conversation, Master ap Rowan. You see me before you, so why speak of such a will?'

'Curiosity, Kate. But I'll speak no more on this matter now. If you have finished your supper, no doubt you'd like to go to bed. You must be weary.'

'Aye! But…' His usage of her shortened name made her feel that everything had shifted again. Were they back to where they had been on the ship? If so, who was she pretending to be now? She licked her lips. 'Where do we sleep?' she croaked.

His deep blue eyes held hers. 'They believe us newly wed,' he said softly, 'so it should not surprise you that the crone has offered us the bed in the loft. No need to look apprehensive, Lady Kate. No doubt what happened earlier was due to a need to warm our chilled bodies, as well as the joy of finding ourselves still alive.'

Is that what he really thought? She doubted it and said in a mocking voice, 'I will remember your words next time I find myself in danger of dying of the cold, Master ap Rowan.' She rose and with a *Bon nuit!* to the crone she made her way to the ladder and climbed up into the loft.

She lay on the bed, still wearing the homespun tunic. The mattress rustled beneath her, making a sound similar to the wind blowing through the rushes on the edge of the great mere. Such a yearning for home, her mother and her brother swept over her that tears filled her eyes. Would she ever see them and Merebury again? She buried her head in her arms and wept until exhausted. Yet despite being weary to the bone, she remained awake, reliving those moments on the beach. Was it just lust she felt for Owain ap Rowan or was it love?

When she heard Owain climbing the ladder, she decided to pretend to be asleep. Yet her ears were alert to every sound he made. He did not approach the bed and, after a short while, she opened her eyes to see where he was. Through the open shutters she could see a full moon sailing in the sky. By its light she was able to make out Owain lying on the bare boards with but a single blanket for his comfort. She felt compassion for him, remembering how he had taken such care of her. But before she could speak, there came the sound of scampering tiny feet. She stifled a scream by burying her head beneath the blankets.

'Scared of a mouse, Kate?' Owain's voice sounded loud.

'Aye. It could have fleas and they bite.' Her voice was muffled as she still had her head beneath the covers.

'Doubtless it's more scared of you than you are of it and will keep its distance.'

'That is something I've told myself many times, but to my shame I still wish there was a cat up here,' she wailed.

'You would have me fetch the cat from downstairs?' There was a smile in his voice.

'Nay. You might disturb the old woman and I would not have that. If only I could sleep, then I would not care about mice.'

'Are you uncomfortable? Or is it the moonlight keeping you awake? Perhaps you'd like me to close the shutters.'

Her head popped out from beneath the blankets and she saw him making his way over to the window, fully dressed. How sensible, she thought wryly even as she called, 'Leave them open. I don't like the dark.'

He turned and stared in the direction of the bed. 'It is an understandable fear. But why does the dark scare you?'

She sat up, hugging her knees and setting the straw in the mattress rustling. 'Too many tales of ghosts and ghouls told on a winter's evening.'

'I remember hearing many a tale of hell's demons and the little people intent on mischief told by my father. Couple that with sleeping in a room that is pitch black and it is easy to imagine danger lurking in every corner.'

'You understand,' she marvelled.

'Aye.' He came over and sat on the bed. 'Poor Kate. I would ease your fear.'

Her heart leapt, for he was so close she could see the gleam of his eyes. 'In what way?' she stammered.

'You tell me.'

She hesitated and heat suffused her body. 'If you give me your word of honour…not to—to touch me… then you could share this bed.'

'I accept,' he said with alacrity. 'This floor is damnably hard and I give you my word of honour that I will not lose my head as I did on the shore, my lady.'

Relief should have been the uppermost emotion caused by those words and yet…

Without more ado he climbed into bed, causing the straw mattress to rustle. She resisted the urge to slip her arm about him and instead turned her back on him. A smile feathered the corners of her mouth as she closed her eyes. Somewhere a mouse scrabbled, but it no longer bothered her and she allowed her weariness to have its way and drifted into sleep.

Owain lay awake, his sword close at hand and a dagger under the pillow. So far all was well, but he had not survived so long by not being aware of the ploys people could trick travellers with. The old woman and her fisher son could truly be honest and generous folk in providing him and Kate with food and shelter. Yet he had no intention of being caught off guard as he had on the beach. He knew the men could have killed them both if that had been their intention. Even so, who was to say that they would not change their mind when the boats returned. He did not want his throat slit while he slept and Kate raped. As soon as she was asleep, he intended keeping a watch at the window. Perhaps, too, it would be best if they slipped out of the house before dawn. He would leave coin on the table for the hospitality they had received.

The straw rustled and the soft swell of Kate's buttocks nudged up against him and, despite the rough homespun separating their bare flesh, he was aroused. He supposed he should have expected to discover fire in a Stanley bastard. There were two questions he would like answers to. One was whether her mother had told her that she was Sir Thomas's cousin, Sir Arthur Stanley's daughter; the other, was did she know the contents of Lady Catherine's will? Her natural father had died six months ago, but she would not know of that. For the time being, he intended keeping quiet about it. But did she know whether the death of the man she believed to be her father was an accident or murder? It had been passed off as an accident, and yet…

He needed to solve the mystery of Sir Roger's death. To find a culprit who would satisfy Sir Thomas and the King—if he was to regain his wits—so as to bring this whole affair to a satisfactory conclusion. Could the Comte d'Azay with his Welsh aristocratic connections be the guilty party? The thought of him roused memories he would rather forget. Yet he had a task to complete so must put personal feeling aside. And needing to think clearly, he was best removing himself from Kate's bed. With great reluctance he did so.

* * *

Kate woke and for a moment she could not think where she was until the sound of rustling straw caused her to reach out cautiously to the space beside her. But there was no one there. For a moment she feared that Owain had deserted her, then she heard her name being whispered and forced her eyes open. In the pearly light that preceded dawn, she could make out his face a few inches from hers.

'You must get up,' he said in a low voice.

'Why? Has something happened?' She threw back the blanket and at the same time noticed he had donned the homespun tunic he had worn when she had first set eyes on him.

'Nay. But I'm not taking any chances. I want to be away from here before folk are stirring.'

'Do you know the way? And why are you dressed so?'

'Towards the sunrise is as good a direction as any. And two pilgrims might travel more safely through Normandy than ordinary travellers. Now hurry. I've packed your gown, although it is so stiff and stained with saltwater that I question whether you'll ever be able to wear it again.'

'It is a great pity,' she stated sadly.

He agreed, but added that she must hurry.

They descended the ladder and were able to make out the hump of the old woman curled up in a blanket, asleep on the floor in the grey light. Presumably her son had not come home last night. Holding her breath, Kate tiptoed across the room in Owain's wake. He had already saddled Merlin and attached the saddlebags. He signalled to her to open the front door. It squeaked, and the crone muttered in her sleep, but did not waken. In seconds they were outside and he hoisted himself up into the saddle before reaching down a hand and swinging Kate up behind him. The salty tang of the sea filled their nostrils. Streaks of silver and apricot flamed the eastern sky and somewhere a cockerel crowed.

Kate took a firm hold on the back of Owain's belt as he dug his knees into the horse's flanks. There was the clatter of hooves and they were away. A shutter was flung back and a woman's voice cried out, but they had left the village behind. The road they took was of beaten earth with deep ruts made by cartwheels; yesterday's storm had softened the soil and there were puddles here and there, making the ground treacherous in places. Owain kept Merlin's speed in check for safety's sake, so that they travelled at little more than a trot at first. Suddenly the sun burst over the horizon, dazzling them, so that for a moment the horse seemed to check before continuing along the road.

They stopped to buy food and wine at a village in sight of Mont St Michel and ate and drank sitting by a river, where Merlin could crop the grass and drink his fill. They spoke little as both were still weary and had much on their minds. Then they took to the road again, still heading east.

The sun grew hot and Kate's head drooped and she would have dozed if she had not been conscious of the danger of falling from the horse. They passed through wooded forest and fortunately all was silent. Eventually they left the trees without having encountered any trouble. They came to a crossroads where Owain frowned and hesitated before deciding on the left fork.

They travelled some way before stopping briefly in order for Merlin to rest again and drink from a stream. There they stretched their legs and Kate would have asked where they were heading, but was put off by Owain's louring expression. Something was obviously bothering him, but she refrained from giving voice to her curiosity and concern.

They continued their journey at little more than a walking pace through a landscape marked by granite outcrops, waterfalls and copses. The sun began to sink in the west and Kate was weary to the bone. She told herself that at least the air was cooler now. At last they came to a river tumbling down a hillside, on which sprawled a town and looming over all was a castle.

'Do you know this place?' murmured Kate as the horse made its weary way beneath a gateway set between towering walls.

'Aye! It is Mortain, I was here with my brother shortly before he was killed.' His voice was so grim, she refrained from asking any more questions.

As they made their way through narrow, winding streets, she felt as if they were being watched and reminded herself Normandy was now under the rule of the King of France. Owain informed her that they would seek shelter at the Cistercian lodging house. She sagged with relief, thinking that there they should be safe—after all, they still had their scallop badges and signed pilgrim passports to open such doors for them. It proved so. They were shown to the guest house. The food provided was simple but nourishing, washed down with the local cider. After attending compline they were allotted single cells.

Kate had difficulty sleeping on the narrow, hard bed.

She was stiff and sore from having spent the day on horseback and dreaded the morrow. Her thoughts darted hither and thither, but uppermost in her mind was why Owain had come to this place if it held such sad memories for him? How had his brother died? Perhaps there had been a battle between the French and English. Could he have been taken prisoner and perished in the castle's dungeon? Maybe Owain might be persuaded to talk about it once they were on the road again.

She drifted into an uncomfortable sleep and heard the bell in the middle of the night calling the monks to prayer, but was too exhausted to leave her cell.

It was not until the bell rang for matins that she roused herself and made her way to the chapel. There she looked for Owain, but could not see him. As she prayed and listened to the plainchant of the monks, she began to worry over his whereabouts. Perhaps he had heard her confession after all and decided to escort her to this place and then leave her? Panic gripped her. Then she told herself firmly that Owain was not the kind of man to do that. He had shown her kindness and cared about her safety. Besides, whether he believed her to be the Lady Catherine or Kate Fletcher, he still wanted answers from her.

She made her way to the refectory, but when the simple meal came to an end, there was still no sign of Owain.

Chapter Six

Kate hurried across the stable yard, hoping to find Owain with Merlin. But when she reached the stables, it was to discover that the horse was missing. She enquired of the lay monk in French as to whether he had seen Owain or his horse that morning. He told her that he had only just come on duty and seen neither horse nor man. Her spirits sank, remembering Owain's dour expression last even. Could his brother's death have aught to do with his absence? Or was it possible Owain had been recognised by an enemy and been spirited away, killed and his horse stolen? For a moment she despaired. Then she pulled herself together, knowing she must not allow her imagination to run away with her. Owain's absence must be reported to the abbot and hopefully he would instigate a search.

Immediately she set out for the abbot's quarters, only to be hailed by Owain as she crossed the courtyard. Her head turned and she saw him approaching on Merlin. Relief surged through her, but that emotion soon turned to anger. 'Where have you been? What were you thinking of going off without a word to me?'

'There was no need to worry about me, sweeting,' he murmured. 'And keep your voice down if you're going to speak in English.'

His just rebuke following on the tail of the endearment caused her cheeks to flame. 'I am not your sweeting,' she hissed. 'Besides, I wasn't worried about you, but myself. I did not fancy walking all the way to the Channel. Where have you been?'

'Hunting.'

'Hunting?' She stared at him in disbelief.

'I thought a nice juicy fox wouldn't go amiss, and they are in abundance round here.' His voice was light.

'A—a fox? You jest.'

He winked. She opened her mouth to ask him what he meant, but he placed a finger against his lips, silencing her. 'Are you ready to continue our journey? If we are to make Caen before they close the gates for the night, we must set out immediately.'

'Caen. We're going to Caen?' she asked in surprise.

'*Doucement, ma chérie,*' he murmured against her ear as he stopped by the mounting block. 'Come, I'll take you up before me so that if you tire then you'll be able to rest against me.'

Kate was not sure if being held against him was such a good idea in the circumstances. But as she had no choice in the matter, she climbed on to the block and accepted his help to mount the horse. She winced as she tried to make herself comfortable, felt his arms brush her sides, causing her pulses to quicken. Then he clicked his tongue and dug his heels into the horse's flanks. 'Let's put as much distance as we can between us and this place,' he breathed against her cheek.

* * *

It was not until they had left the town and its brooding castle behind that she asked him what he had meant by hunting a fox. He did not answer directly, but instead asked, 'The Comte d'Azay has foxy red hair, does he not?'

Kate stiffened. 'Are you saying he is the fox you talk of and that he lives here in Mortain?'

'Not Mortain. But he has kin living close by. In '48 I encountered Sir Roger and the Comte at the castle at Domfront.'

She drew in her breath with a hiss. 'My la—' She changed what she had been about to say swiftly. 'My *lord* husband and he seemed to have much to talk about extremely late into the night. Please tell me why you were there with your brother?'

'The nobleman who lives at Domfront is a horse breeder and dealer. Martin and I were delivering a couple of horses for his breeding stock. We were asked to stay several days, as is customary, to make sure that all was well with the horses.' He paused. 'What I didn't know until I arrived was that Friar Stephen, the uncle of my stepmother Gwendolyn, would be there. In truth, I didn't even know she had an uncle at the time, nor did I know he was involved in the black arts. Within a couple of years, though, I was to discover that our meeting was to lead him to my stepmother. He was also to become acquainted with the priest who served the manor at Nether Alderley in the Palatine of Chester, where kinsmen of Sir Thomas Stanley hold sway.'

'I should have known the Stanleys would come into this somewhere,' she said tartly. She felt his harsh breath stir the mantilla, tied like a veil about her head and neck. Glancing up, she noticed the lines of strain about his eyes and mouth. 'I beg your pardon. Pray, go on,' she urged.

He nodded tersely. 'I can only remember snatches of what took place. At first the talk was all of horses and my brother's skill in handling them. Martin had such a gift that Sir Roger even accused him of using magic. I could see my brother was angered and hurt by such talk from a man he had spoken of with admiration at first. After we had dined the conversation veered into darker channels; black magic and demons and whether the Comte's ancestor had been possessed of the devil.'

Kate gasped. 'I can see why Sir Roger would be interested in such talk…but why should they think that of the Comte's ancestor?'

'His wickedness was legendary in an age when cruelty was commonplace. He once starved three hundred prisoners to death during Lent and there were plenty of other examples of his disregard for human life. He's reputed to have imprisoned his wife after she had given birth and gouged out the eyes of his own godson because he hated the boy's father!'

Kate cried out in distress, 'Such wickedness.'

'Aye. But Sir Roger suggested he must have doubted the paternity of his lady's child. That perhaps his godson's father had bedded his wife due to his spending so much time away with his men in Wales.'

Kate's eyes widened in amazement. 'Was Sir Roger in his cups?'

'Certainly, he behaved recklessly. He was asked to leave for making such a slur on the legitimacy of the

Comte's forebears. He was annoyed and asked that Martin and myself accompany him. My brother and I refused. Three days later, when we departed, we were set upon. Our attackers seemed intent on separating us. I was knocked unconscious and left for dead. If I had not been found by a monk on his way to Mortain, who put me on his mule and took me to the apothecary, most likely I would have died.'

'And your brother?' whispered Kate.

Owain said in a grim voice, 'He was found several days later, still alive but having been cruelly used. I will not describe the unspeakable injuries he suffered—to a lady. He died the next day.'

Kate placed a hand on Owain's hand that held the reins. 'How terrible. You must have blamed the Comte and his kinsmen for your brother's death.' Her eyes were dark with anxiety. 'Owain, I understand your wish not to allow your brother's death to go unpunished, but if you have now killed that fox, the Comte, then your life could be forfeit. Should we not be travelling with more speed so you can escape?'

'My dear Kate, I appreciate your concern.' Owain's voice was warm. 'But I have not killed the Comte d'Azay—he is not at Domfront. I visited the grave of my brother, who is buried in the churchyard of Notre-Dame sur l'Eau nearby.'

Her brow puckered in bemusement. 'So you came only to visit your brother's grave.'

'Nay. I wanted to see if the Comte was here. Apparently he had visited, but left for Angers several weeks ago. It would be interesting to know why he visits the capital of Anjou.' He smiled. 'Now you know almost

as much as I do about the man, so we will leave the subject alone and move on to another matter—how came
you by those scars on your wrists, Kate?'

Her mind was still partly occupied with what he had
just told her, so, instead of putting him off, she said,
'They planned to sacrifice me.'

He stilled. 'Was that up by the old stones?' She was
silent. 'You might as well tell me all, if justice is to be
done,' added Owain persuasively.

She cleared her throat. 'Aye. I was fortunate. God
sent a mist…as well as a rescuer. He was dressed in a
devilish fashion, but he was flesh and blood.'

He said casually, 'Have you any notion who he was?'

She shook her head. 'And I would not tell you if I did.'

'You think this devilish figure killed Sir Roger?'

She shrugged. 'Perhaps. It happened only a couple
of months before his death. But as I know not his identity, it seemed pointless speaking of him to anyone but
my—' She stopped abruptly.

'Your?'

'It doesn't matter. It can make no difference now.'

'So you don't fear for his life?'

'I imagine him to be a man well able to take care of
himself. I never saw him again and can only believe he
left Merebury after achieving his aim.'

After that exchange they were silent, absorbed by
their thoughts.

They stopped once or twice to refresh themselves
from a stream and to stretch their legs before continuing the journey northwards. Having slept badly, Kate
dozed off only waking when Owain shook her gently

and told her that the towers of the white-walled donjon at Caen were in sight. As they approached the city, he pointed out the great Abbaye-aux-Dames, which had been founded by William the Conqueror's wife, Matilde. 'There outside the city walls is her tomb,' informed Owain, 'whilst the Conqueror's bones lay in the abbey he founded in the city.'

'It is a strange thing that they chose to lie separate in death,' murmured Kate. He agreed. She changed the subject, 'Will we be staying the night at the pilgrims' hostel?'

He shook his head. 'I am hoping to find my friend, Master Nat Milburn, at his kinswoman's house. If he is here, then it's possible he has a rendezvous with one of his ships, sailing for Yorkshire. If that is so, then I am certain he will take us aboard.'

Kate's weary face brightened. 'That would be fortunate indeed…but this kinswoman you speak of, will she be able to offer us shelter?'

'Most likely.' He fell silent.

As the sun sank in the west, they crossed a bridge spanning the River Orne, which was guarded by the fort of St Pierre. Soon they wended their way between tall houses with steep tiled roofs. At last Owain brought Merlin to a halt. He dismounted and lifted Kate down. He set her on her feet and then had to place an arm round her as she stumbled.

Before he could bang the wrought-iron knocker on the front door, it opened and on the threshold stood a giant of a man, tawny haired and pleasant of face. He stared at them in surprise, but then his grey eyes brightened. 'Owain. I hoped to see you here, but did not really expect it.'

Owain's face broke into a relieved smile. 'I was hoping to see you as I'm in need of your help.'

'Just say the word.' Nat clapped him on the back before turning to Kate and scrutinising her from top to toe. 'Who is this?'

Kate had no illusion about her appearance and wished the ground would open up and swallow her. She darted an anguished look at Owain. 'I think you have met before, Nat, but she would have looked very different then. This is the Lady Catherine Miles,' he responded instantly with a smile. 'Be kind to her, Nat, because she has suffered much.'

'I beg the Lady's pardon…but must ask what happened to the gown I sold you for her?'

Owain said ruefully, 'Alas, it was ruined. We were shipwrecked and barely escaped with our lives.'

Nat's eyebrows shot up. 'God's blood, Owain! I can't wait to hear your tale.' He beamed down at Kate.

She held out a hand, which was immediately enveloped in a large, warm grasp. 'I am pleased to make your acquaintance again, Lady Catherine.' He gave her another of those intense stares. 'I don't suppose you remember us meeting at my aunt's house in Liverpool? You were much younger then and accompanied by your serving woman and her children.'

Kate's face, already flushed by the sun, deepened in colour. Of course, she remembered him now! Thank God, he had taken little notice of Kate Fletcher…but she seemed to recall his giving her mother more than one glance. 'Of course, I remember now. I had forgotten your name.'

'What of the family, who accompanied you? The Fletchers?' He still held her hand.

'Dead,' she said starkly.

'I'm sorry to hear that,' said Nat.

Owain pressed her shoulder gently. 'Perhaps you can continue this conversation indoors. The Lady is weary. Is Marguerite within? If she cannot provide us with shelter, then we'll need to seek elsewhere.'

'Once she knows Owain ap Rowan is here, she'll insist on your staying,' said Nat confidently. 'But putting her aside, I needs must tell you that you are in for a surprise as your brothers are here in Caen.'

Owain's dark brows shot up and his hand tightened on Merlin's reins. 'My brothers?'

'Aye. I told them I'd met you in Spain and had hopes of seeing you here. They've gone with one of the stable lads to deliver a couple of yearling colts to some lord or other and to show him their paces.' He clapped Owain on the shoulder again. 'Now hurry. Since I told Marguerite of our meeting in Spain, she has talked of nobody else but you.'

Aware of Kate's eyes on him, Owain muttered something incomprehensible and turned away. An irritated Kate wondered how well he knew this Marguerite. She had an urge to follow him to the stables and demand an answer. Instead, she was ushered into the house by Master Milburn but once inside, she asked about his kinswoman.

'She is a widow with a small son and her husband has left her and the boy well endowed.'

'But what is Owain to her?' she demanded.

Nat smiled down at Kate from his great height. 'You

have become fond of my young friend whilst thrown in his company, Lady Catherine?'

She was taken aback by the question and felt the colour rise in her cheeks. Then she remembered that she wore his ring. 'Aye. We have a fondness for the other. Have you not noticed I wear his signet ring, Master Milburn?'

Nat gaped. 'By God's blood and the Holy Trinity, I had not.' His eyes fixed on the hand she held out to him. 'I didn't think he would act so speedily. Marguerite will not best be pleased.'

Kate's eyes sparkled and she tilted her chin. 'Why should your kinswoman be displeased that I wear Master ap Rowan's ring? Maybe she has a fancy for a young hot-blooded suitor. Methinks I should go to the stables and suggest to him that we stay at the pilgrims' hostel,' she said angrily.

'Nay, nay. Forget what I said. Perhaps she will not notice the ring if you do not flaunt it,' he whispered, sounding embarrassed.

She raised her eyebrows, but decided that silence was probably the best course to take now.

Nat ushered Kate into a well-appointed parlour where a log fire provided a welcome blaze. A woman, dressed in grey and mauve, sat on a cushioned chair, with a child on her lap. She stared at Kate from large, protuberant eyes and rattled off some words to Nat in French.

He answered in English. 'It is the Lady Catherine whom Owain was seeking in Spain. He will be with you presently.'

'She does not look like a lady nor does she smell like

one,' said Marguerite in broken English, wrinkling her nose. 'She stinks of horse.'

Kate's control over her temper was already precarious, but she managed to hold on to it and explain in French the reason why she was dressed so simply and stank of horse.

Marguerite held a kerchief to her nose. 'I comprehend. Master Milburn told me that you were on a pilgrimage to Santiago de Compostela and that you, too, are a widow.'

'That is true,' lied Kate.

'Have you children, Lady Catherine?'

'I do not,' she replied, startled by the question.

'I have a son,' stated Marguerite with a great deal of satisfaction. 'A man needs to have sons.'

'I would not deny it,' said Kate politely, irritated by her manner.

'Where is Owain? Why is he not here now?' asked Marguerite, turning to Nat.

Kate answered for him. 'He is stabling his horse. Surely you know how he puts his steed before his own welfare?'

Marguerite frowned. 'I do not like what you say. You mention only one horse? What of the family that accompanied you on pilgrimage? Where are they?'

'Dead. My horse was stolen crossing the mountains by brigands…and the family was killed.'

Marguerite looked put out. 'You have no chaperon—no maid with you?'

Kate drew herself up to her full height and said in honeyed tones, 'I have already explained, madame. They were murdered by brigands. Fortunately Master

ap Rowan came in search of me and I thank the Trinity
and all the saints that he found me. I do not know what
would have happened to me, otherwise. He has taken
great care of me.'

Marguerite scowled at her before turning to Nat and
speaking rapidly in French. Kate understood very little
of their conversation and her opinion that the woman
was rude remained unchanged. Suddenly she heard the
door open behind her and saw Marguerite's expression
change. 'Owain, *mon cher*! It ees so good to see you!'

'*Bon soir*, Marguerite,' said Owain, glancing briefly
at Kate's stony profile as he crossed the floor. He took
the hand Marguerite offered and raised it to his lips.
'My condolences on the loss of your husband,' he said
in French.

'*Merci!*' She fluttered her eyelashes at him in what
Kate considered a ridiculous manner. 'It seems so long
since I have seen you, *mon cher*, but I have never forgotten you.'

'Yet you wed another,' he said drily.

'Ahhh! But you had only dreams to offer. But times
have changed and life has proved the decision I made
was sensible. My husband has left me and the boy well
provided for…and with no stipulation in his will about
my giving up the portion he left me if I remarry. This
time I can choose my own husband.'

It was obvious to Kate what was behind her words
and she was impatient to hear Owain's response. She
prayed he would speak in English.

He did. 'I congratulate you. But now I pray that you
will extend your hospitality to the Lady Catherine
Miles. No doubt Nat has told you that the Lady is wid-

owed and has just accomplished a pilgrimage to the shrine of St James. But I wager he has not told you that I was commissioned by the King of England, himself, to seek her out and bring her home.'

Kate smiled, satisfied. Those words would certainly give Marguerite something to think about.

'The King of England, himself?' Marguerite looked impressed. Obviously Nat Milburn had not told her that Henry VI of England had lost his wits. 'Lady Catherine tells me that you have travelled alone without maid or chaperon, *mon cher*.' The Frenchwoman placed a podgy hand on Owain's sleeve. 'This does not please me, Owain.'

He raised his dark brows. 'There were companions on the way, Marguerite, but then we were shipwrecked and barely escaped with our lives.' He glanced at Kate. 'An unforgettable experience, wouldn't you agree?'

She marvelled at his audacity and felt quite breathless as his eyes met hers. 'We will spare her the details, Master ap Rowan,' she riposted.

'Of course.'

Nat said, 'No doubt it was a terrifying experience.'

'Terrifying,' agreed Owain, the corner of his mouth twitching.

Kate wanted to laugh and had to bite hard on her lip to stop it quivering. Hastily, Nat said, 'You're both lucky to be alive. What with the King of England taking an interest in your well-being, Lady Catherine, Owain's life could have been forfeit if he returned to England without you.'

'But Owain does not have to return to England,' said Marguerite firmly. 'The Lady could travel with you, Nat, or his brothers.'

Kate darted a look at Owain to see how he responded to that suggestion. 'Ahhh, but, *ma chérie*, I am honour bound to see that she is safely delivered into the King's hands, but that does not mean I will not return to France some time in the future.' Swiftly, he changed the subject. 'Tell me, have you seen much of my brothers whilst they've been in Caen?'

She did not reply immediately, but continued to stare at him. 'You will give me your word that you will return?'

His black brows drew together. 'You doubt me, Marguerite, after what we once were to each other?'

'No, but...' She shrugged her plump shoulders. 'Your brothers...I was happy to provide them with hospitality, but they do not have the understanding of my language that you do. No doubt they will have much to say to you—especially about the Lady.' She flashed Kate a look of disdain. 'You will wish to refresh yourself and change your garments, Lady Catherine. I will show you to a bedchamber, where there are several gowns that belonged to my husband's dead sister.' She turned to Owain. 'You, too, will wish to refresh yourself before supper.'

He kissed her hand. 'You have my undying gratitude for your kindness to myself and the Lady.'

'I want more than gratitude before you leave, *mon cher* Owain!' she said, her eyes narrowing as she tapped him on the cheek.

Kate wanted to slap her. She did not want to believe Owain could be tempted by all that the Frenchwoman had to offer—her dead husband's fortune, a house and proof that she was fertile.

Marguerite rang a bell and a maid entered. She handed her son to the girl and rising from her seat, moved gracefully towards Kate. '*Bienvenue*, Lady Catherine.' She took up a candlestick and, with an imperious gesture, indicated that Kate follow her.

Marguerite led the way to a landing on the first floor and then up another flight of stairs. Here, she showed Kate into a bedchamber. By the musty smell that hung in the air, it was obviously not often used. Simply furnished with an unmade, narrow bed, chest and a couple of hanging poles, it was not what an English lady was used to. Marguerite placed the candlestick on the chest and left her alone.

Glad to be relieved of her presence, Kate went over to the window. Despite it being evening, the room beneath the eaves was stifling. She struggled to open the shutters and, after a few minutes, managed to prise them apart. A cool breeze wafted into the room. She gazed down through the gloom on to a stable yard. Suddenly she noticed Nat Milburn and Owain with their heads together. What were they discussing? She was tempted to call down to them, *See where that woman has put me*. But that would hardly be seemly.

After a few moments she moved away from the window and shifted the candle in its holder from the chest to the floor so as to open the chest. She breathed in the sweet scent of faded lavender and reached inside. Her hands found several blankets and she lifted them out before delving deeper into the chest. She discovered a couple of plain gowns, a chemise and a full-skirted corset with a tight-fitting laced bodice. She poked a finger through a hole in one of the gowns. Obviously the moths had made inroads into the garments despite the lavender. They must have been here for some time.

Was she supposed to wear one of these gowns?

Kate flung the garments on the bed and sat down, wincing as she did so, and gazed about her. Was this the only bedchamber available, due to Master Milburn and Owain's brothers' presence? Or was Marguerite deliberately insulting her? Where had she put Owain? Most likely as far away from this chamber as possible. She sat there for a while, absently twisting his signet ring round her finger. A blush warmed her cheeks, remembering the expression in his eyes when he had spoken of them being shipwrecked.

A knock on the door interrupted her thoughts and she called, *'Entrez!'*

A young girl entered, carrying a bowl and a pitcher of steaming water. Over her arm hung a drying cloth. She smiled nervously. *'Excusez-moi, madame. Votre eau.'*

Kate smiled with relief, thinking that at least she could make her toilet. She took the bowl from the maid and placed it on the chest before filling it with water from the pitcher. The girl placed the cloth on the bed along with a tablet of soap. *'Merci,'* said Kate, and would have ushered her from the chamber, so desperate was she to rid herself of the perspiration and dust of the journey. The maid pointed at the bed and exclaimed, *'Le lit?'*

'Plus tard,' responded Kate, ushering her out of the room and closing the door on her. She undressed and washed not only her face and body but her hair, as well.

Then she rubbed herself dry until her skin tingled and her hair was merely damp. She turned to the garments she had removed from the chest.

What would Owain think if he saw her clad in any of these? She mourned the beautiful gown ruined by seawater. With a slight pucker between her fair brows, she reached for the corset. At least the holes in this would not show and it did not smell of horse. She pulled it over her newly washed body and laced up the bodice before picking up a gown of russet homespun and dragged it over the corset. Through the various moth holes, glimpses of the cream-coloured corset showed, but both garments fitted snugly so that they clung to her shapely figure. She smiled, considering that perhaps she might start a new fashion. Picking up her mantilla, she draped it over her hair and round her neck. Then, taking several deep breaths, she left the bedchamber.

She entered the hall, which was bright with many candles, to find Marguerite and the two men already seated. Her efforts were rewarded when she saw the startled expression on their faces as they stood up. She smiled at Owain, whom she presumed was wearing garments lent to him by Nat Milburn, and looked good enough to eat. She remembered the tangy salty taste of his skin beneath her tongue and her insides melted. She prayed that her feelings did not show in her face.

'Where did you get those garments?' Owain demanded, coming over to her.

'They were all I could find in the chest in my bedchamber. Perhaps holes will become fashionable. What think you, Master Milburn?' She turned to Nat with a smile.

He was looking genuinely horrified. 'I could have given you another of the gowns meant for my sister if—' He did not finish his sentence because Marguerite interrupted his words with a stream of French.

Kate glanced at Owain with raised eyebrows. After a few moments he said quietly, 'She says it is the maid's fault. She was supposed to have brought you fresh garments from her own *armoire*. She begs your pardon and says the girl will be whipped.'

Kate knew she lied, but decided that there was little point in saying so. 'I accept her apology, but I don't want the maid whipped.'

'Do you wish me to ask her to have a gown taken to your bedchamber and we will wait while you change?' asked Owain.

Kate shook her head. 'It is on the top floor and I would not delay your meal.' With a proud tilt of her chin, she led the way over to the table.

Owain murmured against her ear. 'Nat thinks we are betrothed. Congratulations, Kate.'

She flushed and said in a low voice, 'I did not say we were betrothed. Did you not explain to him why I wear your ring?'

Before he could answer, Marguerite bade him to sit beside her. Nat sat the other side of her and Kate was placed next to him. Her stomach had been rumbling for the last hour, and she had to restrain herself from pouncing on the food set on the table. There were cheeses, pickled fish and slices of ham, as well as crusty bread and a jug of cider. She thought of her Lady and ate with decorum. Yet it was but a short time before the cider set her senses swimming and she had difficulty concentrating on the conversation. She was so sleepy that her eyes refused to stay open. Owain spoke to her, but his voice seemed far away. Then she was being lifted and carried, was barely aware of the pettish feminine voice calling shrilly. She did not like its tone and buried her head against his broad chest.

She stirred only when he placed her on the bed and managed to force her eyelids open. Unexpectedly the remembrance of the last time he had put her to bed the worse for drink surfaced. 'You do not have to disturb yourself further, Master ap Rowan. I can manage myself,' she said, slurring her words.

'Are you sure, little sweeting?' His words seemed to mock her.

She blinked at him through the darkness and fumbled for his face. She grasped it between her hands and sought his mouth. For a moment he did not respond, but then she felt a change in him and the pressure of his mouth against hers hardened. Her lips parted beneath his, allowing his tongue to caress the inside of her mouth as he crushed her against him. She clung to him as if her life depended on it. Who knew what might have happened next if Marguerite had not spoken outside the door? For another moment Owain's mouth held hers and then he drew away and bid her goodnight.

The door clicked shut behind him. A delicious warmth wrapped about her as she curled up on the bed, dreamily thinking about what had just taken place. Without doubt she knew her feeling for Owain was love and she fell asleep with a smile on her lips.

* * *

The sun was streaming into the bedchamber through the open window when Kate was wakened by the sound of men's voices. They were speaking in English and it took her a few moments to realise their identity.

'What is it to be, Owain? Do you sail for Chester with us on the morrow and tell our father the truth about his whore of a wife or do you sail with Nat Milburn?' demanded a deep voice.

Hearing the word *Chester*, Kate sat up in bed.

'Why do you persist in believing that Father will believe anything I have to say?' asked Owain, sounding exasperated.

'But she is carrying a child and we know she has played him false,' said a younger, excitable voice.

'Then take your proof to him,' said Owain firmly.

'We have tried, but she has bewitched him. He accuses us of being jealous of her. Only you can break her spell, Owain, only you are strong enough to face Gwendolyn,' said that same excitable voice.

Gwendolyn, thought Kate. Was not that the name of his stepmother?

'Gwendolyn is no witch,' said Owain emphatically. 'She has cast no spell over Father, except that of her beauty.'

'She would have him disinherit you and give all to the child she carries. A child, we believe, begat by that Comte d'Azay on another of his visits to Father's manor in November. Don't you care about that either, Owain?' asked that deep voice.

Kate shot over to the window at the mention of the Comte.

'Of course I care,' said Owain. 'Do you know if he was staying at Nether Alderley when you left home?'

'We've no idea. He comes and goes…as does that uncle of hers, who's bleeding Father dry.'

There was a brief silence before Owain said, 'I will think on what you say. Now hush your mouths.'

'Nat Milburn told us that you mean to marry the Lady to gain her manor, so you can breed your own stock. If that is so, then you must believe her innocent of her husband's murder?' said the excitable one.

'Nat Milburn needs to guard his tongue. What else did he tell you?' Owain's voice had dropped, so a trembling Kate had to strain her ears to hear what was said next.

'That King Henry has promised her and her manor to the man who finds not only her husband's murderer, but returns his money to him.'

Kate gasped and pressed both hands to her mouth.

'The situation is far more complicated than you can ever know,' rasped Owain. 'And as the King has lost his wits, we waste time speaking of the matter. Now I'm hungry so I'm going indoors. You must say nothing of this to the Lady.'

'Lovely, is she, Owain?' asked the excitable voice.

'You'll see for yourself. Now, when does the *Saint Werburgh* sail? Even if I don't go with you, I'll come and see you off.'

'First light tomorrow morning, but we need to be aboard this evening.'

Kate heard their footsteps coming towards the house. She leaned against the wall, so shocked that she could not move. At least now she knew there was more to

Owain's search for Lady Catherine than he had told her.
She had been mistaken in him. He was just as greedy
to possess Merebury as Sir Thomas.

Chapter Seven

A miserable Kate decided she must leave the house straight away. She thought deeply about what to do as she donned her homespun tunic. She still had her scallop badge and pilgrim passport and hopefully would be able to beg a staff from the hostel in the city, having left hers in Spain. Her eyes filled with tears as she gazed at Owain's ring. Then she wrenched it from her fingers and placed it on the chest.

She went down the back stairs, past the kitchen and into the yard. She hurried out into the street and made her way to the quays, hoping to find the ship mentioned by Owain's brothers.

It was busy down by the quayside with ships being loaded and unloaded and merchants and mariners standing in groups talking. Fortunately, it did not take her long to discover where the *St Werburgh* was moored. She noted the flag of a white horse on a green-and-white background fluttering from one of its smaller masts and stood in the shade of a warehouse, watching barrels, baskets and packets being carried aboard. After a while she decided she had seen enough and made her way to the Abbaye-aux-Dames and spent time in confession and prayer, not only for the good of her soul, but also that of her Lady.

Her heart was heavy, knowing that she still loved Owain. She imagined his anger when he discovered her missing, and prayed that she would be able to avoid him if he came seeking her. But perhaps Marguerite would ensure that did not happen, if she was intent on having Owain for a husband, she thought bitterly. For a moment she remembered the sweetness of his kisses and the thrill of being held safe in his strong embrace. Then she told herself that she must stop thinking of him and concentrate all her efforts on being reunited with her mother and Diccon.

Yet, as she went in search of the hostel, she could not help wondering how differently matters might have turned out, if he had heard her confess she was not the Lady Catherine. But as he, obviously, still believed her to be that lady, she must adhere to her plan. When evening came she would make her way to the quays again. Once there, she would smuggle herself on board the *St Werburgh*. Naturally, she could not escape discovery once the ship was at sea, but hopefully the brothers would take pity on a pilgrim, and let her stay with the ship until it tied up at Chester.

A moon flittered fitfully through the scudding clouds, reflecting off the surface of the water. Kate darted out of the shadows and across a street, into the lee of a warehouse, overlooking the river. There she paused to catch her breath, gazing in dismay at the ship rocking at anchor a little way out; a lantern was tied to the top of its main mast and a flag with a horse on a white-and-green background fluttered from one of the smaller masts. She could see the dark outline of two men and hear the murmur of their voices. Her spirits plummeted even further. Earlier that day the ship had been moored at the quayside and mariners had carried goods aboard, simply by walking up a gangplank. Why had they moved the ship?

A light puff of salt-laden air fluttered a strand of golden hair before it settled on her forehead. Her teeth worried her lip as she debated what to do. The distance from the quay to the ship was not great, but if she attempted to swim it she might be seen, but still she must try. Aware of the raucous laughter coming from a nearby tavern, she waited for the moon to go behind a cloud before making her way to the quayside.

There she paused because the night was black as pitch in the shadows. The moon reappeared and she scurried along the waterfront, darting a glance every now and again in the direction of the tavern. Frowning, she realised that if she managed to reach the ship then she was going to have difficulty dragging herself aboard. To climb up from a small boat might be easier. She would have to wait until those frequenting the tavern had settled for the night, though, if she was to steal a boat. She retraced her steps and almost immediately realised she would have been wiser staying where she was, because she had been spotted by one of the mariners outside the tavern, who was weaving his way swiftly towards her.

She ran. The moon went behind a cloud again and

plunged the quayside into darkness. Frightened of falling into the river, she changed direction and headed towards the warehouses, hoping to hide in their shadow. But the mariner had been joined by his drinking companions and her escape route was now cut off; they were obviously looking for sport. She had no illusions what they would do to her if they realised she was a woman.

Her hand tightened on the staff, given to her by a nun, and she swung it in an arc in front of her; only for it to be grabbed by one of the men. He pulled hard, catapulting her against him. A scream was jolted out of her and she kicked the man in the shins. He would have wrenched the staff from her, but she sank her teeth into his hand. He yelped and stepped back and she brought up her staff and whacked him across the head with it. He staggered, cursing her.

She was seized from behind and rough hands grabbed her breasts. 'What have we here? A nice little pilgrim,' sneered a voice as she was lifted off her feet.

She dropped her staff and dug her fingernails into the back of the man's wrists and raked his skin. He swore and, loosening his grip, aimed a blow at her. She felt her ear stinging and flung her head backwards and heard him groan as her skull made contact with his nose. Then suddenly she was free and immediately she bent to pick up a staff. As she did so, out of the corner of her eye she saw two men running towards her and her heart sank. Then a voice she recognised commanded her to get out of the way.

She felt quite indignant at his ordering her around, but as that moment her assailants decided that escape seemed a better option when faced by two men armed with swords, they fled.

She leant against a wall, taking deep breaths, staring at Owain and his companion. 'Who'd have believed a lady could be so good in a fight, Owain?' She recognised the voice this time as belonging to one of the brothers in the stable yard.

Breathing heavily, Owain gazed down at her as he leaned on his sword. 'Little fool, don't you ever learn?' he said in a harsh whisper. 'If I had not been keeping a watch out for you, they could have done for you.'

'What are you doing here? How did you know I'd be here?' she demanded.

'But of a surety I guessed. Where else would you go if you needed a ship to take you home?'

'Then—then why did your brothers make it d-difficult for me by moving the ship?' she retorted crossly.

He raised his eyebrows. 'You'd have them make it easy for an enemy to sneak aboard after dark?'

'Nay, but if you knew I would come, then you could have watched for an enemy,' she snapped.

'Hadn't we better bring this debate to an end, Owain?' said his brother. 'Before those two rouse the rest of their shipmates. Let's aboard and be on our way.'

Kate looked questioningly at Owain.

'This is Davy, who's persuaded me to go home and see my father.' He grabbed her by the shoulders and brought her against him to whisper in her ear, 'You could have saved us both a lot of anxiety if you'd thought to speak to me before running away, Mistress Fletcher.'

He did not give her time to recover from the effect of his words, but frogmarched her along the quay and down steps into a rowing boat. Her heart was beating so heavily in her breast, she thought she might swoon. So he had heard her on the beach in Brittany... Then why had he continued to treat her as if she was the Lady Catherine? Was it because he believed he could trick her into making a slip, believing she had killed Sir Roger? At that moment it was the only reason she could think of for his deception. She kept her eyes averted from his face as the boatman took the oars. Soon Davy was hailing the *St Werburgh* and she saw a rope ladder being lowered.

Once aboard, no time was wasted in lifting the anchor and setting sail. Soon the *St Werburgh* was drifting silently along the river. Owain escorted Kate to a cabin and left her there without a word. She sank onto her knees on the floor, gripping the wooden rim of the lower bunk, and thanked God and the saints for her deliverance from the hands of the mariners. Her emotions were in turmoil, but she could not help but be glad that the pretence was over. She finishing praying and climbed into the lower bunk and fell into an exhausted sleep.

Owain stood on deck, drinking cider and watching the bank slide by. What was Kate thinking of at that moment? He had left her alone because he didn't trust himself, wanting to give her a spanking for worrying him so. When he had entered the house after speaking to his brothers in the yard, he had not been too concerned when she was not at breakfast. But then the maid had appeared and told them that the Lady Catherine was not in her bedchamber and that she had found a ring on the chest. He had snatched it from her, recognising it as his own.

Despite Marguerite's shrill protests he had shot upstairs. As soon as he had spotted the open shutters at her bedroom window, he guessed she had overheard the conversation between himself and his brothers. The extent of his fear for her safety had shaken him to the depths of his being. He had known he had wanted her, but had not realised how Kate, the woman, had wormed her way into his heart. She was loyal, quick-witted, courageous and uncomplaining; the words must have angered and frightened her into running away from him. He sighed. Well, he would talk to her in the morning when they had both calmed down and explain his plans and pray that she would be willing to help him.

He drained his tankard and moved from the side of the ship to greet the helmsman. Then he made his way across the deck to where his horse was quartered. Merlin snickered a welcome. Owain spoke to him softly, stroking his neck. He decided that as there was plenty of straw he would sleep here beneath the stars. As he made himself comfortable, he thought about the Kate who had responded to his lovemaking, and how she might have enjoyed sharing the straw with him and gazing up at the stars. But the Kate who believed he only wanted Lady Catherine for Merebury would repulse him. No doubt she would remind him that she was just plain Kate Fletcher when he told her that he needed her to continue in the role of Lady Catherine for the foreseeable future. He was praying that his betrothal to a Lady might soften his father's heart towards him and the breach between them could be healed. Hopefully, his reason would be strong enough for her to agree.

* * *

Kate gazed out over the shimmering surface of the English Channel, resisting looking at Owain, whose elbow pressed against hers as they stood at the side of the ship. 'I'm sorry if you were upset by my brothers' thoughtless words, Kate.' His voice was low.

She gasped. 'It is your behaviour I find reprehensible, Master ap Rowan. But I suppose you're neither better nor worse than other men out to make their way in the world. Besides, I deceived you, so in truth, I have no right to complain. But before you ask why I pretended to be Lady Catherine, may I ask you why you allowed me to continue with my deception when you knew I was Kate Fletcher?'

'If you recall…we were in rather a predicament at the time.' His amused blue eyes met hers.

She flushed. 'Even so there were other opportunities for you to speak out.'

He cocked an eyebrow. 'I could say the same about you, Kate. Perhaps we should admit that it suited us both to carry on with the deception. And, aye, I would like to know the reason why you pretended to be the Lady in the first place.'

'My reason was plain and simple: I believed you would treat me with respect if I stepped into my Lady's shoes.'

'You do me a discourtesy, Kate,' he said mournfully. 'I would have treated Kate Fletcher just the same.'

Her colour deepened and she toyed with her fingers. 'How was I to know that? But now I'm wondering if you already had your doubts about me before I blurted out the truth.'

'I have to confess that I did.'

'Before, or after, you wanted to lay the blame for Sir Roger's murder on the Fletchers?'

'From the moment you mentioned your brother.'

She sighed. 'It was a stupid slip…and most likely gave you cause to believe me guilty of Sir Roger's murder.'

'I doubt you are capable of cold-blooded murder,' he said softly. 'But I was informed that you and your mother are wise in herb lore. Do you know of a plant that could kill and show no sign of what caused death? Be honest with me, Kate.'

Should she trust him? After the barest of hesitations, she nodded, 'Yew berries. The poison contained within them is slow working. Mixed with some other fruit, stewed and sweetened and served in a tart, Sir Roger could have eaten his fill, entered his chamber, locked the door and died an hour or so later.'

Owain stared at her thoughtfully. 'It could have been so, but it does not explain the look of horror on his face.'

Perhaps as he was dying he had a vision of his devilish master coming to claim him,' she said lightly.

Owain smiled faintly. 'Maybe he saw your rescuer.'

Kate shook her head. 'How could he have left the chamber when the door was locked from the inside?'

'He did not have to be inside the room. A ladder. A face at the window,' suggested Owain.

'He'd be taking a great risk in daylight.'

Owain decided to change the subject. 'I would ask of you a boon.'

His words surprised her. 'A boon?'

He gazed at her intently. 'My brothers have no idea of your true identity. They believe I am betrothed to the Lady Catherine. I want you to continue in that role.'

'Why do you ask this of me?' she demanded, unable to tear her gaze away from his. 'They must know I ran away from you.'

'I told them I had been less than honest with you. That you believed our betrothal to be a love match and were deeply hurt when you overheard them mention my plans for Merebury.'

'They—they believed you?'

He took one of her hands. 'They trust me. That is why they want me to return home and speak with my father. You heard what they said about my stepmother, Gwendolyn?'

'She cuckolded your father by taking the Comte as her lover…and is trying to oust you from your position as his heir so her child can inherit. How did they meet?'

He shrugged. 'I do not know exactly.'

'Why should she do this?'

'My father killed her sire, but she did not realise it at the time. Her uncle discovered the truth and determined to have his revenge on my father for his brother's death. Friar Stephen is not your normal holy man. First he knew that he needed to drive a wedge between me and my father. Gwendolyn did this by convincing him that I schemed to kill Martin and had my eye on her.'

'How could he believe you would kill your own brother?' She was shocked.

'She is a beautiful woman. Her uncle told Gwendolyn that he could see my envy and dark heart during that meeting in France and then to back up his foul claim he introduced her to Sir Roger and he colluded with him to lay the blame on me. Of course I did not have all this information at my last meeting with my father. I thought that if I presented you to him as the lady I am going to marry and you told him of the kind of man Sir Roger was, then he might soften towards me and the breach between us could be healed.'

'I understand.' She was thinking it was too much to hope for that he might love Kate Fletcher and wish to marry her.

'But—' She stopped abruptly, knowing she needed to consider carefully before agreeing to what he asked. The fact that he was toying with her fingers did not make it any the easier for her to concentrate. 'If the Comte d'Azay or Friar Stephen were to see me, they would know me for who I am,' she said slowly.

'Then we'll have to make sure that doesn't happen.'

Suddenly she was distracted by a wayward thought. 'Perhaps you wish to return home so you can revenge your brother's death by killing the Comte?'

Owain stared at her before raising her hand to his lips and kissing each of her fingers. 'I never said I believed him to be responsible for my brother's death, sweet Kate. But perhaps we can prove he and that wily friar guilty of other crimes. Wouldn't you enjoy helping me to bring them to justice?'

'Aye, but…' Another thought struck her. 'You haven't asked me what happened to Lady Catherine.'

'I believe she is dead, otherwise you would not have stepped into her shoes.'

Kate's eyes were suddenly moist. 'She died of fever and exhaustion. She is buried in the graveyard at Villa-franca.'

'But your mother and brother are alive? Otherwise you would surely not have leapt to their defence.'

Kate lowered her eyes and withdrew her hand from his grasp. 'I will trust you so far, Master ap Rowan, but no further,' she said with dignity.

He frowned. 'They know something that causes them to go in fear of their lives?'

She gripped the side of the ship with trembling hands. 'You ask too many questions.'

'That is the task to which I have been appointed by Sir Thomas,' he countered. Her reaction to his questions convinced him that her mother and brother were indeed alive.

The mention of that knight immediately brought a scowl to her face and, without another word, she walked away.

Owain watched her go, torn between frustration and desire. Even in the pilgrim tunic he found her appealing. Her hips swayed seductively, causing his loins to react to what he saw. He remembered the gift that Nat had handed to him before he left Marguerite's house. Hopefully when he gave it to her she might agree to his proposal.

Kate sat on the bunk. Why had he had to remind her that he was in the pay of a Stanley? She might have done what he asked if he had kept silent about that family. Although… She glanced down at herself. What a fine lady she made dressed in a smelly, homespun tunic, forsooth. What must his brothers think of her dressed so? What had one of them said? *Lovely is she, Owain?* And what had he said? *You'll see for yourself.* She determined to keep to her cabin until the ship arrived at Chester.

* * *

But that was not to be. An hour or so later, Owain brought her a gown of midnight blue, without sides. It was to be worn over a fine wool kirtle of the palest blue; the latter was designed to fit snugly from shoulder to hip. Her pleasure was immediate and she could not conceal her feelings as she fingered the fabrics. 'I appreciate your gift, but I deem you were not given these garments by Master Milburn's kinswoman?'

Owain grimaced. 'Her rudeness embarrassed us both.'

'Yet you kissed her hand and, from what she said, you were once fond of her.'

'I am no saint. There have been women in my life…but what I felt for Marguerite died when she plighted her troth to another man.' He smiled faintly. 'I'll leave you to dress…and if you would agree to wear this, too?' He took his signet ring from his pocket and held it out to her.

She made no move to take it. 'A betrothal is a serious matter, Master ap Rowan. It was different when we pretended to be married whilst travelling amongst strangers. But to deceive your brothers and others…what reason will you give when the time comes to end it?'

'Allow me to worry about that, Kate.' Reaching out for her left hand, he slipped the ring upon her third finger. Then he brushed his lips against hers before leaving the cabin.

She ran the tip of a finger where his lips had touched so tantalisingly briefly. He had left her wanting more…and perhaps she would not have to wait long be-

fore he kissed her again. After all, love making was part
of the game they played. Removing her soiled garments, she donned the new ones. The woollen fabric of
the kirtle was warm and soft against her skin, but, most
importantly, it did not smell. She shrugged on the gown,
which fell in folds to her ankles. Her spirits rose until
she noticed her shabby sandals and pulled a face. She
was also in need of a headdress and veil, but knew she
would have to make do with the mantilla Owain had
given to her. Not for the first time she wished for a looking glass, but, as there wasn't one available, she was
dependent once again on Owain's reactions to her appearance.

She went up on deck. The catch in his breath and the
desire in his eyes told her more than she could have
asked. Which made it imperative that she put a guard
on her feelings for him. 'You look very much the lady,'
he murmured against her cheek as she went and stood
next to him.

'I've had some practice.'

He laughed and suggested they resume their games
of chess. She decided to stop worrying about the future
and to make the most of the present. Although, due to
the presence of his brothers, it would be different from
the last time they had sailed together.

Hal, the youngest of the three brothers, who was as
fair as Owain was dark, came to watch them play. Several times she caught him looking at her with a curious
expression on his freckled face. But, as soon as he realised that she had noticed him staring, his eyes would
light up in a mischievous, boyish smile. She could not
help but be amused.

* * *

A few days later when Owain was in deep conversation with Davy, Kate was gazing across the sea to where she could make out the south coast of England, Hal came and stood next to her. 'When you and Owain are married, do you think you could persuade him to allow me to live with you?' The question took her unawares and for a moment she was at a loss how to reply. Then she murmured, 'That will surely be up to Owain. You're not happy at home?'

'Not since Father married that witch, Gwendolyn.'

Kate remembered his words back in Caen. 'Witch?'

'She has cast a spell on Father, and he can see no wrong in her, whilst all the time she deceives him. Owain is the only one who can deal with her.'

'Why is that?'

'The blood of seers runs in our family and he has inherited the gift. Because of that she fears him and accused him of deeds most foul.'

His words surprised her. 'Owain is a seer?'

He nodded his head vigorously. 'He would deny it, that is why he hasn't mentioned it to you.'

'Of a surety,' she said swiftly, more interested at the moment in his stepmother. 'Owain said she is beautiful.'

'Her beauty is a lure. She accused Owain of scheming to have our eldest brother, Martin, killed. She lies. He loved him. She sought out your husband, having learnt that he was staying at Domfront at the same time as my brothers. She told Father that Sir Roger revealed to her that Owain had blurted out such a scheme whilst in his cups.'

Kate said softly, 'If your father had known Sir Roger as I did, he would not have believed aught he said.'

'Gwendolyn persuaded him that he was a knight to be trusted more than his heir, by telling him that Owain had tried to rape her.'

Kate's eyes widened.

'It is not true,' said Hal hastily. 'She lied because she wanted Owain completely discredited in Father's eyes. She blamed Owain for Martin's death before she even met Sir Roger. She loved Martin and would not accept that he only cared for her like a brother. Whilst he lived, she never gave up hope of persuading him to marry her. But once he was dead, her grief was terrible to behold.'

'Tell me about Martin?'

'He was handsome and charming and with a rare gift for handling horses, which was useful to Father. If my brother had a fault, it was that he was easily led. Unlike Owain, who could never be led by the nose, Martin was placid and did what Father said, Owain would argue if he thought he was in the right. That angered Father, and yet because he knew Owain was the stronger of the two…despite his being the younger…he trusted Owain to take care of his heir.'

'I see,' murmured Kate.

Hal glanced in his brothers' direction. 'Owain would not like my speaking of this to you, but I thought you should know what Gwendolyn is capable of before you meet her. Owain does not believe she is a witch with magical powers, but she would kill him if she could.'

Kate felt as if an icy hand gripped her heart and, for a moment, her fear for Owain dried her mouth. Then she pulled herself together. 'I'm glad you've told me this as I have some knowledge of women such as your stepmother. Tell me more about her now?'

Hal shook his head and said gruffly, 'Owain and Davy have finished talking. You will find out for yourself if Father permits it and you stay at Rowan Manor. If he does not, will you speak to Owain about my living with you? I will be a great asset, for I have a way with horses, too.'

Kate said gently, 'I can make no promises but, if the opportunity should rise, I will do what you ask.'

He looked delighted and pressed a kiss on her cheek. She smiled at him before shooing him away. He left her, a solitary figure, gazing towards England, considering all that had been said.

Owain touched her shoulder. 'We'll soon be dropping anchor at Southampton.'

She darted him a glance. 'But we'll be sailing on to Chester, once we've taken on fresh water and provisions?'

He nodded. 'It's no more dangerous than if we went by land. Now fortunes can no longer be made in France, there is a soldiery here with weapons for hire and with a need to look elsewhere for booty.' For a moment there was silence, then he said, 'You and Hal appeared deep in conversation.'

'He wants to come and live with us after we're married,' she said with a droll expression.

'And what was your response?'

'I said the decision was yours. Didn't you say I was to leave any difficulties that arose from us being betrothed to you?'

A grin creased his face. 'Aye. Did he say why he wanted to leave home?'

'At length…but he assures me that he'll be a great asset as he, too, has a way with horses.' Her tone was light. 'Isn't that what you told me about your brother, Martin?'

'You have an excellent memory, Kate. I wonder what else Hal told you?' he rasped, his eyes narrowing. 'I guess he mentioned our stepmother.'

'Yes. Tell me, how did your father kill hers?'

Owain gazed towards the coast. 'It was in a disagreement over a field…it was a fair fight and took place at a local tournament. Her mother was dead, as was mine, and, as far as I knew, Gwendolyn had no other kin. So she was brought to our house and brought up as one of the family. Until Martin's death and her meeting with her uncle she was a sweet girl, if a trifle fey and wild at times. She teased and flirted as young maids do, favouring one or the other of us younger brothers depending on her mood, but we knew it was Martin she had her eye on. Also, she adored my grandmother, who managed to keep a rein on her wilder behaviour. Then Grandmother died and six months later Martin was dead, too.' His voice was emotionless but Kate could see the pain in his eyes.

'Hal said her grief was terrible.'

'So he did speak of her,' said Owain grimly.

'A little. Please, continue.'

He hesitated. 'She greeted Martin's death with a storm of tears and then a passionate tirade against me, saying that I'd always wanted to be Father's heir. I denied it, of course, and told them both that I suspected Sir Roger of conspiring in Martin's death.' Kate gasped. But he did not give her a chance to speak, only saying,

'Let me finish. She wanted to know why I believed that was so, but I could not tell them my reasons. Anyway, I had to return to France and Father encouraged me to look for evidence against Sir Roger whilst I was there. At the time I had no idea that he was interested in alchemy or that the King had spoken to him about Merebury and its Lady.' He paused, as if expecting her to comment, but she remained silent. So he picked up his tale and carried on. 'Due to the war, I was in France longer than I intended and had no opportunity to find the evidence I sought. I was wounded and that delayed my return further. When I returned, Gwendolyn had not only married Father, but had turned him completely against me. He was coldly condemning and refused to listen to a word I said.' Owain's blue eyes were hard as sapphires.

Silence.

'You have nothing to say?' he rasped. 'You must realise now that I had reason for wanting Sir Roger dead?'

'Does Sir Thomas know this?' asked Kate.

He nodded. 'I told him of my suspicions, knowing he had the ear of the King. In my naïveté, I thought Sir Thomas would see justice done as he had known my brother as well. It was then I discovered that Sir Roger was married to the Lady Catherine and his experiments into changing base metal into gold were being funded by the King and others. Sir Thomas told me that the King wouldn't listen to any accusation of murder against Sir Roger without definite proof.'

'So what did you do?'

His eyes darkened. 'I had to find a way of supporting myself. Sir Thomas offered me a position working

with his stud and I accepted it. My time was divided between his manors of Lathom and Knowsley.'

She was disappointed. 'I didn't think you'd have
given up.'

He shrugged. 'What else could I do? My father had
told me never to darken his doors again. My grandmother had left me a little money, but that would soon
go if I couldn't earn a living.'

Her brows knitted. 'You say you were at Lathom.
I don't ever remember seeing you and I often tres-
passed on Sir Thomas's manor in search of wild
herbs.'

'Sometimes he would send me to other parts of the
country, as well as abroad, to inspect a horse and decide whether it was worth purchasing.'

She stared at him and said uncomfortably, 'It seems
strange to me that Sir Thomas should choose you to
solve the mystery of Sir Roger's murder, knowing how
you felt about him.'

His expression was quizzical. 'Do you really believe, Kate, I would be such a fool as to kill Sir Roger,
knowing Sir Thomas was aware of my feeling towards
that evil knight?'

She felt the colour rise in her cheeks and pressed her
hands against them. 'You could be doubly clever making him believe that you weren't such a fool.'

His eyes sobered. 'Believe me, Kate, I did not kill
Sir Roger. But knowing of my interest in him, as well
as my need for land and money, Sir Thomas decided I
was the best man to find the person—or persons—responsible for his death, as well as the King's treasure.
So far, I have found only you. Although, if I were to

come face to face with the Comte again, there are several questions I would wish him to answer.'

Kate was silent, tempted to tell him what her mother and Diccon had witnessed on the fells. But she had been sworn to secrecy and would not break her vow. Instead, she gazed towards the harbour wall a few yards away and changed the subject. 'It will be strange hearing so many people speaking our own tongue after being away from England for so long.'

'Perhaps you should make a few purchases whilst we are ashore. Buy some hose, gloves, cloth, needles and thread to make yourself more clothes,' he said rapidly. 'I would have you look your best when you face my father and stepmother.'

'If I do so, then I'll be even more indebted to you than I am already,' she said mildly.

Owain shook his head. 'You owe me nothing but a promise that you will enjoy yourself. As your betrothed, it is my right to shower you with gifts. I can borrow clean raiment from my brothers, but you cannot go on wearing the same gown until we reach Chester.'

'I could don my pilgrim garb,' she said, with a humorous twist to her mouth.

He laughed. 'You would do me a disfavour if you did so. I would have you throw it into the sea.'

'That would be a foolishness for someone reared in ways of thrift. Now, tell me what you know of Southampton?'

'According to legend, it was here that one of the old kings of England, Canute, ordered the waves to retreat.'

'I wager he got his feet wet.'

He smiled and drew her arm through his. 'Let us go ashore.'

As she walked down the gangplank, of their own volition her fingers caressed his arm, enjoying the feel of the muscle through the fabric of his sleeve. Now they were in England, parting from him was the last thing on her mind.

Chapter Eight

The streets of Southampton were busy and they soon realised why when they saw the stalls set up in the market square. 'It appears we have arrived on a market day,' said Owain.

Kate was fortunate in finding a stall with just the fabric she was looking for and asked Owain's opinion of a cloth of the deepest green linsey-woolsey. He agreed that it would be suitable for a gown, and also suggested that she buy a length of the red Venetian cotton for a kirtle. 'And what of this saffron silk?' He fingered it and asked the cost of both off the vendor.

Kate's fair brows shot up when he named a price. 'I'll not have you spending that amount of money on me just to impress your father and his wife,' she said firmly.

'Do not argue with me, Kate. It is not solely for them I wish you to dress so fine. I would like to see you wearing silk. Have you never felt it against your skin?' His eyes met hers in a teasing glance. 'Then you must do so. Perhaps you should also have a new cloak. What think you of this russet woollen cloth? It will soon be September and you'll need a cloak for travelling.'

She agreed that it would do, and also bought a length of undyed linen to make a couple of simple shifts and a wimple. Next to the fabric stall was one stall selling, not only needles and thread, but also buttons and ribands. After paying for their purchases, Owain encouraged Kate to buy some ready-made leather slippers, as well as a pair of kid gloves. She watched all the goods being carried aboard and placed in her cabin with much satisfaction and pleasure.

That evening they dined on roast pork and creamed leeks, apple tart, cheese and fresh bread, washed down by the local ale and a fine red wine. Splendidly replete, Kate tumbled onto her bunk and fell fast asleep.

When she woke they were under sail. After a breakfast of bread and bacon, apples and ale, she borrowed shears from one of the mariners, whose task it was to repair the sails, and set about cutting out the cream linen to a simple design that she held in her head, having been taught not only by her mother, but also Lady Catherine's seamstress. By the time she lay down to sleep that night, she had made a plain shift. In the morning she would cut the green material for a gown. She planned on its completion by the time the ship reached Chester.

A few days later, she woke to grey skies and a playful breeze. When she went up on deck it was to discover that they were sailing inland. On either side there was woodland and fields. She went in search of Owain. 'Where are we?'

He was grimfaced. 'This is the River Dee and soon we will tie up at Chester. I will see my father, even if it is for the last time.'

A cold hand seemed to grip her heart. 'What do you mean—the last time?'

He did not answer, only placing an arm about her. 'At least I will have you at my side.'

Kate was silent, remembering her plan to go in search of her mother and Diccon when they disembarked at Chester. Now that the time had come for her to escape Owain, she found she did not want to leave him. She remembered what Hal had said about Owain being a seer. Had he seen the future and, instead of trying to escape his fate, had decided to face it head on, even if it meant his death? She must pray for his safety and bring to mind all that her mother had taught her about doing battle with such women as Gwendolyn, the so-called witch.

Kate sat on a small, sturdy Welsh pony, hired to carry herself and her baggage. She wore the green gown she had made on the ship, and her short hair was concealed beneath a plain linen wimple. Owain rode beside her on Merlin. His brothers had gone ahead to prepare their father for the imminent arrival of his estranged son and the woman they believed to be his betrothed. She gazed about her, half-hoping to catch a glimpse of her mother or Diccon as they made their way through the bustling streets of Chester, although she was unsure what she would do if she did see them. As it was, she and Owain reached the Northgate of the city without her doing so.

Kate glanced at Owain's brooding profile. Was he thinking of the beautiful Gwendolyn who had once been like a sister to him? Perhaps he was not as indifferent to her attractions as he appeared to be? 'Hal said you were a seer. If that is true, could you not have prevented your father's marriage?' she asked.

Owain frowned. 'Just because I have foreseen how certain events would turn out, it does not say I have the sight. Most folk with sense can do the same…but Hal likes to believe otherwise. Do you understand?'

She nodded, wondering whether now was the time to ask about his home, but he had turned away and appeared absorbed in his own thoughts once more. She gazed about her at the other travellers and the scenery. Trees had been cut well back from the road to deter sudden attacks from outlaws. Brambles grew in the grassy verges, and she could see ripening blackberries peeping out between the leaves. She had always enjoyed this time of year when the harvesting began and food was plentiful. Suddenly she became aware of a horse approaching at speed and saw a rider galloping towards them. She recognised Hal.

'You must put on all speed, Owain,' he yelled. 'Father's fallen from his horse and is lying as one dead. Gwendolyn has gone off somewhere to weave her spells at a distance, believing she can get away with what she has done.'

'You believe she is responsible for your father's fall?' cried Kate, urging her mount forward.

'Aye. She looked scared and then furious when I told her Owain was on his way here with his betrothed, the Lady Catherine of Merebury. She accused you of your husband's murder and of being an adulteress.'

Kate gasped. 'That is slanderous talk.'

A muscle in Owain's jaw tightened. 'What did Father say?' he demanded.

His brother turned his horse. 'He repeated her words. Davy said he was talking nonsense, but Father told him to shut his mouth and continued to rage, blustering and threatening to throw you off his land as soon as you showed your face. Davy tried to get him to see sense, but he was not prepared to listen.'

'So how did he come to fall from his horse?' asked Owain, digging his heels into Merlin's flanks.

'It was just as he mounted his horse that it happened. No sooner was he in the saddle than he slipped sidewards and fell. There was no one near him at the time and the horse did not move. It can only be that she put a spell on him.'

'Did he bang his head?' asked Owain.

'Davy rushed forward and broke his fall.'

Owain said no more, but urged Merlin into a canter. Kate followed suit, but had difficulty keeping up with the two brothers. Inside her head echoed the words *your husband's murderer and an adulteress*. Obviously the accusation of adulterer in connection with Lady Catherine had never occurred to Owain.

As they passed fields, where men laboured at the barley harvest and horses and cattle grazed, she caught sight of what must surely be Rowan Manor. From a distance its walls appeared rosy red as the sun caught the sandstone; the building appeared to be a fair size. It was not long before they were riding beneath an archway into a courtyard. Hens scattered before them and from somewhere nearby came the grunting of swine. A serving man, several stable boys and an elderly woman came hurrying out of various buildings.

'Master Owain, you're home at last and not a moment too soon,' called one of the men.

'Where are my father and brother?' asked Owain, dismounting.

'Master Davy is sitting with Sir Hywel in his bedchamber. The physician came swiftly, but he says there is nothing he can do and that the priest should be sent for. Megan has gone to fetch him.'

'Let us not give up hope yet,' said Owain. Lifting Kate down from the pony, he introduced her to the members of the household. 'This is the Lady Catherine, my betrothed. You will see that she receives every courtesy in your power.' He turned to the woman. 'Agnes, show the Lady to the best guest bedchamber.'

'Aye, Master Owain.'

'Edward, bring the baggage in. Robbie, see to the horses and send one of the lads to Chester to return the hired one.' Owain hurried up the steps that led to the entrance and disappeared inside. Hal raced after him.

Accompanied by Agnes, Kate climbed the steps more slowly. She paused inside and gazed about the hall. Its walls were hung with tapestries, depicting various scenes from the chase and beneath her feet was rush matting. In an enormous fireplace, flames embraced what appeared to be half a tree trunk. But she had no time to note the rest of the furnishings as Agnes scurried towards a staircase at the far end. 'This way, my Lady,' she called.

Kate followed her and was soon shown into a spacious bedchamber, furnished with a large bed, an *ar-*

moire, a carved chest, a washstand and a cushioned chair. A fair chamber, she thought, worthy of an honoured guest. But how long would she be here? And where was Gwendolyn? She went over to the window and looked out over the vegetable and herb gardens.

'You have no maid with you, my Lady,' said Agnes. 'Will I send the head groom's daughter, Megan, to you when she returns?'

Kate turned and faced her. 'Of a surety. Tell me, Agnes, have you any notion where your mistress has gone?'

The woman's rheumy pale blue eyes dropped beneath her gaze. 'Would she tell the likes of me, my Lady?'

Kate stared at her intently. 'Why not? No doubt you have lived here most of your life and were here when your mistress came as a girl. Perhaps you were even given the task of tending her every need as a child. Maybe you do know where she is and she has set you to spy on us whilst she keeps her distance.'

Agnes's eyes darted to her face and she wailed, 'He must have told you that, for how else would you know?'

'He? You mean Master Owain ap Rowan?'

Agnes chewed on her lip with toothless gums. 'He has the sight. That's why he's useful to them,' she mumbled.

Kate seized on the last word. 'Them?'

A crafty expression came over the woman's face. 'You knows the ones I mean. Methinks you be another like him. Although the mistress says you don't have the power…that it is the woman who was your nurse and her daughter that have knowledge of the old ways….as did the nurse's man before he met with his death.'

Kate was stunned. Who had told Gwendolyn that she and her mother knew the ancient rhyming spells? They had always kept that knowledge to themselves. Could her father have told Sir Roger? She frowned. And what had the crone meant about Owain's gift being of use to them? 'Name me one name,' she demanded abruptly, fixing the old woman with a stare. 'If you don't, I will inform Master ap Rowan that you have been insolent and he will turn you from his gates to beg for your bread.'

Agnes gasped. 'He would do no such thing. I was here when he was born. I served his mother and grandmother.'

'I am to be his wife. He would let me have my way. I will keep quiet if you give me a name,' demanded Kate, her tone inflexible.

Agnes looked uneasy. 'My Lady Gwendolyn, the Frenchman and the friar will not like it.'

'So they have been here recently.' Kate controlled a shudder. 'For what purpose?'

The old woman mumbled, 'Always they want money and news.'

'News of whom? Master Owain?'

The old woman chewed on her lip. 'Aye! As well as the King's half-brothers, the Earls of Pembroke and Richmond. There, I've said it. But you must not tell anyone that I told you.' She shivered and glanced over her shoulder.

Kate dismissed Agnes and sank on to the bed. Why were the Comte and the friar so interested in the King's half-brothers? She must speak to Owain as soon as possible, but knew his father's needs must come first.

* * *

Owain gazed down at the man in the bed, regretting the rift between them. A large, burly figure, his father had emanated power and arrogance all his life. Now he appeared to have aged ten years. The corner of his left eyelid looked as if pulled by an invisible string and he was drooling from the corner of his mouth. His left hand lay, seemingly lifeless, on the richly embroidered blue coverlet. Sir Hywel had opened his mouth ten minutes ago, but his speech had been slurred and the words incomprehensible.

Much to Owain's irritation, Hal had declared that their father was possessed and in need of exorcising.

'What are you going to do?' asked Davy from the other side of the bed, his dark eyes meeting Owain's.

'What would you have me do?'

Hal broke into the exchange. 'Have the priest come or find Gwendolyn and make her lift the spell,' he said firmly.

A derisive laugh rumbled in Davy's throat. 'If she wanted to persuade him to change his will in her and the child's favour, it does not make sense to put Father in a condition where he is unable to make his wishes known.'

Owain murmured, 'I have seen a man struck down like this before where some spoke of devilry, but then he recovered and all claimed a miracle had taken place.'

'You sound as if you don't believe in miracles,' burst out Hal.

Owain said gently, 'I'm sure they do happen.' He was reminded of Kate pretending to be dumb and her claim to a miracle later. He smiled faintly at the memory.

'We should try and find Gwendolyn so as to keep an eye on her,' stated Hal. 'I'm sure you could tell us where she is if you wanted to.'

Owain could hazard a guess as to his stepmother's whereabouts, but had no intention of going in search of her. 'I must speak with Lady Kate before I make a decision,' he said, getting to his feet. 'Hal, you stay with Father. Davy, you'd best get back to your work.'

'How long must I sit with him?' said Hal, frowning.

'Until either I or Davy take your place,' ordered Owain, heading for the door with his middle brother just behind him.

Once outside Davy said, 'What say you to the accusation that you murdered the Lady's husband and have committed adultery with her?'

'I say that Gwendolyn had it in mind to accuse me of such before my arrival. Instigated, no doubt, by the Comte d'Azay or her uncle, who must know of my search for the Lady and the Fletchers. When were they last here?'

'I don't know. You forget, brother, that I've been in France, too.'

Grimfaced, Owain said, 'At least he won't get any more money from Father now.'

'You think he will die?'

'He is in God's care. I will say no more than that.'

Silently, they walked to the top of the staircase before going their separate ways.

Owain made haste to his old bedchamber. His baggage had been brought up and the bed made, and he was glad to see a fire burning in a brazier. He felt cold. It had been a shock to see his father laid so low and he only hoped that he would regain his speech long enough for them to heal the rift between them. He delved into one of his saddlebags and removed a package wrapped in oil-skin. He went over to the wall next to the bed and re-moved a block of sandstone a few feet from the floor. Behind was a cavity in which he placed the package be-fore replacing the stone. That done, he went over to the carved chest at the foot of the bed and flung up the lid, hoping that his father had not got rid of all his posses-sions.

He was relieved to find some of his old clothes within its depths and took out undergarments, a linen shirt, a dark green doublet and rust-coloured hose. All were clean and smelt of lavender and he knew that he had Mistress Carver to thank for that.

He must change and find Kate. Sweet Kate! He wanted to tell her the secret that Sir Thomas had im-parted to him, but had sworn an oath that he would leave the telling to her mother. He did not doubt that sooner or later Kate would lead him to Beth Fletcher. He guessed that his love would react angrily at first. Hope-fully, she would soon realise the benefit of the change in her circumstances. Remembering her response to him when he had held her naked in his arms on that Brittany beach, he felt a heat in his blood and had to force himself to veer his thoughts away from her and concentrate on his father. The next twenty-four hours could bring about such a change in his own position that he could offer for Kate's hand and, hopefully, Sir Thomas would consider him worthy of her and would not withhold his permission if matters went his way.

He combed his windswept black curls and went in search of Kate. Not finding her in the house, he went outside to search for her. Eventually he heard her voice imparting wisdom concerning the healing property of comfrey, also known as boneset and bruisewort. He entered the herb garden by a picket gate in the bay hedge to see her talking to Megan. At the sound of his footsteps, Kate turned a smiling face towards him. His heart seemed to turn over in his chest.

'How fares your father?' she asked, her expression becoming grave.

Owain gained control of his emotions and covered the distance between them. 'He has gained consciousness but is not himself.'

'I will leave you, my Lady,' said Megan, and hurried away.

As soon as she was out of earshot, Kate said, 'Will you have to stay here?'

'That decision will be made for me in the next few days.' He took her hand and drew it through his arm and began to walk along a path set between low-growing thyme and pennyroyal. He was aware that her fingers quivered as they rested on his sleeve. 'Hal would have me go in search of Gwendolyn.'

'You know where she is?'

'Chester or Nether Alderley…but I see no sense in pursuing her. She will return of her own volition and no doubt she will not come alone.'

She looked at him. 'Agnes told me that the friar and the Comte are often here, asking for money and news of the Earls of Richmond and Pembroke.'

Owain's stride faltered and he slanted her a searching glance. 'I guess she did not volunteer that information,' he murmured.

She pulled a face. 'Not immediately. She also said that, because you have the sight, you're useful to some unnamed persons. Does she mean Sir Thomas?'

He shook his head as in disbelief. 'What other fodder did she throw your way?'

Kate hesitated and whispered, 'She knows that Mother and I have knowledge of the old rhyming spells. I can only believe our enemies found this out from Sir Roger before he died. I want to believe that my—my father would not have willingly revealed it, knowing such information could be used by our enemies if they decided to get rid of us by bringing a charge of witchcraft against us.'

'That's why now they must not suspect your real identity,' said Owain, thinking it was vital they both played their roles as a betrothed couple to the hilt. The least suspicion that it was a hoax and she was not the Lady Catherine Miles could prove fatal.

'I'm sorry to worry you with such things when your concern for your father is so great,' said Kate, rousing him from his reverie.

'I am glad you feel you can trust me with your worries.' Owain raised her hand to his lips and planted a kiss on her palm. All sensible thought fled as she felt that tingle that never failed to thrill. Here was magic enough for her without any need to ensnare with love potions or spells.

'I shall order a watch be kept for the Comte and the friar and any sighting of either to be reported to me before they are allowed into the house. Shall we take another turn round the garden before we dine? Regretfully, I will have to leave you to your own devices afterwards. I must sit with my father.'

* * *

Dinner was a sombre meal. People spoke in hushed voices and Kate was aware of being the focus of numerous pairs of eyes. She was introduced to the local priest, who congratulated her on her betrothal. She thanked him, although convinced it would all end in tears. Conversation was spasmodic. The priest questioned Kate about her pilgrimage. Davy talked to Owain about the brood mares in foal and the barley harvest. As soon as the meal was over, Owain excused himself and the priest accompanied him from the hall. Kate went to her bedchamber and took up her sewing. She was making a kirtle with the scarlet Venetian cotton and settled comfortably to her task.

Shadows were filling the corners of the room when there came a knock on her door. 'My father is failing and I want you to come to his bedside before he dies,' called Owain.

'Then I will come,' she said, opening the door.

He took her hand and hurried her along a passageway lit by torches in sconces every few yards. Both were silent as they rounded a corner and sped along another passage until Owain stopped in front of a massive door. He ushered her into a vast, candlelit bedchamber.

Kate's eyes were immediately drawn to the large bed set against a far wall. Its curtains were tied back and Hal and Davy were seated on one side of it and the priest on the other.

Owain drew Kate forward. Her heart thudded in her breast as they stopped at the foot of the bed. She gazed down at the dying man, observing that one side of his face was dragged down and his breathing was shallow.

'Father!' called Owain. There was no response, so he repeated the word. Slowly one of the man's eyes opened and he fixed it on his son. 'This is the Lady Catherine, my betrothed,' said Owain earnestly. 'She will tell you the truth about Sir Roger. We are both innocent of the accusations Gwendolyn levelled against us.'

With obvious difficulty Sir Hywel opened the other eye, but there was no sign of recognition in his face, although he continued to stare at them both for what felt like an age without moving. There was something about his immobility that caused a cold shiver to run down Kate's spine. Suddenly his breathing stopped.

A haggard-faced Owain hurried to the side of the bed and placed two fingers against his father's neck. 'He's dead,' he muttered.

The priest reached past him and closed the dead man's eyes, chanting as he did so. Owain's hand crushed Kate's and, turning away from the bed, he drew her from the bedchamber.

'I'm so sorry, Owain,' she said gently.

'In my heart I knew there was little chance of him making a recovery. Yet I had to try to heal the breach between us.' His voice was raw with emotion. 'I will pray that God will forgive him, reunite his spirit with Martin's and my mother's and give him peace.'

'I will join my prayers with yours.'

He thanked her and accompanied her to her bedchamber. There he kissed her briefly on the lips. 'Don't allow what has just happened to keep you from your sleep, Kate. May the Holy Trinity bless you this night.'

She watched his retreating figure, longing to go after him. But there was something about the way he held himself that told her now was not the time to offer him comfort. She went inside her darkened bedchamber and removed her outer clothing and, clad in her linen shift, climbed into bed. She remembered what Owain had said on the ship about seeing his father for the last time and how she had worried that he might have foreseen his own death. Uncertain about how much time there was left to spend with him, she had been prepared to do what he wanted. It was obvious now that he would have to stay at Rowan Manor, at least until his father's funeral was over and his legal affairs sorted out. But there was a limit to the time she could linger here. She must seek out her mother and brother and reassure them of her well being. There was so much she had to tell them before she could decide what to do next. Her heart ached at the thought of saying farewell to Owain, but it had to be done. For a little while longer she lay, thinking about how he had planned on marrying the Lady Catherine so he could have Merebury to breed his own horses. Now he no longer needed that manor so desperately, would he be prepared to marry plain Kate Fletcher? Sooner or later their betrothal would be declared null and void. On that sad thought, she drifted into a shallow sleep.

She was wakened by a rat-tat-tat on her door. 'Who is there?' she called, propping herself up on an elbow.

'Owain! I must speak with you.'

Scrambling from her bed, she hurried over to the door and opened it just a crack. Owain was dressed in black and for travelling. 'Where are you going?' she asked, thinking how attractive he looked even in black.

'I'm for Chester to see the family lawyer. I will be back in time for supper.'

For a moment she wondered if he would also seek out Gwendolyn, but more immediate in her thoughts was that here was a chance to leave the manor without dispute and seek out her mother and brother. 'May I come with you?'

He shook his dark heard. 'Not this time, Kate. Agnes has disappeared, Davy has gone off somewhere and I must leave immediately. Could you talk to Mistress Carver, who holds house here, and see if there is anything you can do to help her.'

'But…I was thinking of leaving. Now your father is dead you no longer have need of me here.'

His face fell. 'But I do need you here, Kate. Please stay a little longer,' he pleaded.

She was touched by his plea. 'But, Owain, our betrothal is a pretence,' she said with a catch in her voice. 'I will have to leave sooner or later.'

'But not just yet. It will look extremely odd if you were to leave before the funeral. I know you want to find your mother and brother, but will another week make that much difference?'

'I have not said they are alive,' she cried.

'Not in so many words but I believe them to be.'

She was silent.

He sighed. 'Stay and meet Mistress Carver. You didn't see her yesterday because she was visiting her niece, who has just given birth. Her husband is head cook here. The Carvers were never blessed with children, so she took over the running of the household after my grandmother died. I have known her all my life.'

'But what of Gwendolyn? She is your father's widow—surely she will still be mistress here?'

'You must not think of running away because of Gwendolyn,' he said firmly and seized her by the shoulders, kissing her with such ardour that, when he released her, she had to cling to him, otherwise she would have fallen. 'Promise me, Kate, that you will be here when I return.'

'I promise,' she whispered, her lips throbbing with the force of his kiss.

He smiled. 'Do not fear, you will be more than a match for Gwendolyn. Now I must go.' He bent his head and this time his kiss was as gentle as a butterfly landing on a flower. Then he strode off down the passageway in a manner very different from that of last even.

She touched her lips briefly, watching him until he turned the corner. Then she went over to the wash stand, where a pitcher of fresh water, soap and a drying cloth had been placed. She presumed Megan had crept in while she slept. Kate washed swiftly, only to dither over what she should wear. Eventually she decided on the dark blue gown and kirtle of pale blue that Owain had given to her on the ship.

Downstairs she found Hal eating white cocket bread and bacon. 'I'm having a second breakfast,' he said, smiling up at her and getting to his feet. Pulling out a seat for her, he added, 'I'm glad you didn't go with Owain.'

'He asked me to stay behind and see if I could help Mistress Carver,' said Kate, arranging her skirts so they did not crease as she sat down.

'Good. With both my brothers away for the day, I'll be glad of your company when Gwendolyn returns.' He signalled to a serving man.

Kate's brows puckered. 'Do you know where Davy has gone?'

He did not answer her immediately, but asked whether she wanted bacon or butter and honey with her bread. She decided on the latter and he spoke to a serving man, who hurried behind a screen to where she presumed lay the kitchen, still room and pantry. She repeated her question.

Hal said in a low voice, 'He's gone to tell Joan that Father is dead. He's wanted to wed her since last harvest, but Father wouldn't allow it. At least life will be easier now the old man's gone and Owain has returned.' She shot him a surprised look. Hal grinned. 'It's no use my pretending that I'm heartbroken. Father wasn't an easy man to live with and showed weakness by falling under Gwendolyn's power. Our lives will be the happier now he has gone to his rest—but I'll put on my mourning face when folk arrive for his funeral and so will Davy.'

A boy appeared at Kate's elbow with a bowl of water and a napkin. She washed her fingers and dried them, ready for when the serving man appeared with a tray bearing food and a tankard of small ale. She thanked him and he bowed with a smile before leaving them.

'Tell me about Mistress Carver,' asked Kate, spreading butter and honey on the bread.

'Gwendolyn could not manage without her…but where you'll find Mistress Carver at any given moment is not easy to answer. She could be in the buttery, the storeroom, the stillroom, the pantry, the dairy, the brewery or bake house—she organises all.'

His answer filled Kate with trepidation. Mistress Carver sounded formidable; a woman capable of spotting a fraud a league away.

* * *

So it was that when she went in search of the woman whom both brothers spoke well of, Kate was filled with trepidation. But her fears were to be soothed when she entered the dairy to find a woman she presumed to be Mistress Carver talking to a maid working a great cheese press. Kate cleared her throat to attract their attention, hoping she did not sound as nervous as she felt.

The woman's head turned and Kate found herself the focus of a pair of keen, grey eyes. The dark hair that escaped from her cap was streaked with silver and she was dressed neatly in a black gown; from her waist hung a chain holding several keys. Kate smiled. 'Mistress Carver?'

'Aye. You must be Master Owain's lady,' she said warmly. 'What can I do for you?'

'Master Owain suggested that I make myself known to you…and to ask if there is anything I can *do* for *you* in the Lady Gwendolyn's absence. If I can make your task easier, I will willingly do so.'

The woman beamed at her. 'Gladly, I accept your offer. Everything's in such a muddle since Sir Hywel's sudden death.'

'Surely our priorities will be food and drink during this coming week?' said Kate hesitantly. 'And no doubt we need prepare bedchambers for any guests coming from a distance for the funeral.'

'Aye, my Lady. Although I cannot see there being many. Since Sir Hywel wed Mistress Gwendolyn, guests have been few and far between—and those who have shown their faces the old mistress would have disapproved of, just as she would the marriage.' She added in a rush, 'It was downright improper of Mistress Gwendolyn to turn her charms on for the master. But could he see what she was after? Nay! The master could never admit he was in the wrong and was downright cruel to Master Owain, believing her side of a story before that of his own son.'

'I am pleased to find those who will support him during this difficult time,' said Kate in heartfelt tones.

The woman blushed. 'I feel as if a dark cloud has been lifted from this household now that Master Owain is home—bringing his future bride with him. You are very welcome, my Lady.'

Now it was Kate's turn to blush. 'I thank you for your welcome. Perhaps you can show me what foodstuffs and drink you have in store?'

'Gladly, my Lady. But firstly, perhaps you can approve my husband's choice for this evening's meal. He suggests pottage for the first course, then—seeing as how it's a fish day—a couple of eel pies and carp and pike with sauce galentyne. For dessert, we've some pears from the orchard— he'll stew them in a wine syrup and accompany them with some green cheese.'

'That sounds very satisfactory, Mistress Carver. Please tell him so from me.'

'I will, my Lady. If you'll be pleased to accompany me. I'll do that and then show you around.'

Kate decided she had to continue as if it was her right to ask questions, express approval and make suggestions. She found much to interest her during the next hour or so. Mistress Carver showed her the storeroom and the stillroom, where there were jars of fruit in syrup, sacks of flour and dried fruit; onions, herbs and garlic hung from the ceilings. Drink ready to be served was kept in the buttery and the smell of baking bread teased the nostrils as one passed the bakery. The house-keeper told her of the meat on hoof and claw, took her to the stew ponds, which held carp and roach—these were tended by the Carvers' nephew, Jonathan.

'He's a bit backward in some things, Lady Catherine, seeing as he came into the world the wrong way round, which did for my poor sister,' explained Mistress Carver. 'But he's a good worker and worships Master Owain. Jonathan was born a few months after him and, when they were boys, would trail after him. Master Owain never chased him off, even when he must have irritated him excessively. Master Owain was a bit of a scamp, himself, nevertheless, he has always had a kind heart.'

Kate could not argue with those words, remembering how he had cared for her. When Mistress Carver suggested that she might like to see the rest of the house, she accepted with alacrity. First, Kate was shown the parlour, which overlooked a walled garden at the back of the house. 'This was Master Owain's grand-mother's favourite place, but it's been sadly neglected. Lady Gwendolyn will not use it, has said it holds too many memories of the old lady.'

The parlour was full of sunshine, which had faded the fabrics on chairs and the cushioned settle. Kate imagined sewing here in the evenings whilst Owain read to her from a book and smiled wistfully, before signalling she was ready to move on.

Mistress Carver took her upstairs to the bedchambers. There she bemoaned the state of the curtains and hangings. 'Sir Hywel never liked spending out on furnishings. Any spare money would go on horses to improve the breeding strain. As for the Lady Gwendolyn—she was content as long as her bedchamber was the way she wanted it—she did not concern herself with the rest of the house.'

Kate made no comment; when the tour was over, she thanked Mistress Carver.

'It was a pleasure, my Lady. Is there aught else I can do for you?'

'I wonder if you could spare Megan this afternoon to help me with some sewing?'

'Certainly, my Lady. I'll send her to you once she's finished her chores.'

Kate thanked her and they parted.

After the midday meal, she returned to her bedchamber to resume her sewing and await Megan's arrival. She had not been there long when the door burst open and a woman stood in the opening. Instantly Kate guessed she was the Lady Gwendolyn, although she was shorter than she had imagined. But her face was, indeed, beautiful—a perfect oval with skin as pale as moonlight. She had lustrous brown eyes, a delicately shaped nose and a cupid- bow-shaped mouth. A few wisps of dark hair had escaped the confines of her butterfly headdress and the scarlet velvet gown that clung to her body did little to conceal her swollen belly and the agitated rise and fall of her breasts.

'I wouldn't make myself too comfortable, Lady Catherine,' she said huskily. 'I wager Owain never told you that he and I were once lovers.'

Chapter Nine

'This child I carry is his!' cried Gwendolyn, advancing on her.

Immediately Kate sprang to Owain's defence. 'That's ridiculous. His father banned him from this manor more than a year ago. Besides, Owain would not betray his father in such a way. He is an honourable man. You speak falsely.'

Gwendolyn flushed. 'You seem to know much about him. You've no right to come here. You seek to oust me. Leave now or it will be the worse for you.'

'Make me no threats, Lady Gwendolyn. You do not scare me,' said Kate, looking down on her with disdain.

Gwendolyn fixed her with a stare. 'I have known strong men tremble and beg for me to release them from my spell.' Her voice was silky soft.

'How many strong women have you encountered? I say fie to you!' Kate snapped her fingers and advanced on her. 'If you try to cast a spell on me, I would counter it with one of my own.'

Gwendolyn's jaw dropped and then, abruptly, she turned and rushed out of the bedchamber.

Kate took a deep breath. She should not have allowed herself to be provoked. Her mother would have boxed her ears if she had heard her speak in such a way. She should have remained calm in her role of Lady Catherine. After all, her enemies might have managed to worm themselves into the house with Owain and Davy absent.

'Can you cast spells, Lady Catherine?' whispered a voice.

Roused from her reverie, Kate stared at Megan. 'You heard?'

'Aye!'

'Then you must forget what I said,' said Kate, a quiver in her voice.

Megan's face fell. 'It isn't true?'

Kate hesitated a little too long. 'Of course not.'

'I'll not breathe a word to a soul, Lady Catherine,' she whispered, stepping into the bedchamber and closing the door behind her. 'I just want to make widower Evans fall in love with me. He's plenty of money and a well-made house with good solid furniture and only two children…but there's several who've got their eye on him.'

Kate shot the bolt on the door. 'Will a love potion do?'

Megan beamed at her. 'Aye! But when'll I give it him?'

'You'll have to be patient, Megan. Have you forgotten Sir Hywel has just died? I'll deal with such matters once the funeral is over.' She forced a smile. 'Now you must help me finish this kirtle, Megan.'

'Certainly, my Lady. Just show me what you want done.'

'In a moment. But first tell me…is Friar Stephen or the Comte d'Azay downstairs?'

'They were not there when I came upstairs.' Megan shuddered slightly. 'I've always made myself scarce when either of them comes. I do not like the way they look at me…but if you wish, my Lady, I will go and see.'

Kate shook her head. After all, Owain had left orders that both were not to be allowed inside the house. She had to trust that they had been obeyed. Still, she would not take any chances, but stay here in her bedchamber until he arrived home.

Later as they sat sewing, Kate wondered if Gwendolyn and Owain really had once been lovers. Maybe when that first stirring in the blood had signalled the onset of fertility, they could have been tempted. Hadn't he mentioned his stepmother flirting with him and his brothers when she was a girl? She sighed, hoping it was not true, knowing she could never ask him.

Owain returned to the house just before supper and immediately came face to face with Gwendolyn in the hall. She was sitting on a settle in front of the fire, swathed from head to foot in black. On her breast hung a large silver crucifix, which she caressed with slender pale fingers, whispering to the saturnine-faced friar bending over her. Fortunately, the cleric had not been left alone to wander the house. Jonathan sat a few feet away from him, a hand resting on the neck of a large hound, watching them.

'Good news travels fast,' said Owain, barely able to control his fury that the friar had managed to worm his way into the house.

Gwendolyn and her uncle turned to stare at him. 'How can you speak to me so?' she said reproachfully, holding out both hands to him. 'We are both sorrowing and needs must comfort the other.'

'You don't have to pretend with me, Gwendolyn.' He wrenched off one of his riding gauntlets. 'Although my father's death is a sadness to me, I do not expect you to keep vigil with me and my brothers in the lady chapel during the night before the burial.'

Her eyes flashed fire. 'I have met your Lady Catherine. I was telling my uncle of your betrothal. He is delighted for you.'

'Indeed,' said the cleric, stretching his thin lips into a smile. 'As you well know, Master ap Rowan, her disappearance and that of the Fletcher family caused quite a stir. What news of that family?'

'They were killed in an attack by brigands whilst crossing the Pyrenees,' said Owain. If he had not been watching the cleric so intently, he might have missed the flash of relief in the man's eyes.

'May God have mercy on their souls!' He crossed himself and then placed his palms together. 'Lady Catherine must be deeply upset and in need of spiritual succour. Perhaps I can help.'

'I think not. She has me to care for her now, and there is our own priest to see to her spiritual needs.'

There was a taut silence and then the friar said, 'As you wish…but allow me to speak on behalf of the Lady Gwendolyn on a matter she does not wish to mention to you herself. She is worried that in the excitement and cost involved in your taking a bride that you will be distracted from your duty to her, Master ap Rowan.'

'I do not need reminding of my duty to my father's widow,' said Owain coldly. 'I see no need for you to be here on this manor. I want you off my land within the hour.'

The friar's thin lips tightened and his hand fastened on the rope that served as a girdle at his waist. 'I am concerned only for the Lady Gwendolyn. Your brother tells me you have been to Chester to visit the family lawyer. You should have consulted with your priest first and he would have gone with you. One cannot always trust these lawyers.'

Owain raised his dark eyebrows. 'You think not? Our priest has no need to fear and I am certain he knows that. He will receive the legacy that my father promised for the repair of the church roof, as well as one of our finest mares. Now if you'll excuse me, I must find the Lady Catherine.' He strode from the hall.

'See, Uncle, it is as I said and she is all he can think about. No doubt, despite his fine words, he intends cheating me out of what is mine.' Gwendolyn's voice carried across the hall.

Owain turned on his heel and returned to where she and the friar were seated. 'As his widow you are entitled to a third of my father's estate, Gwendolyn. Although it will not be as much as you might have hoped for—it appears that my father has been spending large sums of money without explaining what they were for. No doubt you know where the money has gone?'

Two spots of colour appeared on her cheeks. 'I am not his man of business, so how should I know what he's done with his money?' she cried. 'Or is it that you want an excuse not to include the child I carry in the payments? As Sir Hywel's son, surely he is entitled to a share of his estate?'

Owain's eyes glinted with anger. 'A decision about the child is best left until it is born. As for you, Friar Stephen, if you are still here when I return, I will have great pleasure in removing you bodily.'

He did not wait to see the effect of those words on them, but left the hall to seek out Kate. He took the stairs two at a time and hurried along the passageway until he came to her chamber. He rapped his knuckles on the door and called her name. Immediately she answered and he heard the bolt being drawn. The door opened to reveal Kate and Megan. Instantly he dismissed the serving maid.

As soon as Megan was out of earshot, Kate said lightly, 'You would let the servants know that you visit me in my bedchamber without a chaperon, Owain? What will that do for my reputation?'

'I'm glad you're still able to jest, Kate.' He closed the door and rested his back again it. 'Despite my orders, the friar is with Gwendolyn down in the hall.'

Kate gasped. 'I am glad I bolted the door. Does she suspect I am not the Lady Catherine? She angered me and I said what I aught not have done.'

'She referred to you as Lady Catherine, so I think not. I told them that the Fletchers were killed crossing the Pyrenees and I could see in the friar's eyes that news came as a relief to him. Perhaps you can tell me why later. I want you to stay here until we know for certain he has left. The speed they arrived after my father's death convinces me that he was most likely staying in the abbey lodging house in Chester and that Gwendolyn knew where to find him. It is near enough for Agnes to go there with the tidings of my father's death and to enable Gwendolyn and the friar to return here the same day. God only knows where Comte d'Azay is, but no doubt a message will have been sent to him.'

'She must have taken a different route, otherwise we would have passed her on the road yesterday,' said Kate.

Owain nodded. 'There are other paths, although on horseback they would be hazardous for a woman in her condition. What did she say to upset you?'

Kate hesitated, twisting her hands together. He reached out and took hold of her fingers, stilling them. 'Come, sweeting, there is no need to fear telling me the truth.'

His touch and his use of the endearment sent delight trickling through her veins like warm honey and encouraged her to be honest with him. 'She told me you were once lovers.'

He cocked a devilishly dark eyebrow. 'Never!'

'Also that the child she carries is yours.'

He laughed. 'Impossible! Besides, she has just told me she carries my father's son and wishes to lay claim to part of his estate for him. Whether that is true or not…'

Kate smiled. 'I told her that I did not believe her child was yours—that *you* would not have betrayed your father.'

His eyes held a flicker of appreciation and he bent and kissed her mouth. 'Sweet Kate. Now bolt the door after me. I will return as soon as I can.'

Owain hurried away but instead of immediately

going down to the hall, he went to his own bedchamber, not only to change his travel-stained garments, but also to see whether his hiding place in the wall had been interfered with. In the past he had never been certain whether Gwendolyn had knowledge of the hidey-hole where he had kept his boyish treasures: a peacock's iridescent feather, a pebble with the remains of some long-dead creature embedded in it, a Roman coin he had found whilst fishing in the Dee.

The stone was slightly out of alignment and he sat back on his heels, relieved that he had made the decision that morning to hand the copy of Lady Catherine's will over to the family lawyer for safe keeping. He had sent a message to Sir Thomas, bringing him up to date with most of what had happened on his travels, as well as the news of his father's death.

He rose to his feet and made haste to the hall, half-hoping to find the friar there, so he would have the excuse to throw him out. But Gwendolyn's uncle was gone and so had Jonathan and the hound. She still sat on the settle; the expression on her pale-skinned face caused him to wonder what she was plotting now. She appeared completely oblivious to the preparations going on about her for the evening meal. He did not speak to her, but made his way to the stables and asked one of the grooms whether the friar had gone.

'Aye, Master Owain. He left a short while ago and appeared to be in a foul mood, kicking out at the stable lad as he mounted.'

Owain nodded, glad to be rid of the man, although he did not doubt they would confront each other again.

* * *

'So tell me, Lady Catherine, how did you and Owain meet?' asked Gwendolyn, moving restlessly in her chair. Two days had passed since the death of Sir Hywel, but it was the first time she had sat at table with the rest of the family and Kate.

'You were there when Davy told Father that Owain had met her in Spain where she was on pilgrimage,' said Hal, reaching for more bread. 'And your question proves that you lied when you accused Owain of murder and adultery.'

'My thanks for reminding me, Hal,' she said in a silky voice, fixing him with a stare.

He shifted uncomfortably and seemed to have trouble looking away. Guessing what the other woman was trying to do, Kate leaned forward to block Hal from her vision and changed the subject. 'Have you ever been on pilgrimage, Lady Gwendolyn?' Her voice was icily polite.

Gwendolyn's mouth tightened; picking up her spoon, she dipped it into the bowl of pottage. 'My uncle is my spiritual advisor and he says a pilgrimage is an indulgence and an excuse to escape one's duty.'

'Even so, you should consider a pilgrimage—one is never the same afterwards,' said Kate.

Gwendolyn flashed a honeyed smile. 'I have no wish to be someone different. As for travelling abroad to St James's shrine—surely it was a foolish notion of yours so soon after your husband's death? No wonder there were rumours.'

'No more foolish than your behaviour at this table,' rasped Owain. 'You forget your manners, Gwendolyn.

Also, it strikes me that you know too much about what happened at Lady Catherine's manor that day. No doubt your so-called spiritual advisor and your lover were in the vicinity and had their own reasons for wanting Sir Roger dead.'

'How dare you accuse me of having a lover?' cried Gwendolyn, her face twitching as she lumbered to her feet, clutching her belly. 'You have no consideration for me at all. You ordered my uncle to leave just when I was most in need of spiritual succour. I deem that it will be I who will be asked to leave my home next. Your father welcomed him and you had no right to alter his orders.'

'He has every right,' rumbled Davy from the other end of the table. 'He is Father's heir, not that bastard you carry in your womb.'

'So it is you I have to blame for such falsehoods.' Gwendolyn shot out an arm and pointed a finger at Davy. 'I will curse you and that slut you would marry.'

Owain banged the table with the hilt of his knife. 'Enough! The servants are listening. Gwendolyn, you should be resting. Your time is near and we want nothing to befall you or your child.'

'You mean that you do want that. You threaten me!' Her eyes were wild. 'I will curse you, too. You and your…'

'Stop it!' roared Owain. 'No one is threatening you, you foolish woman.'

'She is a threat to me! I will curse her.' Gwendolyn turned on Kate, only to double up and clutch her stomach. 'Ahhh! The pain. She wants to destroy me and my child.'

Exasperated, Kate got to her feet. 'It is obvious that

your travail has started. I will fetch Agnes and she will accompany you to your bedchamber.'

'Nay! I do not want you having any part in this.' Gwendolyn backed away and turned to one of the serving men. 'Fetch Agnes.' Even as he hurried away, she held up an arm between herself and Kate as if to ward her off.

Owain swore under his breath and his brothers exchanged glances and rolled their eyes. Kate whispered to Owain, 'I do not envy the midwife and Agnes. All I can do is to pray for a safe delivery for her and her child.'

He nodded. 'Best for all of us if she had joined her lover. As it is, I will ensure that the midwife and Agnes receive all the help they need in seeing her through her travail.'

Kate was woken about eight the following morning by screams. Megan informed her that the Lady Gwendolyn had laboured all night, but that the midwife considered it would not be long now before the baby was born. Kate washed, dressed and went downstairs, to find the three brothers breaking their fast.

Afterwards Kate, accompanied by Megan, sat in the parlour and sewed. Owain joined them there, sitting at a small table and reading the answers to his invitations to his father's funeral on the morrow. Shortly before ten o'clock the screams ceased. Kate's hands stilled and she glanced at Owain. He raised his eyebrows. She turned to Megan, 'Run up and see whether the baby has been born and how fares the Lady Gwendolyn.'

Megan wasted no time in doing as asked.

* * *

A short while later the maid returned, accompanied by the midwife cradling a baby wrapped in a blanket. She looked past Kate to Owain. 'The Lady Gwendolyn has given birth to a daughter, Master Owain, but she has told me to let her die,' she said, distressed.

He was amazed. 'Is there aught wrong with the child?'

'Nay, sir. She's strong in wind and limb. But the lady wanted a son and refuses even to hold the child.'

Kate went over to the midwife and drew back the blanket to reveal a small screwed-up face topped by a mop of red-gold hair. Owain rose and gazed down at the child. With a helpless gesture, he murmured, 'With such hair I cannot help but think…'

The baby whimpered and pity smote Kate's heart. 'But who is to say that in your father's ancestry there wasn't someone with such hair?' she whispered.

'That is true,' he said, sounding relieved. 'She has survived what must have been an arduous birth, so should have her chance. But if Gwendolyn will have naught to do with her—what do we do?'

'The midwife could place her with a wet nurse if she knows of one.' Kate turned to the woman.

'The smith's wife has recently given birth, Master Owain,' said the midwife with a smiling nod. 'Shall I take her to her?'

'Aye,' said Owain, 'and see that she is baptised.'

'What name shall we give her?' asked the midwife.

Owain exchanged a glance with Kate. 'What was your mother's name?' she asked.

'Anna,' he murmured.

'Then shall she be Anna?' asked the midwife.

He nodded and dismissed her and Megan.

As soon as they left, he turned to Kate. 'The babe is easily dealt with, but Gwendolyn is a different matter altogether. If she recovers from the birth, I have no doubt that once she is up and about then she will be hell-bent on making trouble for us.'

Kate said seriously, 'Then you must get rid of her. Once she gets her hands on her widow's portion, she should set up her own establishment in the company of a sensible, older woman, and have naught else to do with her uncle or the Comte.'

Owain's expression was sombre. 'I doubt she will do that—she is too much under their influence. Besides, it could be that they will want her to stay on here as their spy.'

'Why do they need to spy on you? What is it they want from you?' asked Kate, a tiny crease of worry between her fair brows.

He smiled faintly. 'Perhaps they think I know more about their affairs than I do.' He took her hand and clasped it firmly. 'Then there is you, Kate. They might believe the Fletchers dead, but Lady Catherine could still be a threat to them. She might have heard them plotting against the King when Sir Roger was supposedly turning base metal into gold.'

Kate's eyes widened. 'You believe them traitors?'

'These are uncertain and dangerous times. Even if the King recovers from his sickness—as I hope—there are those who would rather see England ruled by someone stronger. There are many who believe there are others of the royal blood who have more right to the throne than Henry of Lancaster.'

Kate paled. 'The King's half-brother, the Earl of Richmond, could he be one of these men?'

Owain shook his head, toying with her fingers. 'They share the same mother, so it's in his interest to support Henry.'

Kate nodded. 'I was not thinking clearly. I spoke his name, only because Agnes mentioned it. But perhaps his life could be in danger because of his closeness and influence on the King.'

Owain smiled. 'It is possible. But we have discussed this enough for now.' He drew her hand through his arm. 'Let's go outside. There's a mare, no use for breeding, that I wish to show you.'

'Why is she of no use for breeding?' asked Kate.

'A stray stallion ran amok amongst the mares and covered one before we could capture him. The off-spring of that union is not pure bred, but she has nice manners. We'll go through the orchard, so you can pluck an apple for her and make friends.' He smiled down at Kate with such warmth in his eyes that her heart was filled with love for him.

As they walked beneath trees heavy with fruit, she wished that she did not have to leave this place. The air was filled with birdsong and when the sun came out from behind the clouds, sending beams of pale golden light through the branches, she experienced an explosion of pure happiness. Yet she was going to have to leave and soon, thought Kate, bending to pick up a windfall apple.

Owain opened a gate and they went through into a meadow where there were several horses. He caught and brought a dapple-grey mare towards her. Kate realised that the horse was no beauty—her head was too large for her body and her legs seemed too short. Wisps of grass hung from the mare's mouth as she ambled towards her as if in a dream. Kate held out the apple on the palm of her hand and the mare blew gently down her nostrils, lipping her fingers before taking the fruit gently in one gulp.

'Her name is Epona,' said Owain with a twinkle in his eye. 'She is the perfect lady's mount, so if you wish to ride at any time…'

Kate thanked him with a laugh in her voice. 'Epona was an equestrian goddess, worshipped by those who followed the old religion. Whoever named her was surely jesting. She does not have the appearance of a goddess.'

'I named her. I wanted to make up to her for her ill appearance.' He patted the horse's neck.

A slight pucker formed between Kate's brows as she stroked Epona's muzzle. 'But you must have learnt something of the old religion to know the goddess's name.'

'It pays to know as much as one can about our enemies' interests,' said Owain lightly. 'But I question whether Sir Roger really believed in the existence of the old gods and goddesses. I believe what attracted him was that they were worshipped at a time when men discovered that by applying great heat to lumps of different rocks, they were able to extract metal from the stone. You will have seen a smith hammering red hot iron into shape…imagine the excitement felt by those ancients when copper, tin, silver and gold ran in liquid form separate from the rock.'

'It must have been exciting, unbelievable…magical,' said Kate, trying to picture the scene.

'Some would definitely believe it magic.' Owain smiled. 'And think about those ancients mixing iron with tin and making bronze…copper and zinc and discovering brass.'

'But even those metals corrode,' said Kate.

Owain nodded. 'Silver, too.'

'But not gold…and that's why the King and other gullible fools are prepared to hand over chests of coin to Sir Roger.' Kate nibbled on her nether lip.

'So you know there was more than one chest?'

Kate hesitated. 'It would make sense. Coin is heavy and easier to carry in small chests, rather than one large one. Do you think Sir Roger was murdered for the coin he had collected?'

Owain hesitated, then said smoothly, 'It's as good a reason as any. Who knew about the money?'

'My father, of course…but as he was already dead he could not have murdered Sir Roger. What about Sir Thomas? Surely he would have known about the chests,' said Kate.

Owain shrugged. 'Perhaps. But I doubt Sir Roger would have told him where the coin was hidden. Besides, Sir Thomas has too much to lose to betray the King.'

Kate could only agree. 'Most likely the friar would know…and the Comte perhaps.'

'Naturally. There is one other person who would have known about them…and that's the Lady Catherine. She might have even had one of her servants take one and hide it away.'

Kate stared at him in astonishment. 'I never considered her doing such a thing. Surely she would have mentioned it to Mother or myself if she had.' She gave Epona a final pat and made for the gate.

Owain followed her. 'Someone might have put the idea into her head. I presume she gave you no hint of such a thing when she was dying, although you must have discussed what the other would do if one of you were to die? She had no husband, children or kin.'

Kate froze in her tracks. When she spoke her voice was husky with emotion. 'We have spoken of this before. I'm certain she made a will before she left England, although she made no mention of it until she was dying. Even then I was unsure whether I heard her aright.'

'What did she say?'

Kate dragged her gaze away from his and looked down at the ground. 'She was too sick to speak clearly. Her mind wandered in her fever. There were odd snatches of lucidity when I managed to understand her. If I am right, then she left her will with the rector at Walton-on-the-Hill.' Kate sighed. 'But what does it matter now? The King has laid claim to Merebury, so it is unlikely her wishes will be met.'

'They won't be if you're not prepared to claim what is yours, Kate.'

Kate felt the colour rush to her cheeks and lifting her head, she gazed at him. 'You have seen the will?'

He nodded. 'Who else would she leave her property to but her faithful companion? No doubt Sir Thomas's lawyer will be in touch with the rector when I write to him about this.'

'No doubt Sir Thomas will accuse *me* of murdering my Lady as soon as he knows I am her main benefici-ary,' she said bitterly.

Owain frowned. 'Calm yourself, Kate. You do both Sir Thomas and myself a discourtesy. My message will inform him that the Lady Catherine is buried in the graveyard at Villafranca. If there are those who would accuse you of murder, then he will send someone to ver-ify your word.'

She flushed. 'You truly believe that he will do that for me?'

'I would not write to him otherwise,' he said pa-tiently.

Her temper flared and her eyes sparkled with anger. 'I don't know why you have to send word to him at all! I suppose you've already written to him and told him that you suspect my mother and brother are alive?'

He nodded. 'Part of the task appointed to me was to find the Fletchers. Once my father's funeral is over then you will take me to them.'

I will not, thought Kate rebelliously. She did not have his faith in Sir Thomas and was determined to speak to her mother and Diccon alone before making any decisions that could endanger their lives. Tomorrow she would attend the requiem mass, but, during the fu-neral meal, she would pretend to have a megrim and leave the hall. She would go on horseback and as she would be travelling alone, would wear her pilgrim's garb, and hope to pass unnoticed.

Chapter Ten

Kate urged the dappled grey mare through the North-gate of Chester. An autumnal nip was in the air, but at least the rain held off during her journey, which had passed without incident. All she had to do now was find the quickest route to her uncle's house, which she had not visited in years. She called to a boy carrying a basket of rushes and asked the way to the street of the shoemakers. He directed her to the abbey and along East Gate Street. Not far from the city wall, overlooking the river, was Souters Lane.

In no time at all, she came to a lane plunging steeply towards the Dee. She dismounted and led the horse between the open fronts of houses where shoemakers laboured. Some were cutting out leather, others sat cross-legged, stitching soles to uppers or mending shoes on lasts. Suddenly she recognised a face and pounced on a youth brushing up offcuts of leather and thread into the street. 'Diccon!' she cried in delight.

'Gerroff!' The brown-haired youth pushed her away.

'Diccon, it's me, Kate!' she cried.

He dropped the besom and stared at her in disbelief. 'You can't be Kate. You're dead.'

She laughed. 'I can understand you deeming that so…but here I am alive and well.'

His hazel eyes washed over her. 'What happened to your hair?'

'Never mind that now.' She hugged him. 'Where is Mother?'

'She is off some place with our aunt,' he said, freeing himself from Kate's embrace, flushing red with embarrassment to the tips of his ears. 'They'll probably swoon when they see you.' Diccon stared at her as if he still could not believe she was there in front of him. 'You look…older.'

She laughed. 'I am older…and I could say the same about you. You've grown up.'

He grimaced. 'You wouldn't believe it—the way our uncle treats me. But forget him for now. What of the Lady Catherine? Is she well?'

Kate's expression altered and her eyes were sad. 'She died of a fever.'

His freckled face fell. 'Mother will be upset.'

'It was a great sadness to me, but there was little I could do to help her. All the spirit went out of her after we were attacked in the mountains by brigands. We lost all that we possessed and she cut off my hair so men would believe me to be a youth. She wouldn't eat, and travelling on foot with little respite exhausted her.'

He shook his head slowly. 'It is a great pity. She and her father were good to our family.'

Kate agreed with a sigh. 'It was difficult for me to continue after she died, but I made her a promise. It's a long tale and I'd rather tell you and Mother together. Suffice to say that I met someone, whose home is less than half a day's journey from here. He gave me permission to ride this mare.' She patted the horse's neck. 'Epona is her name.'

Diccon's lips twitched as he stared at the horse. 'There's little of the goddess about her.'

Kate put her hands over the horse's ears and said in mock reproof, 'I'll not have you hurting her feelings. She is the perfect horse for a lady.'

Diccon raised his eyebrows. 'You—a lady?'

Kate raised her chin and assumed a haughty expression. 'On Master Owain ap Rowan's manor they believe me to be the Lady Catherine Miles.'

He gaped. 'You jest?'

She shook her head. 'He mistook me for her whilst we were in Spain.'

Diccon's eyes narrowed. 'What have you been up to, sister? I want to hear all.'

'Later I will tell you everything. Mother—she is well?' asked Kate, her eyes filled with concern.

Diccon said glumly, 'She's not happy here and neither am I—but where can we go? I would return to Merebury, but Mother says it is too risky.'

'Master Owain ap Rowan's manor,' said Kate without a second thought.

Before Diccon could reply, a man came out of the house behind him and growled, 'Stop wasting time with that lad and get on with your work, boy.' He clouted Diccon across the head, causing him to drop the besom.

Kate was indignant and would have voiced her feelings. But as Diccon bent to pick up the besom, he whispered, 'Don't let Uncle know it's you.' As he straightened, his expression was sullen as he looked at his uncle. 'He was asking if I could recommend a tavern for his master and mistress, who have not visited Chester before. I told him to try the Falcon on Bridge Street, not far from the Friar's Gate. He'll need to turn left at the top of the lane and carry on in that direction.' Diccon jerked his head at Kate.

She mumbled her thanks and led Epona back up the lane, puzzled by her brother's behaviour. But, by the time she reached the top of the lane, she concluded that he meant her to go to the Falcon with the intention of meeting her there later. On the way to the inn, she gazed about her, hoping to catch sight of her mother, but with so many people thronging the streets that proved impossible. She found the inn without difficulty and prayed that she would not have to wait long before Beth and Diccon joined her. She thought with longing of Owain and wondered if he had missed her yet.

Owain's head throbbed. What with the noise, the smoke from the fire, the wine and ale, he'd had his fill of people and longed for them all to go. At least Gwendolyn was still abed, so he was not plagued by her dark stares, complaints and threats. He wondered if she'd had second thoughts about her daughter, but he was more concerned about Kate. He had not seen her since she had excused herself, saying she felt a megrim coming on and needed fresh air. His need to attend his guests had made it difficult for him to accompany her, although at the time he had seen no reason to doubt that she did indeed have a megrim. Even so, he wanted to find her. She had scarcely spoken to him since their conversation yesterday. He wished he could have been completely honest with her, but it would have meant breaking his word. He must find her and assure her that she and her family were in no danger from Sir Thomas and that it was vital that he spoke with her mother. He signalled to Davy to take his place and left the hall.

Kate was not in the gardens and neither was she in her bedchamber, where he found the gown she had worn that day on the bed. Where was she? Could she have gone, alone, in search of her mother and brother? Apprehension seized him and he ran down the backstairs and hurried to the stables. As he crossed the yard, one of the stable lads hailed him. 'Master Owain, here is a strange thing, Epona is missing. I could understand if one of the other horses had been stolen, but—'

'Saddle Merlin,' ordered Owain, convinced that Kate had taken the horse. But where was her destination? He thought deeply as he checked his pouch for coin and remembered her asking if she could accompany him to Chester the morning after his father had died. It was only a slender lead, but it was all he had. It suddenly occurred to him that, if she had gone there and could not find her family, she might seek shelter at the abbey lodging house—a building frequented by the friar. He prayed for her safety and, once in the saddle, headed at a gallop across the fields in the direction of Chester, knowing he had to get there before the gates closed at sundown.

Kate was anxious and restless. She had been waiting an age for her brother and mother before it occurred to her that the friar could be staying in Chester and might recognise her. She was seriously considering returning to the house of her aunt and uncle when she caught sight of Diccon and Beth approaching from the direction of Souters Lane. Her mother wore a russet gown and a grey cloak, the hood of which concealed most of her soft brown hair, but Kate would have known her walk anywhere. Her worries evaporated and she hurried towards them.

Tears brimmed in Beth Fletcher's eyes, spilling over and trickling down her slender cheeks. She stopped a foot or so away from Kate and exclaimed, 'Your hair! No wonder your uncle mistook you for a lad. But it is you, daughter...and I never gave up hope of you returning, even when it appeared that I was a fool to carry on believing you would.'

Oblivious to the stares of passers-by, Kate flung herself into Beth's arms and wept. When there were no more tears left, she lifted her head. 'I have so much to tell you, Mother. Some of it good and some bad. But let us get away from here. Friar Stephen stays here at the abbey lodging house and we might be seen.'

Beth paled, darting glances at the faces of those nearby, but fortunately there was no sign of the friar. 'How do you know this?' she asked her daughter, watching as she handed the horse's reins to Diccon.

Kate slipped an arm through her mother's and urged her in the direction of the river. 'I will explain when I reach that part of my tale.'

'Diccon told me of Lady Catherine's death. My heart is sore with grief for she was like a daughter to me,' said Beth, her voice quivering.

'I also grieve…but at least I fulfilled the promise I made to her.'

'What promise was that?' asked Beth, her face blotchy with weeping.

'To pray for her soul at the tomb of St James.'

Beth's eyes brightened. 'Praise the Holy Trinity! Was it wonderful in the city of the saint?'

Kate told her mother about the shrine and the cathedral and the celebration. When she finished, Beth said enviously, 'How I wish that I could have been there. But explain to me, daughter, how you came to be mistaken for the Lady Catherine? This Master ap Rowan…where did you meet him?'

Kate schooled her features to show little emotion. 'Whilst in Spain. At first I believed Owain to be an enemy…and it is true that he was sent by Sir Thomas Stanley to find us and Lady Catherine.'

'So it is as I feared. Our flight has caused him to believe we are guilty of Sir Roger's death.' Beth's face was pinched and drawn.

'Owain denies that, although he has admitted that his commission is to find those responsible for Sir Roger's murder. He is acting on the King's orders.'

'The King is sick in his mind,' said Diccon, who had been listening intently. 'Prayers are being said daily in the Abbey for his recovery and the well-being of his son, Prince Edward, Earl of Chester.'

Kate turned to him. 'Owain told me that the Duke of York is Protectorate of England because of the King's illness.'

'Aye, and he immediately removed Edmund Beaufort, the Duke of Somerset, from his lucrative position as

Captain of Calais and placed him in the Tower, claiming the post for himself,' said Diccon with a laugh. 'Who can blame him when the King favours others above him?'

'How do you know this?' asked Kate, surprised that he should be so well informed.

'The Beaufort lords visited Chester when the Earl of Richmond was here. We feared there might be trouble here in the north.'

'The Earl of Richmond was *here*?' cried Kate.

Diccon rolled his eyes. 'I tell you, sister, I've seen more of the King's relatives here in Chester than I ever did at home.'

'You distract Kate from her tale,' said Beth, drawing her cloak closer about her as a breeze from the river set it billowing. 'She has yet to tell us how she was mistaken for Lady Catherine.'

Kate hesitated. 'It was no mistake, Mother. I decided it was safer for me to pretend to be her. I was alone in a foreign land and decided I would be treated with respect if I claimed to be a Lady.' In her mind's eye Kate pictured herself facing Owain dressed in the new gown he had given to her. Her pulse beat rapidly as she remembered the expression in his eyes as he had stared at her, recalled the feel of his fingers on her neck as he had combed her hair.

Beth nudged her daughter with an elbow. 'Don't stop now. Was your virtue in danger?'

Kate collected herself. 'That is why my hair was hacked off. Master ap Rowan believed me to be Diccon at first.'

Beth groaned. 'And now he believes you are a lady dressed the way you are…and with that hair?'

Kate pressed her mother's arm. 'I told him the truth when we were in France and now he is certain you and Diccon are alive and wants to meet you.' She added in soothing tones, 'I don't think he suspects us of murdering Sir Roger any more.'

Her mother moaned. 'Easy to say that. What else did you tell him, Kate?'

She glanced at her brother. 'I have not told him what we saw the day our father died.'

Beth looked relieved. 'At least in that you have behaved wisely.'

'But it is a reason for the friar and the Comte wanting *us* dead,' said Kate.

Beth crossed herself. 'Praise the Saints that neither has crossed our path since.'

'Comte d'Azay is believed to be Owain's stepmother's lover and the friar is her uncle. He persuaded Owain's father to give him money.'

Beth put a hand to her head. 'Are you saying this *Owain*, this Master ap Rowan, is acquainted with both these men?'

Kate nodded.

'I can't believe it,' wailed Beth, clutched her cloak. 'And you told this man that we are alive?'

A flush darkened Kate's cheeks and she shook her head. 'Don't fret, Mother. He loathes them both. Now let me tell you some good news.'

Beth sighed. 'There is some.'

Kate smiled and squeezed her mother's arm. 'The Lady Catherine made a will and left it in the care of the rector at Walton-on-the-Hill. She has left Merebury to me. If I had perished, then it would have come to you.

Whatever, it does not matter because I survived and where my home is there will be yours also.'

Beth stared at her as if she could not believe her. 'It is indeed a great gift, but what chance have we of taking possession of it?' she said gloomily.

'Owain believes that Sir Thomas will help me,' said Kate firmly.

'Owain! Owain! I tire of hearing this man's name. You are besotted with him and he would lead us into a trap,' said Beth, shaking her head.

Kate's colour deepened. 'I believe it is not in his interest to lead us into a trap. I have trusted him with my life and he has shown me kindness. Merebury is mine and I will fight for it. So what is it to be, Mother? Are you willing to meet Owain ap Rowan? If so, we must leave now before night falls.'

Beth fixed her with a stare. 'No doubt if I refuse to go with you then you will go alone.'

'I have travelled far to get here, Mother. I love you and do not wish to be parted from you so soon,' said Kate in a low voice.

'Then give me time to think, daughter. Let me sleep on it. You have yet to explain, if this man knows you are Kate Fletcher, why those on his manor believe you to be Lady Cathcrine.'

Kate hesitated, knowing she was going to have difficulty explaining what had happened. There was silence, except for the dull plod of the horse's hooves on the path of beaten earth and the sound of the rising wind whipping the surface of the river.

'I'm waiting,' said Beth.

Kate glanced up at the darkening sky. 'I believe

we're in for a storm. So now isn't the time to be leaving Chester. You can have your time to think, Mother.'

'That is all you have to say?'

'I, also, need to think.'

'Then we will go back to your uncle's house and in the morning I will decide what to do,' said Beth, grim-faced.

Diccon looked dismayed and opened his mouth as if to speak, but already his mother was forging ahead against the wind. He glanced at Kate and then led the horse east along the river bank.

As a huge raindrop splashed onto Kate's face, she followed them, knowing Owain was bound to be angry when he discovered her absence. She could only hope he would forgive her.

Huddled beneath his sodden cloak, Owain was in a foul mood as he entered Chester. The storm had broken a short while ago and he was soaked to the skin. As he passed through the almost deserted streets, he knew that only through an amazing stroke of luck would he find Kate that evening. He was so angry with her that if he had caught sight of her then he'd have spanked her. He could only pray that she was safe with her mother and brother and had not encountered their enemy. Merlin's hooves clip-clopped on the cobbles as they made their way through the glistening streets to the Falcon Inn.

He dismounted and went inside and bespoke a bed-chamber for the night before going outside again and stabling his horse. He knew he was in for an anxious and uncomfortable night.

* * *

Kate stood in the lane outside her uncle's house, stroking Epona's neck, turning over in her mind all that her mother and aunt had said about Owain. The sisters had agreed that Kate was far too trusting of Master ap Rowan and it would be best if she never saw him again. They didn't have to say they believed he had compromised her because it was there in their faces. Her mother had wanted her to promise that she would take the mare to the livery stables and ask for it to be returned to Rowan Manor, along with his ring, and then come straight back. Kate was furious at being treated like a child after journeying so far from England and arriving back safely.

'I know I shouldn't say this,' said Diccon, coming up behind Kate, 'but I think it's a mistake returning the horse.'

She whirled round. 'I agree, but you heard what Mother and Aunt said.'

Diccon nodded. 'She's frightened and I can understand that. But I don't see much of a future for us staying here in hiding. I'd probably end up as a shoemaker. Nothing wrong with shoemakers, but I would rather risk trusting your Master ap Rowan and have the chance of returning to Merebury than stay here. We'll have to keep it secret from Mother, mind. She's going to worry when we vanish, but that's what mothers do.'

Kate nodded. 'She'll probably guess where we've gone. But as Owain wishes to speak to her, no doubt we'll be back here before too long.'

Suddenly they heard their uncle's angry voice from inside the house. 'Let's go now,' said Diccon urgently.

'Help me to mount,' whispered Kate.

'Best we go downhill towards the river.' Diccon bent

and laced his hands together for her to place her foot in. He flung her on to the horse's back and wasted no time dragging himself up behind her. Kate dug in her heels and urged the mare down the lane.

Owain stepped outside the Falcon Inn and breathed deeply of the crisp air, tinged with wood smoke and dung. He walked across the street and strode swiftly in the direction of the abbey, gazing into the faces of passers-by as he did so. His concern for Kate was a tightness in his chest, so that when he spotted a youth and a figure, whom he took to be a novice, astride a recognisable, dappled grey horse, he tore after them, shouting, 'Stop, thief!'

Kate was oblivious to the commotion breaking out behind her. That was until Diccon was suddenly dragged from the saddle. Before she could turn and see what had happened, she felt a tug on the back of her tunic and was pulled from the horse. She protested loudly and struggled to free herself, but her assailant was strong and forced her round to face him. Instantly she recognised Owain and her heart leapt with gladness before plummeting into her stomach.

'By all that I hold holy, Kate, I'll wring your neck if you ever run away from me again,' said Owain in a seething voice. 'Have I treated you so badly that you need must don that filthy tunic again and vanish into thin air?'

'Owain, h-how did you know where to f-find me?' she stammered.

'Does that matter? Did you give no thought to the danger? You could have been abducted, tortured, killed.'

A slow smile warmed her eyes. 'You were worried about me.'

'More fool me,' he rasped, shaking her.

She clung to him, only to wrench herself out of his arms when she heard a pain-filled yelp from her brother. She flew at the burly citizen who held a struggling Diccon. 'Let him go,' she ordered, hitting the man with her fist.

Owain pulled her off him and said to the man, 'Release him. I made a mistake. But you have my thanks for acting so swiftly.' He took a coin from his pocket and tossed it to him. The man caught it deftly, thanked him and walked off through the dispersing crowd.

Diccon rubbed his posterior and gazed at Owain. 'Are you Master ap Rowan?'

'Of course he is,' said Kate, frowning.

Owain glanced down at her. 'Where is your mother?'

Kate did not answer. Her emotions were in turmoil.

Diccon said, 'At the house of my aunt and uncle in Souters Lane. We were coming to you, but Mother has lived with fear too long to trust someone who is acquainted with the friar and the Comte.'

Owain stared at him intently. 'Kate told you that… and yet you appear to trust me.'

'I doubt my sister would have arrived safely in Chester if you weren't to be trusted.'

Kate raised her eyebrows, but was silent. Owain smiled. 'Your brother is definitely a youth of some intelligence. I must speak with your mother. Perhaps the news I have to tell her will make her think better of me.'

'News? What news is this?' asked Kate swiftly.

'It is for your mother's ears first,' said Owain. 'Now, up into the saddle with you, Kate.' Before she could prevent him, he seized her by the waist and lifted her on to the mare. Taking hold of the reins, he indicated that Diccon walk beside him. 'Tell me, who do you think killed Sir Roger?' asked Owain.

Diccon gave him a sidelong, wary glance. 'Perhaps the friar or the Comte. Or even one of those knights who gave him money and took part in his evil revels.'

Owain's step faltered a moment. 'You saw coin changing hands?' Diccon nodded. 'Do you know what happened to the money?'

'My father told me he had found the hiding place where they stored the chests of coin. They were not big, otherwise it would have taken more than two men to move them. Father removed one and hid it somewhere else. I believe he knew his life could be in danger and wanted to provide for us.'

Owain nodded slowly. 'No doubt his theft definitely sealed his fate.'

Diccon's head shot up and dark colour stained his youthful cheeks as he glanced at his sister. 'You promised not to speak of that.'

'I didn't! Master ap Rowan is hazarding a guess to make you reveal more.'

Owain's lips curved into a grim smile. 'Not quite the words I would use, Kate.'

Diccon rushed into speech. 'Father wanted to initiate me into the old ways. Kate told me it could lead me into danger, but I did not believe her. Then Sir Roger asked to see me and wanted me to…' The youth paused and swallowed before continuing in fierce tones. 'I believe it was then that my father realised his mistake. He wasn't in it for gold. Sir Roger was bestial and greedy.'

He paused to take a breath. 'The friar was false to his calling; his worship wasn't for nature, but took the form of invoking his—his Satanic majesty as he called Ol' Nick in a way that froze the blood.' Diccon moistened his lips.

'What of the Comte?' murmured Owain. 'I suspect he had a deeper purpose for involving himself with Sir Roger.'

'Murder,' whispered Diccon. 'Although he also was interested in the devil and the old ways. He said that the blood of the ancients ran in his veins.'

Owain said sharply, 'Never mind that now. You spoke of murder. You know for certain he murdered Sir Roger?'

When the answer came it was not from Diccon, but from Kate. 'Nay! Diccon speaks of Father. We found him with his head broken. Of course, we were meant to believe that he'd fallen from a crag, but we had seen what happened from a distance.'

Owain lifted his head and gazed into her sad but beautiful face. 'I knew of his fall, but not that there were witnesses to it. You should have spoken of this to me sooner, Kate.'

'And given you more reason for suspecting the Fletchers of Sir Roger's murder,' she said with a wry smile. 'Besides, I had given my promise.'

'So what happened?'

Diccon answered. 'We saw two robed figures arguing and struggling with each other on top of a crag. We knew one was Sir Roger because he had his hood down. The other we were certain was Father. Suddenly two more robed figures came on the scene. It was difficult to recognise them with their hoods up, but voices carry on the wind and we were convinced they were the friar and Comte d'Azay. They joined the struggle and for a moment I thought Sir Roger was going to go over the edge, but instead it was Father who plunged to his death.'

'I'll never forget his dying scream,' said Kate.

'But we couldn't be sure which one killed him. We were convinced that if we dared to accuse any of them then, they'd find some way to silence us,' said Diccon.

'Could you hear what they were arguing about?' asked Owain.

'Not clearly enough that we could make sense of it,' said Diccon. 'Neither could we be sure whether we had been recognised by them. Mother told Lady Catherine what had happened…but surely *she* wouldn't have mentioned it to Sir Roger?' There was a puzzled note in his voice.

'Yet you suspect she might have,' said Owain.

Kate sighed. 'She could be stubborn and rash. Then Sir Roger demanded the heriot due to him after Father's death. We could not afford to pay it and Mother told him so. He said we'd have to leave Merebury if it was not paid by nightfall of the following day, but he did not live that long…' She paused, expecting Owain to speak, but when he was silent, she continued, 'Lady Catherine insisted that we all went away immediately. She just wouldn't listen to reason when we said that people might suspect us of having a hand in his death by leaving in a rush. She gave Mother some money and insisted she and Diccon stay with my aunt and uncle here in Chester until our return from pilgrimage. I never thought we would be away so long, not knowing she had it in mind to delay our arrival until the saint's feast day. I think we must have stopped at every shrine on the way.'

Owain muttered, 'I wonder if she did speak to him. But we'll never know now. Let's pass over it and tell me, Kate—did Lady Catherine have much to do with the Comte when he visited the manor?'

Kate's brow knitted. 'I remember he tried to flirt with her, but she was not interested. Then something must have happened because, one day, I came upon them talking in the garden. They were so engrossed in what they were saying they did not notice me.'

'Did you hear any of their conversation?' asked Owain.

Kate smiled faintly. 'They were speaking in French and I could not understand all what they said. I did wonder whether she was asking him about his home in France.'

Owain frowned. 'It's possible that your father's death was an accident.'

They stared at him in astonishment. 'Why should you think that?'

'If he'd stolen a chest of money and hidden it away, they'd want to find out where it was before killing him.'

Diccon nodded. 'Of course!'

'You don't know where your father hid the chest?' asked Owain, raising an eyebrow.

Diccon returned his gaze woodenly. 'He wouldn't tell me. I think he considered it too dangerous for me to know.'

'I can understand a father thinking like that. Yet our

enemies might believe you have that knowledge,' said Owain grimly.

Diccon agreed. 'That's why I didn't argue with Lady Catherine when she told us we had to leave Merebury. Our enemies might also believe Mother knows, so I wanted her safe.'

'Of course you did. And yours and her safety is as just important to me as that of Kate. But there comes a time when one has to come out of hiding. I must speak with your mother and persuade her to trust me.'

Chapter Eleven

Owain watched Kate's mother seat herself on the wooden bench in the garden to the rear of the house. He could tell from the way she plucked at her apron that she was not as calm as she appeared on the surface. 'There is nothing for you to fear, Mistress Fletcher,' he said gently. 'I hold you blameless in the matter of Sir Roger's death. It is a different matter altogether that I wish to talk to you about. It concerns Kate.'

She darted him a glance. 'Will you wed my daughter? You have certainly compromised her, Master ap Rowan.'

He raised his eyebrows. 'Is that what she said?'

'No! But I can read between the lines. If you know she has been left Merebury, then perhaps you intended to seduce her from the beginning.' There was a tremor in her voice.

Owain said stiffly, 'There has been no seduction.'

Beth flushed and lowered her eyes. 'I beg your pardon. But you must understand a mother's concern for her only daughter.'

'Of course.' His voice softened. 'But let us put this matter aside for the moment and discuss the reason I wished to speak to you alone.' He paused. 'Sir Thomas told me that you went through a simple form of marriage in your youth with his cousin, Sir Arthur Stanley.'

He heard her sharp intake of breath. 'It was kept quiet. How does he know of this?'

'Sir Arthur was dying and he sent for him. You and his child were on his conscience and he wished to make some provision for you both.'

Beth's eyes filled with tears. 'I thought he had forgotten us,' she whispered.

Owain smiled. 'It seems you were unforgettable. He gave Sir Thomas a gift of money for you both—fifty pounds for you and a hundred for Kate—with the added proviso that Sir Thomas find a suitable husband for his daughter.'

Beth swayed and seemed on the verge of collapse. Swiftly Owain sat beside her and took her hand, patting it. 'Fifty pounds! And a hundred for Kate,' she gasped. 'I always knew Arthur to be a sweet youth, a little weak perhaps, but…' A beauteous expression lit up her face.

Owain was curious. 'How did you meet?'

She turned to him eagerly. 'I was gathering wild herbs for my mother. I didn't know who he was at first because he was dressed in homespun and told me he'd been snaring rabbits for the pot.' Beth's eyes took on a distant expression. 'Naturally I took him to be a poacher…but I didn't hold that against him, although I worried in case he was caught.' A gentle smile played about her lips. 'He wasn't particularly handsome, but he was kind and so different from the lads I knew. He would tell me stories and read tales of chivalry and romance from a book. Eventually he told me who he was and suggested a secret marriage. I was young and innocent and loved him so I agreed. We plighted our troth in front of a wandering priest, both of us knowing that it could be some time before we could tell our parents the truth. We spent what time we could together…always away from prying eyes. Then I discovered I was with child.' She sighed.

Owain could imagine what it must have been like for them both. 'So you had to tell your parents.'

Beth nodded and her face clouded. 'My father beat me and called me filthy names and demanded to know the name of the man, but I wouldn't tell him. When I was able to walk again, I went in search of Arthur and told him about the baby and what my father had done.' She grimaced. 'I thought he could make everything right. It's true he told his parents that we had been married by a priest, but they said it was no true marriage. They already had a bride in mind for him…an heiress. I was wilful as a child and could be stubborn. I insisted that we were truly wed and he stood by my side and agreed. But they determined to separate us and paid my father to agree to my removal to a small manor near Lathom. They paid Richard Fletcher to go through a form of marriage with me. He was a widower and had lost his children to fever. He wasn't a bad man, but I thought my heart would break. Then my Kate was born and she brought light back into my life. She was fair just like Arthur with the same blue-green eyes. No wonder I could never forget him.' She fell silent.

'You will need to tell her about her father,' said Owain.

Beth nodded. 'I will do so now I know that he did

not forget us. Lady Catherine's father was aware that she was a Stanley and allowed Kate to learn to read and write alongside his daughter. He used to say that one day Sir Arthur would remember his first love and Kate would take her rightful place.'

Owain nodded. 'My orders from Sir Thomas are to take you both to Lathom…but first we must go to Rowan Manor. Kate needs to dress in a manner fitting for a lady.' He helped Beth to her feet.

'And what are your intentions towards my daughter, Master ap Rowan?' she asked, cocking her head on one side, her eyes as bright and sharp as a robin's. 'I deem she has a fondness for you. I do not want her heart broken.'

'I will be honest with you, Mistress Fletcher. When I set out on my search, gaining possession of Merebury by marrying the Lady Catherine was uppermost in my mind. My father and I had quarrelled and I needed land to breed horses. Since my return to England my father has died and I have inherited Rowan Manor. Now I wish to marry Kate because…she is Kate. Adorable yet maddening, self-willed but full of courage, beautiful, kind, determined…'

Laughing, Beth held out a hand. 'Enough! You have my consent.'

He gave her a smile of such sweetness that Beth felt a flutter beneath her ribs. 'Hopefully, Sir Thomas will agree that I will make her a suitable husband,' he said ruefully.

Beth's expression sobered. 'That you need his permission is something I cannot be happy about.' She paused. 'Is there aught else you wish to ask me?'

Owain hesitated. 'Diccon told me that your husband took one of Sir Roger's chests of coin and hid it. Do you know where it is?'

Beth's mouth set. 'I did not want to know. I thought him a fool to get involved in such chicanery. My Lady told me that the Comte was using some of the money to pay mercenaries to cause unrest in the Welsh Marches. It is not only his kin that have land there—so, too, does the Duke of York and the King's half-brothers.'

His gaze sharpened. 'Have you spoken of this to anyone?'

She shook her head and said firmly, 'Let the King's relatives and the nobility fight amongst themselves and kill each other. It is nothing to me.'

Owain could see there was no changing her mind and dropped the matter. He suggested they returned to the house.

As Beth and Owain entered the parlour Kate lifted her head and smiled tentatively. She noticed signs of tears on her mother's face. What had Owain said to make her cry? Kate's questioning gaze met his, but he smiled reassuringly and said he must speak to Diccon.

As soon as he had gone, Beth took Kate aside and repeated the tale she had just told Owain. Her daughter stared at her in amazement. 'You were married to a Stanley! Father was not my real father?'

'Aye.' Beth's cheeks were flushed and her eyes bright. 'Perhaps I should have told you when Richard died, but I could see no sensible reason to do so.'

'But you've always spoken against the Stanleys— now you tell me that I'm one of them!' Kate put a hand to her head. 'I can't take it in.' She paused. 'Wait a moment! Owain has something to do with this—otherwise you would not be telling me now.'

'Indeed, he does. Sir Thomas commissioned Master ap Rowan to find us for two reasons. One of them you already know about, but the other was because Sir Arthur died a few months ago. He gave Sir Thomas a sum of money for us.' Beth's eyes shone even brighter. 'Fifty pounds for me, Kate, and a *hundred pounds* for you! Arthur did not forget us! You do not know how happy that makes me.'

'I can't believe it,' said Kate in a daze.

'It is true, daughter. Forgive me for not telling you before, but I thought it best for you. Arthur's remembrance of us has changed matters. I am happy that Sir Thomas sent Master ap Rowan to inform me.'

'Me too,' whispered Kate, still struggling to come to terms with all that her mother had told her.

'Think what a difference this money will make to us, Kate,' said Beth.

'I see that now you have met Owain and he has brought you news that meets with your approval, he appears to have convinced you that he can be trusted,' Kate murmured.

'As much as any man can be trusted,' said Beth drily. 'I feel as if a great weight has been lifted from me. I am glad that I will no longer have to live beneath your uncle's roof. Once you meet Sir Thomas, he will see to it that Merebury will be yours and Diccon and I can move back home.'

'I will need help to hold Merebury, Mother,' said Kate seriously.

'Of a surety, daughter. But no doubt, between them, Master ap Rowan and Sir Thomas will see to all,' assured Beth. 'Now I must not keep Master ap Rowan waiting, but pack my few belongings. Then I must explain all to my sister. Where is she?'

'Upstairs,' said Kate.

Beth hurried out. Kate was amazed by the change in her. But then she, herself, felt a different person from the Kate who had woken that morning. In the past she would not have wanted to accept that the blood of powerful and often ruthless men ran in her veins. Now she was starting to consider what a difference being part of the Stanley clan could make to her life. If she was accepted by them, then she would be in a better position to help not only the poor and the needy, but also Owain. Here was another secret he had kept from her. How many more might he have up his sleeve? She felt a momentary vexation with him, and then shrugged her ill humour away. At least his knowing she was a Stanley made sense of his encouraging her to play the part of a lady. He had been preparing her for the moment when she would have to face Sir Thomas, who was…her cousin! It felt strange thinking of him as such after hating all that he represented for so long.

Kate recalled her mother telling her about the ancestry of the Stanleys. Now she understood why. Not only was she descended from a well-born Saxon lady, but also a Norman knight named Stanleigh. One thing was for certain— what she was wearing now would certainly not do to meet her kinsman, she thought with amusement. How strange it felt thinking of Sir Thomas in such a way. She decided that for her first proper meeting with him she would wear the red kirtle and green gown. Which reminded her—as soon as she was in possession of her legacy, she must repay Owain the money she owed him.

At that moment he entered the parlour, ducking his dark head to avoid a beam. His blue eyes were quizzical as he looked at her.

'You want to know what I am thinking,' said Kate promptly, 'you keeper of secrets.'

His mouth creased into a smile and, reaching out, he eased a wayward flaxen curl behind her ear. 'I would hazard a guess that you are wondering if I am hiding any more secrets from you. Secondly that you can't wait to reimburse me of the money I have spent on you.' He ran a finger down her cheek and over her lips.

'You are a seer. How else can you read my thoughts?' she marvelled. 'What would be your third *guess*?'

His arms encircled her waist. 'That you want me to make love to you.' His lips grazed her cheek, hovered over her mouth and then he kissed her. Kate almost purred with pleasure. He lifted his mouth and said unevenly, 'I'd take you right now if it weren't that…'

'My kinsfolk would be shocked to find us writhing on the floor in the throes of…'

He stopped her mouth with another kiss and then with a sigh thrust her from him. 'I have to swear to Sir Thomas that you are still a maid when I bring you before him.'

'Then you will tell him that we are betrothed.'

His lips twitched. 'What a forward maid you are…but, aye, I will tell him I want you for my wife. Hopefully he will give his permission. Although he might already have someone else in mind for you.'

Her eyes flew wide in dismay. 'I will refuse to marry any other suitor.'

'Then I'll have to convince him that I'm the perfect match for you.' Owain smiled and kissed the tip of her nose.

She was about to go into his arms again when the door opened and Diccon and her uncle appeared. Before anyone could speak, Beth came hurrying into the room with her sister at her heels. As soon as Kate saw her, she guessed that something was worrying her. 'What is it, Mother?'

Beth clasped the handles of her cloth bag with both hands and said firmly, 'I'll not go with you to meet Sir Thomas. I'm not one of them and never could be.'

Kate glanced at her uncle, wondering how much he knew of their business. 'Could you leave us alone for a little while longer, Uncle?'

He muttered something under his breath about being master in his own house and stalked out of the room.

Immediately Kate turned to her mother, 'You went through a form of marriage with my father, so you are a Stanley.' She heard the hiss of Diccon's indrawn breath and knew that their mother had more explaining to do.

'Nevertheless, I will stand by what I've said,' said Beth stubbornly. 'It's different for you—their blood runs in thy veins.'

'But I need you, Mother. At least come with me,' pleaded Kate.

Beth darted a look at Owain. 'Do I have to see Sir Thomas to get my money?'

'He did request that both of you be brought to him,' responded Owain.

She sighed. 'If needs must, so be it.'

'Good. Now there are other matters we need to discuss.' His expression was serious. 'I presume you are aware that Kate is believed to be the Lady Catherine at Rowan Manor. In the light of what you, Diccon and Kate have told me, when we return she must continue in that guise and you, Mistress Fletcher and Diccon, must adopt other names.'

Beth protested. 'I understand your reasoning, but surely this deception cannot continue? Truth will out.'

'Safer later than now,' he said. 'If the friar or the Comte were to hear that the Fletchers were still alive, your lives could be at risk. Not only could they have seen you witness Master Fletcher's death…but there is also the missing chest of money. Until we know their whereabouts, I suggest you pretend to be a widow named Archer, sister to the dead Mistress Fletcher.' He turned to Diccon. 'You remain your mother's son, but perhaps it would be wiser if you were Harry Archer.'

Diccon grinned. 'As you wish, Master ap Rowan.'

'If there is a message from Sir Thomas waiting for me, we will depart on the morrow,' continued Owain. 'So say your farewells and let us be on our way. Diccon, you and your mother will ride the mare. Kate will ride with me.'

Beth kissed her sister and said she must come and visit as soon as they were settled at Merebury.

Soon they had left Chester behind and were travelling in a motley company of peddlers, peasants, clerics and knights. The road would eventually lead to the priory at Birkenhead and the ferry across the Mersey, but before then, they would need to take the turning that led to Rowan Manor. Kate was reminded of the journey to La Coruña and how she had felt such a oneness with Owain. Now she dreamed of the day when he would make her his wife.

Owain was also thinking of the future, but knew that his marriage to Kate was far from cut and dried. Whilst aware Sir Thomas had often favoured him above others, he knew that did not necessarily mean he would welcome him as a husband for a Stanley, even one regarded as a bastard child by many. It could be that Sir Thomas would rather see his cousin in a nunnery and take Merebury for himself, situated as it was so conveniently close to Lathom. Of course, he hoped he was doing Sir Thomas an injustice, but one could never completely trust men of power. At least his father's death meant he, himself, was in a better position to press his suit than he had been when he arrived in England. Also, there was the King to consider. If he were to regain his wits, it did not necessarily mean that he would remember what had gone before. Owain hazarded that his best chance of winning the King over to his side was to find his missing money. With that in mind, he gave some thought to where it might be.

At last they came to the turning that would take them to Rowan Manor. Beth and Diccon gazed about them with interest, murmuring appreciation of the harvested fields, the cattle, horses and orchards and the house as they drew nearer to it. Soon they clattered into the yard to be welcomed by Hal and a couple of stable boys.

Hal's curious gaze took in Kate's appearance. Owain dismounted and murmured in his brother's ear, 'Don't ask. Just tell me if there is a message from Sir Thomas.'

'I have it on my person,' retorted Hal in a whisper. 'I haven't forgotten what you said about leaving important letters and documents in view for all to see. But if you ask me, they'd give themselves away if they tampered with this letter.'

'There are ways, dear brother, of resealing letters,' said Owain, watching his brother delve inside his shirt and draw out a scroll. He took it from him and broke the seal.

Kate heard his sharp intake of breath. 'What is wrong?' she asked.

He glanced up at her with a frown. 'Sir Thomas has had to go south and does not know when he will return.'

With a *frisson* of nervous excitement, Kate said in a low voice, 'Is it that the King has recovered and Sir Thomas has gone to speak to him on our behalf?'

He shook his dark head. 'The King is still not himself, but it is possible that Sir Thomas will go to Windsor where Henry resides with Queen Margaret and Prince Edward. Knowing that my father has just died, Sir Thomas suggests that we stay here until his return.' He lifted her down from the horse. 'This is a blow to our plans.'

'Does he mention the Comte or Friar Stephen?' she murmured.

'Only that I am to continue my search for your mother and to be on my guard,' he said grimly. 'As if I did not know that already.'

'Was there aught else of interest? Did he mention the Earl of Richmond? I heard that he and the lords Beaufort have visited Chester.'

Owain nodded. 'Sir Thomas writes of an alliance between the two houses. Lady Margaret Beaufort is to wed the Earl of Richmond, so uniting two families with links to the throne. No doubt the match will be frowned on by the Duke of York and his allies.'

She placed a hand on his sleeve. 'You sense trouble?'

He hesitated. 'Not for us…but for England…' Rolling up the scroll, he placed it inside his doublet and turned to his brother. 'As you heard, the Lady Kate will be staying with us a little longer. And we are to have the company of Mistress Archer and her son Harry,' he added cheerfully.

'Mistress Archer is a widow, Hal,' informed Kate. 'And kin to my dear companions, the Fletchers, who were killed on pilgrimage. They are the reason for my absence yesterday. I had intended returning last even, but the storm destroyed my good intentions.'

She was relieved when Hal accepted her explanation with a smiling nod and suggested that they all got inside as it looked like rain again.

Kate whispered to Owain, 'I will go up the backstairs. I would not have Mistress Carver and the other servants see me so poorly clad—otherwise they might change their good opinion of me.'

He smiled. 'Best your mother accompanies you. I will explain to Mistress Carver and arrange for a truckle bed to be placed in your bedchamber for her.' He turned to Diccon, who had dismounted and was helping his mother down from their mount. 'You will come with me.' Signalling the stable boys to see to the horses, he climbed the steps with Diccon at his heels and entered the hall.

Trestles and benches were already in place for the midday meal. As soon as Mistress Carver saw Owain, she bustled over to him with an anxious expression on her face. 'Master Owain, here you are at last. I wasn't sure when you'd arrive, but there's plenty to eat and to

spare.' She lowered her voice. 'There have been rumours that the Lady Catherine is missing.'

Owain smiled at her reassuringly, 'She is back, but
has gone straight to her bedchamber. She went to visit
her old nurse's sister, who is a widow and living with
her son in Chester. Mistress Archer and Master Harry
have come to stay with us for a while. He will sleep in
the small bedchamber next to mine. Mistress Archer
will sleep in Lady Catherine's bedchamber, so if a
truckle bed could be placed there?'

'Certainly, Master Owain. I will see to it. Do you
wish for some refreshment now?'

He shook his head. 'Although perhaps the young
master might be grateful for a cup of small ale.' Diccon agreed with alacrity and Mistress Carver told him
to sit down by the fire and it would be brought to him.

Kate had just finished her toilet and was dressed in
her blue gown when a knock at the door heralded the
arrival of Mistress Carver. She was accompanied by a
serving man carrying a truckle bed. He placed it down
and left. Kate smiled at Mistress Carver and introduced
the two women. They scrutinised each other and appeared to like what they saw and shook hands. Kate enquired after the Lady Gwendolyn.

'She is demanding that her uncle be sent for, but
Master Davy said he is not allowed inside the house.'

'Has she asked after the child?'

'Nay. Although she is suffering great discomfort for
its lack, but refuses help.'

'What discomfort is this?' asked Beth, placing
Kate's pilgrim tunic over the foot of the bed.

Mistress Carver said, 'She will not feed her baby and her breasts are sore.'

'Why will she not feed her child?' asked Beth.

Kate shook her head at her mother and ushered Mistress Carver out of the bedchamber. She closed the door and turned to Beth. 'I should have told you more about Owain's stepmother.' On that note she told Beth about the birth.

'Poor deceived lass,' said Beth, sounded distressed.

Kate scowled. 'She caused great trouble between Owain and his father and is in league with our enemies and goodness knows what other evil they have involved her in.'

'I pity her even more. Let's go and see her,' said Beth firmly.

Kate shook her head. 'Mother, she will not want your help.'

'But she is suffering.' Beth's eyes sparkled and she jutted her chin. 'Daughter, I reared you to help others, even those who had no love for us.'

Kate sighed, knowing her mother would give her no peace until she had her way. 'If you must try, then you must. But remember you are Mistress Archer, not Fletcher. I will show you the way.'

She escorted Beth along the same passages that Owain had taken her to see his dying father. When they reached the bedchamber, she knocked on the door. No one bid her enter, so she opened the door and went inside. Immediately she recoiled as the acrid smell of sour milk, blood and burning caught the back of her throat. Amongst the burning wood in the brazier she noticed blackened fabric.

'Come, Lady Catherine, you have coped with worse stenches in the past,' said Beth, who had followed her into the bedchamber.

Kate covered her mouth and nose with her hand and went over to the bed, where the curtains were fastened back. Gwendolyn sprawled on top of the bed. She was clad in a stained black velvet gown, her hair was in disarray and she was singing a mournful tune. Kate said in a muffled voice, 'Lady Gwendolyn, I have brought you a visitor, a Mistress Archer.'

Gwendolyn lifted her head and stared at Kate. 'Agnes said you'd gone,' she muttered.

'Well, I've returned,' said Kate, her compassion overcoming her revulsion. Slowly she removed her hand and perched on the side of the bed. 'We've come to see if we can help you.'

Gwendolyn shrank from her. 'You call me Lady, but you want to rule here. No doubt you'd like to trick me into drinking some foul brew so you could be rid of me.' Her voice broke on a sob.

'Now that's foolish talk,' chided Beth, bustling over to the other side of the bed. 'Lady Catherine wouldn't do that. Now, let me have a look at you. How flushed you are. Let me feel your skin.' Before Gwendolyn could draw back, Beth placed the back of her hand against the young woman's forehead and clucked her tongue against her teeth. 'You are feverish, but I don't think you are in any danger of dying—that's not to say you won't if you carry on acting so foolishly. Your breasts are swollen and painful, are they not?'

Gwendolyn nodded, her eyes fixed on Beth's face as if mesmerised. The older woman patted her hand.

'We'll do something about that. Your child must be sent for, so you can perform your God-given task as a mother and feed her. After that you will feel much better.'

Gwendolyn found her voice. 'Who are you?' she demanded, pushing Beth's hands away and hoisting herself up against the pillows.

'I'm the Lady Catherine's mother and I've come to save you,' said Beth before her daughter could prevent her.

Chapter Twelve

'But the Lady Catherine's mother is dead,' stated Gwendolyn, staring at Beth suspiciously.

'She means that she's been like a mother to me,' said Kate in a rush and would have hustled Beth out of the bedchamber if she had not dug her heels in.

'That's exactly what I meant,' said Beth shortly, shrugging off her daughter's hand. 'Now, where is your babe?'

Gwendolyn did not answer, but continued to stare at her. 'I wanted a son. I told the midwife to let her die.'

Beth gasped in horror. 'Perhaps your mother and father didn't want a girl either, but did they give you away?' She pushed Kate in the direction of the door. 'Fetch the child. The Lady will feel better once she has performed her maternal duty.' She turned back to the bed. 'Think of our Lord's mother and her example of motherhood.'

Furious with both women, Kate slammed the door behind her and hurried along the dimly lit passages. Worried about the outcome of her mother's highhanded behaviour and thoughtless words, her imagination ran riot. She pictured Gwendolyn sneaking out of the house to meet the friar—who would then go to the Comte. Their suspicions roused, they would want to see for themselves the woman who had claimed to be the Lady Catherine's mother. What if they had a band of mercenaries close by and attacked Rowan Manor? However bravely Owain and his brothers might fight, they could be killed. She, her mother and Diccon would be carried off and sacrificed by the Comte and the friar to appease the devil they worshipped.

Kate was relieved to reach the hall where everything appeared so normal that her fears diminished. A watch could be kept on Gwendolyn to ensure that she stayed out of mischief, so there was no need to worry. She caught sight of Mistress Carver and went over and asked where she would find Anna and her wet nurse.

It was with reluctance that the smith's young wife handed the tiny girl to Kate. 'A good feeder and not a scrap of trouble, my Lady,' she said, bobbing a curtsy. 'Less trouble than my own son.'

Kate gazed down into the petal-soft face and the brown eyes fringed with reddish-gold eyelashes and was entranced. Whoever Anna's father was, the child was entitled to a mother's care. If Gwendolyn should reject her daughter this time, she must truly have a heart of stone. Kate thanked the woman and strolled back to the house, enjoying the feel of the baby in her arms and daydreaming of presenting Owain with an heir.

She was halfway along the passage, leading to Gwendolyn's bedchamber, when suddenly she came face to face with him. He caught her by the arms and gazed down at her with a puzzled expression in his eyes. 'What are you doing with that baby?' Despite being startled by his unexpected appearance, Kate was aware of that tingle of excitement his touch always ensured and, for a moment, could not think clearly. 'What is it, Kate? I won't bite. At least…' He lowered his head and caressed the column of her throat with his tongue before nipping her skin lightly with his teeth.

She sighed with pleasure. 'You mustn't.'

'Aye, I mustn't,' he murmured, releasing her and gazing down at the child. 'This is Anna?'

She nodded. 'You will be vexed…Mother and I visited the Lady Gwendolyn.'

He frowned. 'You surprise me.'

Kate flushed. 'We were told she was in pain and when Mother heard a little of her story, she felt sorry for her and wanted to help her. I knew I shouldn't have fallen in with her wishes, but Mother can be very determined.'

'Did Gwendolyn ask for her daughter?'

'Nay, but if she feeds her then her discomfort and pain will ease…and perhaps her heart will soften towards Anna.'

He reached out a hand and touched the baby's cheek with a gentle finger. 'She looks prettier than when I first set eyes on her. I would like it if she was my father's daughter.'

'That would make her your half-sister.'

His lips twitched. 'Thank you, Kate, for reasoning that out for me.'

She smiled faintly and said wistfully, 'I would like a child.'

'Would you, Kate? I'd like to oblige right this moment but it would be somewhat awkward.'

The colour deepened in Kate's cheeks. 'You are a rogue, Master ap Rowan. Now I must be on my way.'

'Wait.' He placed a hand on her arm. 'You said that your mother pitied Gwendolyn. I agree that as a child she was to be pitied because she lost both parents whilst young—but my grandmother did much to make up for her lack of a mother. Gwendolyn is in the position she is now because of her own waywardness. Tell your mother not to be fooled into lowering her guard.'

Kate sighed. 'I have not told you all. Mother let slip that she was my mother.'

His mouth tightened. 'Tell me exactly what was said?'

Kate did so and he swore under his breath. 'Give me the child,' he ordered, holding out his arms. 'Time I visited Gwendolyn. Wait for me here.' She handed Anna over to him and watched him walk away.

Owain felt the baby stir in his arms as he knocked on the door of Gwendolyn's bedchamber. He heard hurrying feet and the door was opened by Beth. Her surprise was swiftly replaced by a look of defiance. 'Kate told you, did she?' she whispered. 'I only wanted to help and I'm not accustomed to telling untruths.'

He nodded curtly and looked beyond her towards where Gwendolyn was sitting in a chair by an open window, combing her hair. He made up his mind then what stance he was going to take. Crossing the floor towards her, he said, 'I have brought my half-sister to you, Gwennie. She is as pretty as a newly opened rose.'

Gwendolyn opened her mouth, but no words came out and it was obvious from her expression that she was struggling with her emotions. 'Obviously, you did not expect to see me.'

Gwendolyn glanced at her daughter and then lifted her eyes to his face. 'You are here because she has told you what this woman said. She thought to fool me, but I am not so easily fooled. You have brought her here under false pretences.'

'I don't know what you are talking about,' said Owain calmly. 'I met the Lady Catherine in the passage and offered to bring the child to you. I was told that Mistress Archer thought it would be good for your well-being if you were to feed her yourself.'

Gwendolyn looked less sure of herself and glanced at the baby. 'I wanted a boy,' she muttered. 'I could have persuaded him if it had been a boy.'

'Persuaded whom?' asked Owain.

She glanced up at him from beneath her eyelids and said with sly smile, 'You know of whom I speak.'

Owain continued to stare at Gwendolyn until she tore her gaze from his and said petulantly, 'Give the child to me. You can both get out. Send Agnes to me.'

Owain shook his head. 'Mistress Archer will stay with you until you have fed the child and then she will take charge of her.'

Gwendolyn's eyes glinted. 'If your father were here, you would not dare to speak to me in such a way. I should decide who is to take care of my child.'

There was a responding anger in his face, but his voice was low and intense when he spoke. 'If my father were here, you would not dare speak of *another*.

You lied and cheated, but this child could still be his and so she will be treated as such. I will not chance you harming her. If you attempt to do so after I leave this chamber, then you will greatly regret it.' He left the room without another word.

He found Kate waiting for him at the top of the stairs. Some of the tension caused by the exchange with Gwendolyn left him and, smiling, he reached for her hand and drew it through his arm. 'Do not look so worried. All will be well. That gown brings out the colour of your eyes.'

She smiled. 'You must know that I am not concerned about my appearance. How went your visit to Gwendolyn?' she asked in a low voice as they began to descend the stairs into the rapidly filling hall.

'I refrained from scolding your mother, but Gwendolyn is suspicious, although I do not think she has grasped the exact truth. I have told her your mother is to take charge of the child. Agnes must not be left alone with her.' He hesitated. 'You must take care and do not wander outside the house without company.'

She nodded. 'How long do you think it will be before Sir Thomas returns?'

'I cannot say. At least his absence means that I have time to get matters sorted out here…and there is the harvest supper to arrange…and I must ensure that the thanksgiving tithes are presented to the priest.'

Kate's spirits lifted. 'I will look forward to the harvest supper.'

'Aye! Despite my father's death we must celebrate and be thankful for a good harvest.'

* * *

So it was that, a week later, trestles and benches were set up in the meadow nearest to the house. For several days Master Carver and his minions had been preparing the feast and delicious smells emanated from the kitchen and bake house. There was a great haunch of beef, as well as roasted geese, a spiced ham, loaves of bread, cheese cakes, buttered leeks, custards and apple tartlets.

Children played 'Hoodman Blind', giggling as they hit one of their number wearing a hood back to front. Some of the adults formed a carol and moved in time to the music. Kate longed to join in, but was unsure whether it was seemly to do so due to the recent death of Owain's father.

But Owain saw the yearning in her face and, taking her hand, brought her to her feet. A thrill raced through her as his arm went round her waist and she looked up into his amused eyes and anticipated the pleasure of being held by him once more. They performed the steps sedately at first, but then pipes and drums increased the tempo of the music and soon they were twisting and skipping and leaping into the air as the movement of the carol took them. They danced until she was breathless and laughingly had to beg him to stop.

Soon after the sky darkened and a bonfire was set alight. More ale and wine was poured and more food eaten. Arm in arm, Kate and Owain watched the burning wood crackle, sending sparks flying heavenwards. The flickering flames cast shadows but also lit up faces. Gwendolyn was present, watched over by Beth, Diccon and Jonathan. From her sullen expression it was clear the Lady was not enjoying herself. Kate wondered how

much longer it would be before Gwendolyn rebelled
and they had more trouble on their hands.

During the month that followed Kate saw little of
Owain during the daytime for he was taken up with the
horses and other business on the manor. Occasionally, he
made time to take her riding but they were seldom alone.

One market day Owain asked if she wished to go to
Chester with him. Gladly, she accepted, having in mind
to re-cover the cushions in the parlour. But as soon as
other members of the household heard of their outing,
they asked if they might join them. Even Gwendolyn
made a pretty request and reluctantly Owain agreed
they might all go and ordered Diccon and Jonathan to
keep a close watch on her.

Whilst in Chester, Owain visited the family lawyer,
leaving Kate and Beth to wander round the market stalls.
Kate had in mind not only to make cushion covers, but
also a new gown of linsey-woolsey to wear at Davy's
wedding. It was only later that Diccon told her that
Gwendolyn had visited the abbey but, as she was never
out of sight of Jonathan, Kate saw little reason to worry.

In the days that followed, Kate, Beth and Megan
gathered in the parlour each afternoon where they mea-
sured and cut, fitted and stitched, embroidered and finally admired the finished results of their handiwork.
Kate had asked Gwendolyn to join them, but she had
sneeringly refused, saying that she had no taste for such
poor company. Kate could have answered just as rudely,
but was relieved not to have to tolerate Gwendolyn's
presence. The three woman discussed Anna, who was

thriving, love potions and recipes and Davy's forth-coming wedding. The latter was to be a quiet affair and would take place on All Hallow's Eve.

Kate woke early on the morning of the wedding and slid out of bed to tiptoe over to the window and gaze out. Mist hung amongst the trees so that the bright colours of the changing leaves could scarcely be distinguished; grey blankets of mist lay over the fields, seeming to fuse with the greyness of the sky. She could only pray that it would lift and the clouds part to allow the autumn sun to shine through on Davy and his rosy-cheeked bride.

Everyone who was able gathered in the nave of the parish church a few hours later; the interior struck chill and the smell of candles and incense filled the air, caus-ing Kate's dainty nose to twitch. The bride wore a green gown trimmed with coney fur; her pale hair hung down her back and was entwined with black and green ribands. She spoke her vows in a firm voice and, as she gazed up at Davy, it was obvious that his love for her was returned.

Kate could not help feeling a little envious, but she swiftly quashed such emotion. Even so her hungry eyes could not resist gazing at Owain. She imagined him naked as he had been on the beach in Brittany. He must have sensed her watching him, because he suddenly looked at her and held her gaze. The expression on his face caused her heart to race and her knees to turn to water. Surely it shouldn't be long now until they received word from Sir Thomas and Owain could claim her as his bride.

After the ceremony, they returned to the hall for the wedding feast. Soon the chatter of voices and the clatter of spoons and knives against bowls and platters vied with the orders barked out by those overseeing the meal to their minions. There was no sign of Gwendolyn, who had refused to have anything to do with the celebrations. She had said that she would keep to her bedchamber until it was over. Beth had agreed to stay with her.

Kate frowned as she gazed about the hall, realising that not only was her mother absent, but also that Diccon was not in his usual place. Knowing that he would never willingly miss a meal, she was concerned. He had been restless of late, chaffing beneath the restraints of the task Owain had given to him—and Merebury seemed to be on his lips more often. She wondered if he could have possibly taken one of the horses and set out there alone?

Again Kate's eyes scanned the hall and she realised that Agnes was also missing. She supposed it was possible that while they had been at the church, the old crone might have slipped upstairs to visit her mistress, but for what purpose?

Kate glanced towards the window and saw that the sun was breaking through the mist. She decided she must speak to Owain about her worries, but he was in deep conversation with the bride's father and she thought it would be rude to disturb them. What should she do? Dismiss her unease as groundless or slip upstairs to see if her mother knew where Diccon had gone. Making up her mind, she piled some food on a platter for her mother and slipped out of the hall.

Even from a distance Kate could hear Anna crying, but when she reached the bedchamber and knocked on the door there was no response. She opened the door and saw Beth lying face down on the floor; nearby was an overturned metal pitcher. Kate darted across the room and fell on her knees beside her mother. She touched the back of her head and her hand came away sticky with blood. Her heart beat rapidly as she fumbled for a pulse, fervently thanking the blessed Holy Trinity when she found a strong one. Hurrying over to the bed, she dragged off the embroidered woollen coverlet and placed it over Beth. Then she kissed her mother's forehead and whispered a prayer before leaving the bedchamber. Lifting her skirts, she ran along the passage with the baby's cries following her.

Heads lifted as Kate burst into the hall. Instantly Owain's gaze reached out to her and he pushed back his chair. Making his excuses to his guests, he hastened towards her. 'What is wrong?' he asked in a low voice and reaching up a hand touched her cheek. 'You have blood on your face.'

'Mother has been knocked senseless and the Lady Gwendolyn is missing.'

Immediately Owain signalled a nearby manservant and gave orders for a search to be made. 'Although, I fear she might have already escaped,' he said in an undertone to Kate.

'Diccon and Agnes are missing, too.' Her face paled as she recalled that not only was it All Hallow's Eve, but also the Celtic festival of Samhain, celebrating the end of the old year and the beginning of the new. A time when the veil between this world and the spirit one is at its thinnest, a time when the natural order dissolves into chaos before re-establishing a new one. Tonight, a high priestess, who had ruled a coven since the feast of Beltane in the spring, would step down to allow a high priest to rule throughout the winter. Was it possible that Gwendolyn was a high priestess?

Owain spoke, startling Kate from her reverie. 'Perhaps Diccon or Jonathan saw her slipping out of the house with Agnes and decided to follow them. We'd best check the stables,' said Owain, grim-faced, and hurried from the hall.

Kate sat beside her mother's bedside, sewing by the light of a candle. Beth had regained consciousness, but had not been able to tell them what had happened prior to being hit over the head. She did have some information for them, though, concerning Jonathan, who, along with Diccon, had been ordered to keep a watch on Gwendolyn. Apparently Beth had come upon them earlier that morning, whispering in a corner.

Instantly Owain had Jonathan brought before him. At first he had been unusually sullen and uncooperative, but then Owain had sent for Mistress Carver and she had taken him aside and spoken at length to him. Eventually he had confessed that the Lady had bewitched him into acting as messenger for her and pleaded forgiveness. He spoke of names and places that caused Owain to summon those men whom he could rely on at such a time. Armed and mounted, they departed as soon as they were able.

Some six hours had passed since they had left in search of Diccon and Gwendolyn and, if Jonathan was telling the truth, Gwendolyn was riding to Nether Alderley to meet with her uncle and lover.

Kate thought about what Diccon had said of the Comte's interest in the old religion and of Friar Stephen's tendency to distort old and new. She feared for her brother's life. He would have needed to follow Gwendolyn closely if he was not to lose her in the mist that morning. His absence might mean that he had been spotted, recognised and captured. Unable to remain passive any longer, Kate put aside her sewing and rose to her feet. She padded softly over to the window and gazed out. The sky was full of stars and the moon was in her ascent. At least Owain, Hal and the men would have light to guide them. She prayed that they would soon return safely.

She was about to turn away when, out of the corner of her eye, she thought she saw a dark hooded shape creeping along the outer wall. Suddenly, it scuttled across the garden and disappeared through the arched opening into the yard. Icy fingers seemed to skate down her spine. Yet, curiosity aroused, she wondered if there was a connection with that figure and Diccon's and Gwendolyn's disappearance.

Kate tiptoed over to the bed and gazed down at her mother's slumbering face. She could hear her steady breathing and decided it should be safe to leave her for a short time. She left the bedchamber. The whisper of her skirts brushing the floor seemed loud as she hastened along the passage lit by flickering torches. She rounded a corner and saw a small hooded figure limping towards her, muttering as it did so. Kate drew in her breath with a hiss. The low sound caused the figure to stop and lift its head. She recognised Agnes and hurried towards her. On closer inspection she saw that the old woman's face was bruised with one eye swollen and half-closed.

'Agnes, what has happened to you?'

The crone held out both hands beseechingly. 'They've taken my Lady and young Harry. They beat me until I almost lost my senses. Otherwise I would have been here earlier.'

Recognising her brother's pseudonym, trepidation coiled in the pit of Kate's stomach. 'Who—who has captured them?' she stammered. 'We believed Lady Gwendolyn to have arranged to meet the friar and the Comte at Nether Alderley?'

Agnes trembled. 'Maybe, maybe…but she did not get that far. Men in dark robes…hidden in the trees they were. The friar was there, too, and in a furious temper, accusing her of betraying him. She denied it, but I could see he did not believe her because he hit her, too.'

Kate paled. 'Do you know where they took them?'

Agnes looked uncertain and muttered, 'I couldn't keep up with them. Perhaps you should fetch the Master—he might know where they've gone. It being Samhain, it could be the Devil's Graveyard.'

Kate's heart sank. 'What and where is the Devil's Graveyard?'

'It be a cave in the forest. You will fetch him, my Lady? He's no need to be afeared of Ol' Nick or the dead. He has power.'

'Master Owain has already set out in search of them—but I don't know if he is aware of this cave you speak of. Perhaps you should lead me to it. Unless I rouse Master Davy…but it is his wedding night and I would not disturb him and his bride unless you deemed it necessary.'

Agnes's mouth worked and her body shook. For a moment Kate thought she was going to swoon, but then the old woman seemed to pull herself together. 'Best leave him be. He hasn't the gift. We must save my Lady Gwendolyn. The friar wants a sacrifice. Perhaps two sacrifices.'

Kate fixed her with a stare. 'I hope you would not trick me, Agnes. It will be the worse for you if you were to try.'

'Nay, nay! We must make haste.' She licked her lips. 'Unless, my Lady, you could fly there?'

Kate had every intention of acting with speed—but fly? She knew there were those who claimed to do so after taking aconite or drinking absinthe, the latter a rarity, but her mother had forsworn such dangerous foolishness. She shook her head. 'We will go on horseback. I doubt a broomstick could bear us both,' she said drily.

Kate did not wait to see Agnes's reaction, but went in search of Megan to ask her to sit with Beth. After that, she planned on taking a sharp blade from the kitchen for protection and donning a pair of Diccon's breeches beneath her skirts so she could ride with speed.

To Kate, the open countryside, all black and silver, looked beautiful in the moonlight. She was riding eastwards with Agnes clinging onto her from behind. When the old crone was not muttering she was squeaking out directions. Every now and again she would glance up at the sky and ask Kate if she could she see that witch on a broomstick, but Kate could only see owls, swooping on silent wings before the squeals of their prey disturbed the peaceful landscape.

They had been riding for some time when Agnes tugged on Kate's sleeve. 'We are approaching the great mere of Radnor, whose waters feed the giant watermill of Nether Alderley, my Lady. Now we must take care for there will be some watching this night.'

'So the caves are close to Nether Alderley?'

'Aye!'

'Where exactly?'

'Amongst the trees that cover the roots of the mighty rock at the edge of Alderley,' whispered Agnes. 'We will soon be there.'

'Then hush,' said Kate, managing to keep her voice under control. She felt sick with apprehension, hoping to have seen some sign of Owain and his men by now. She could only pray that they had not been taken by surprise and killed.

As they approached the rock, the mare sniffed the air and whinnied. There came a responding horsy snicker from somewhere above them. Kate started. Could that noise have come from one of Owain's horses or did it belong to the enemy? She hesitated and then dug in her heels and urged the mare into the trees. The moon filtered through branches, almost denuded of leaves, but it was still difficult to see clearly and the horse stumbled over damp roots and leaves. Her heart beating rapidly, she prayed the beast would not break a leg and they be flung from its back. She decided it might be safer to dismount and ordered Agnes to do so.

'Perhaps it would be wiser to go back, my Lady,' she said in a tremulous whisper. 'I should not have brought you here.'

'Have faith, Agnes. You want to save the Lady Gwendolyn, don't you?'

The old woman did not answer, but Kate could hear her gulping convulsively. Then came a voice on the air that caused her to stiffen with fear. She pressed her knees against the horse's flank and prayed that the cave was near. The midnight hour was close and she sensed death in the air.

Chapter Thirteen

Owain lay flat on his stomach, close to the edge of the sandstone rock face overlooking the moonlit Cheshire plain in which lay Nether Alderley. Almost below him in the shadow of the rock was the village of Chorleigh and its neighbouring hall belonging to a kinsman of Sir Thomas Stanley. To his rear his men were concealed behind rocks and trees, awaiting his summons. He had chosen those who performed best at the butts during archery practice on Sunday. They had been there for a number of hours and a short while ago he had watched several men go into the village church, amongst them faces he recognised.

Suddenly he tensed as a hooded figure bearing a torch emerged from the darkened church. He was followed by others. From where he was lying he could not make out whether Diccon or Gwendolyn was with them. He wondered where they were going and, after a short while, decided they were making for the woods at the base of the rock. Soon the column would disappear from sight. His dark brows creased in thought. If they had Diccon and Gwendolyn, then he must make his move now. The height of the moon told him that it was not long till midnight.

Owain signalled to Hal and his men and gave orders for two of them to stay with the horses. The rest he led silently towards a track that would take them through the woods at a different level until they plunged on to the path that led to the caves, rumoured to have been created when men had first mined for copper here. One was larger than the other and legend claimed an army of knights lay sleeping there from Arthur's time, waiting to be called if England was in danger.

The other cave was smaller, its entrance narrower. Some believed that if one walked round the cave seven times whilst reciting the Lord's Prayer backwards, then the devil would appear. He grinned. By the Holy Trinity, if either the friar or the Comte were of a mind to perform that evil rite, as well as offer a human sacrifice, then they were in for a surprise. On his back he had a pack containing a costume he had not worn for quite a while. Kate came suddenly to mind and he could sense her loving concern and felt warmed. His thoughts reached out to her, attempting to reassure her.

At last they reached the caves. There was no sign of those robed figures and Owain gave orders to his archers to conceal themselves in the trees. He guessed he had little time to prepare a welcoming party, but decided to make a quick search of the Devil's Graveyard.

'Are you sure about this?' asked Hal, looking uneasy when Owain explained his plan.

'You just keep a watch out for the enemy,' ordered Owain.

He found it a bit of a tight fit, squeezing through the entrance of the cave, but once inside it widened out. He stilled, waiting for his eyes to become accustomed to the darkness and, in the quietness, he heard the sound of breathing. He glanced round and was able to make out a dark shape on the ground. He took the knife from his belt and walked stealthily over and bent over it. A search with his hand told him that perhaps he had found Diccon. He was gagged and trussed up like a chicken. He pulled the rag from his mouth and immediately his guess was proved right when a voice croaked, 'Master ap Rowan?'

'Aye! Have they hurt you, Diccon?' He cut through the ropes binding the youth's arms and hands to his sides.

'A few bruises and scratches. The Comte said that the friar was saving me for later...talked about slicing off my nose and then an ear and a hand before killing me if I didn't tell him where my father had concealed the chest he'd taken.' Despite all Diccon's efforts to keep his voice steady it shook.

'A truly holy man,' said Owain lightly, sawing through the ropes that tied his ankles together. 'What else did you hear?'

Diccon said with a catch in his voice, 'The Comte boasted of being a high priest and summoning up the devil, but the friar argued with him, saying that it was he who should perform the ritual. Then they began to argue about money. The Comte said that he needed a bigger share of the money so he could pay more mercenaries.' He took a deep breath. 'The Comte hates the King, says he's weak and is not fit to rule, but he has no liking for the Duke of York either. He fears him because he proved in the wars in France that he was a good soldier. If he were to continue as Protectorate, then he believes he would rule with an iron fist.'

'Was any mention made of the Queen?' Owain, his eyes sweeping the cave, helped the youth to his feet, steadying him as he stumbled.

'The Comte seems to think that she would be happy to have the help of his mercenaries. According to him she hates and distrusts York, fearing that if the King does not regain his wits then York will take Prince Edward from her and rule in his stead,' continued Diccon.

Owain nodded, noticing a spur of rock protruding at the back of the cave. Perhaps there was room there to conceal himself. He walked over to it and disappeared behind it, tripping over something in the dark. He sank on to his haunches and ran his hands over the object. A smile creased his face as he recognised the shape of a money chest, locked and bound with a leather strap. 'Eureka!'

'What have you found?' asked Diccon, limping towards him.

'A chest. Most likely it contains money which *my* father handed over to the friar,' murmured Owain. 'But it'll have to stay here for now if I'm to surprise our enemies.' It was doubtful the friar would bring his followers in here—much too small. Most probably he and the Comte together would perform the ceremony believed to rouse Old Nick himself and then they would go outside with the sacrificial victim, he thought grimly. No doubt as soon as they realised Diccon was missing, a search would be made of the cave. No matter! The element of surprise was on his side.

Swiftly, he told Diccon what he planned and, unfastening his pack, removed a horned mask, a doublet, hose and a long, swirling sleeveless cotehardie. 'I got the idea for this when I heard about the mummers who visited Merebury.'

The lad chuckled and helped him don the garments and mask before leaving the cave.

Owain did not have long to wait. In no time at all, the reflection from the flickering flame of a torch lit up the sandstone walls of the cave entrance. He heard the shuffle of feet and the sibilant sound of low voices. The Comte and the friar appeared to be arguing, but this dispute was cut short when they realised that Diccon was gone.

'Where's the sacrifice?' demanded Friar Stephen, enraged. 'You couldn't have tied him up properly.' The Comte swore that he had fastened his bonds extremely tightly. There was an uneasy silence. 'What of the chest?' asked the friar. 'Has that vanished, too?'

Owain knew he could wait no longer and his mouth eased into a genuine grin. Depending on how much they believed, the Comte and Gwendolyn's uncle were in for a shock. He loosened his blade in its scabbard and left his hiding place. Immediately he noticed that a flaming torch had been jammed between two rocks, so lighting the scene as if on a stage. His costume would not have passed muster in the daylight, but here…

He spoke in a booming voice. 'I have come to claim what is mine. Thou hast displeased me and I will dispatch thee to Hell!'

The friar's eyes bulged and his chin sagged. It was as good a reaction as any Owain could have planned but, what happened next he did not expect. The cleric suddenly seemed to have trouble breathing and he clutched at the fastenings about his neck, staggered about before falling to the ground. For a moment Owain was too stunned to act. As for the Comte, he was staring at him in wonder. 'My lord,' he breathed, going down on one knee. 'You are most welcome.'

'Get up, man!' ordered Owain irascibly. 'You know as well as I do that the Lord's Prayer hasn't been said yet.'

The Comte's expression changed and he scrambled to his feet. 'You have erred foolishly in interfering with my plans, Owain ap Rowan,' he hissed.

'I'm flattered that you recognise my voice.'

'You would think to fool me?'

'I did for a moment.' Owain smiled behind the mask. 'As for the friar he appears to have swooned with fright.'

The Comte pulled a dagger from his girdle and lunged at Owain, who managed to seize his wrist and ward off the blade. They grappled a moment before moving back. Owain drew his knife and they circled each other warily. Then the Comte sprang at Owain, who was having some difficulty seeing clearly because his mask had slipped. He felt a sharp pain in his arm and swore beneath his breath. But, instead of retreating, he advanced, forcing the Comte backwards. Suddenly the Frenchman slipped on the sandy floor and his head caught a spur of rock and he slid to the ground.

Owain gazed down at him, alert for any sudden movement, but when the man remained still, he picked up his dagger and thrust it in his own belt. He checked both men for signs of life and discovered that the friar was no longer breathing. Frowning, Owain strode outside.

There was a concerted gasp from those gathered there and then a hush fell on the clearing. Owain's eyes rested on a smaller robed figure at the centre of the group. Gwendolyn had thrown back her hood and was gazing at him. He pushed up the mask so it rested on his dark curls and she screamed.

'It is only I,' said Owain in a mocking voice.

For a moment she did not move and then she seized the knife from the belt of the robed figure beside her and launched herself at him.

Kate could see lights shining through the trees. There came a piercing scream and she was filled with terror. Leaving Agnes and the horse, she ran as if her life depended on it. She burst on to a scene that was pure pandemonium. Arrows whizzed through the air and robed figures scattered in all direction, tossing torches aside as they went. In the moonlight she could see two figures locked in a struggle near the rock face and caught the gleam of a blade. She realised that it was Gwendolyn and Owain. But, before she could move nearer, she was knocked to the ground by one of the robed figures as he sought to escape. She picked herself up and was just in time to see an arrow thud into Gwendolyn's back. Owain caught her and yelled to his archers to stop loosing their arrows.

Kate ran. She stopped a couple feet away and watched as Owain broke off the shaft at the base of the arrow head before lowering Gwendolyn to the ground. She could not take her eyes from the horned mask that crushed his dark curls. 'You,' she said through stiff lips. 'It was you who rescued me at Merebury.'

Owain lifted his head and stared at her. 'What are you doing here?' His voice was ragged.

'Agnes brought me. Where's Diccon?'

'Safe.' With difficulty he removed the bloodstained cotehardie and covered Gwendolyn with it. 'Stay with her whilst I fetch the Comte. Perhaps there is time for them to say their farewells.'

Wearily, he went inside the cave. Instead of doing as she was told, Kate followed him. By the light of the torch she saw the friar's body lying on the ground. Owain swore softly and cautiously crept over to the back of the cave to see if the Comte was concealed behind the spur of rock, but no one was there. He searched with a hand for the chest and was relieved to discover it remained. He knew himself incapable of lifting it; Gwendolyn's blade had pierced the hollow just beneath his collar bone and the wound was disabling. He searched the friar's body, aware of Kate's eyes on him, knowing that sooner or later he would have to give her answers. He removed a key on a chain from about his neck, tried it in the lock of the chest and sighed with satisfaction when it fitted. He left the cave with Kate on his heels.

Outside they found a wailing Agnes cradling Gwendolyn in her scrawny arms whilst Diccon and Hal looked on. 'Gwendolyn's dead,' said Hal in a muted voice.

'So is her uncle,' replied Owain, wiping sweat from his brow with a bloody hand.

'The Comte?' asked Diccon.

'He must have only been stunned and escaped in the confusion. No doubt we'll be seeing him again. But now we must take Gwendolyn's body home with us for burial.'

'I have a horse here,' said Kate, gazing at the growing dark stain on Owain's doublet in shocked dismay.

'See to it, Hal,' he ordered, pressing a hand over his wound. 'Then you and Diccon can fetch the chest from inside the cave and that, too, shall go home with us.'

'Diccon? Who's he?' asked Hal, looking about him.

Diccon hesitated and glanced at his sister. 'I am.'

Hal looked puzzled. 'I thought your name was Harry.'

'That was my...my idea,' gasped Owain. 'Had to keep his identity and that of his mother from Gwendolyn. Kate's his half-sister.' He staggered suddenly.

Kate and Hal hurriedly propped him up. 'No more talking. We need to get you home,' she said firmly.

'Perhaps the nearest village would be better,' suggested Hal.

'Nay! Best we put as much...distance...as we can... between us and...' Owain's voice faded as he slipped into unconsciousness.

Kate cried, 'Put him up on my horse. There's no time to waste. Lady Gwendolyn's body must go on another.'

Between them, Hal and Diccon did as she ordered. 'Someone will have to ride with him so he does not fall,' said Hal.

'I'll do that,' said Diccon firmly. 'He saved my life. We mustn't forget the chest of money hidden in the cave, either.'

Hal nodded. 'I'll see to that. Later you can explain just why my brother felt he had to lie to me.'

'Best Owain tell you himself,' said Kate hastily. 'Now let us hurry!'

* * *

Only once did they stop on the return journey so Kate—with Agnes's aid—could search for some sphagnum moss on the fringe of the great mere of Radnor. She was fortunate in finding some almost immediately, and after squeezing the moisture out of a handful, placed it inside Owain's shirt against his wound. Often she had gathered the moss for her mother and so knew that it would act as an absorbent healing dressing.

By the time they reached Rowan Manor the sun had risen and Owain had regained consciousness. Even so he had to be helped from his horse and into the hall. Mistress Carver and Megan exclaimed in horror when they saw him. Immediately Kate said, 'See that his bed is warmed and a brazier placed in his bedchamber. I need a fire in the parlour, hot water, poppy juice and wine. Also, steep me some ground elecampane root in water…and I'll need bandages and goose grass salve. Tell me, how fares Mistress Archer?'

'She has been asking for you and her son,' replied Mistress Carver. 'And has threatened to leave her bed if you both did not return soon.'

Kate smiled faintly. 'Then she must be feeling better.'

'What of the Lady Gwendolyn?' asked Megan.

Kate turned to her. 'She is dead.'

The maid's eyes widened with shock and Mistress Carver gasped. Kate said in a low voice. 'It was she who was responsible for your master's wound. She tried to kill him. Agnes's grief is deep, so you must be kind to her.' The women murmured agreement.

Kate hurried to where Hal and Diccon had placed Owain in a chair near to the fire. 'We must send for the physician,' said Hal, facing her.

Owain's eyelids lifted slowly. 'Nay! I have no faith in the man. I'm sure my Lady Kate can do all that is needful for my healing.' He looked at her with such a sweet expression on his pain-racked features that the confusion in her mind, caused by seeing him with that devil's mask, eased.

'Light the fire in the parlour and give him some brandy,' she said, squeezing Owain's hand before leaving the hall.

She dragged herself wearily upstairs and found Diccon already with their mother. Beth was looking so much more like her old self that tears of gratitude sprang to Kate's eyes. 'I am glad you're so much improved, Mother.'

'Diccon tells me that our secret is out and that the Lady Gwendolyn is dead,' said Beth, shaking her head sadly.

'Did he tell you that she tried to kill Owain?' asked Kate, wiping away her tears. 'I cannot grieve for her. She left you unconscious and her child screaming, and if Owain were to...' Her voice trailed off and her hands gripped the carved wooden board at the foot of the bed.

There came a knock on the door and Kate was thankful to see Megan with a pitcher of hot water. Kate asked Diccon to leave them. She removed her riding gloves, undressed and laved her face and hands before donning the blue kirtle and gown she had fashioned on the ship. From a chest she took a length of old sheeting and wrapped it about her waist. Then she tidied her hair and concealed it beneath a clean veil.

'You will tend Master ap Rowan yourself, daughter?' asked Beth.

Kate nodded. 'He does not trust the physician and I am of the same mind. They kill as many as they cure.'

'I do not doubt you are able to do what is necessary, but remember, a careful watch must be kept on the wound over the coming days. Any sign of swelling or badness and you will have to burn it out.'

The muscles of Kate's face quivered, but her voice was controlled when she spoke. 'I will do all that is needful, Mother. Your wound will also need tending and I will see to that later.'

Beth said gently, 'Do not concern yourself with me, daughter. Megan is proving apt at doing exactly what I tell her. Now tend your man.' She leaned back against the pillows and closed her eyes.

Kate hurried downstairs to find Davy keeping an eye on Owain. He was sprawled in a chair in front of the parlour fire and his bloodied garments lay on the floor along with the clump of moss, revealing an ugly wound that was bleeding afresh. His eyes were closed and he was singing what appeared to be a marching song in a slurred voice. The pewter goblet on the table contained but a few dregs of brandy. She wanted to run her hands over his body, to press her lips against his skin and soothe him; instead she was about to inflict pain. She was conscious of Davy's scrutiny and guessed Hal would have told him of Diccon being her half-brother. Right now it did not matter what he made of that information, but no doubt sooner or later he would have something to say about it. Lowering her head, she asked the Trinity's blessing on what she was about to do.

She took the jug of elecampane water, poured it over the wound and allowed a few moments to pass before gently swabbing most of the liquid away. Owain drew in a breath with a hiss and, knowing she was hurting him, she felt her stomach clench. She paused a moment before smearing goose grass salve on the wound and then, taking more sphagnum moss, she pressed it over the wound. He groaned and she felt a pain at her heart and needed to swallow the sudden lump in her throat. She glanced at Davy and, without a word, he handed a clean binding to her. She bound the sphagnum moss into place; once that was done, she dealt with the ugly scratch on his arm. Then she suggested to Davy that he fetch Hal, so that between them, the brothers could help Owain to his bed.

Once he had gone, Kate mixed poppy juice with elderflower water and then gently touched Owain's arm. The black lashes that fanned his damp cheeks fluttered open and he stared at her from pain-filled eyes. Neither of them spoke, but he took her free hand and brought it to his lips and kissed it. Tears filled her eyes at the gesture and she thought how he had such power to move her. 'You must drink this,' she said in an uneven voice, holding the cup out to him.

'What is in it, Kate?'

'Poppy juice and elderflower water.'

'No yew berries?'

The question shocked her. 'You jest?'

'A very poor joke,' he said wearily. 'But it has occurred to me that perhaps Gwendolyn knew that yew berries were poisonous and she shared that knowledge with her lover.'

She puzzled over his words as he took the cup. 'Are you suggesting the Comte wanted Sir Roger dead and Gwendolyn provided the means to kill him?'

'I think they both wanted him dead,' he murmured, his eyelids drooping as he drained the cup.

'Why should Gwendolyn want Sir Roger dead?' asked Kate, taking the cup from his slack fingers.

Owain's answer seemed a long time coming and when it did, the words were spoken barely above a whisper, his voice slurred. 'Perhaps the Comte told her of Sir Roger's taste for men and boys and that he forced himself on Martin.'

Kate was shocked—yet had she not known of Sir Roger's unnatural desires? It seemed highly probable that Owain's guess was right and he had discovered the identity of the murderer.

Kate put down her sewing and rubbed her eyes. The bedchamber was filling with shadows and there was a slight chill in the air. Noticing that the fire in the brazier had burnt low, she rose to her feet and placed more wood in the burner. Then, taking the candle from the chest at the foot of the bed, she tiptoed to its head and gazed down at Owain where he lay on his back. He had slept for more than twenty-four hours and for most of that time she had been by his bedside. His brothers had taken turns in watching over him and, on one occasion, Kate had told them the reason why she had pretended to be Lady Catherine Miles and why Owain had insisted she continue in that role. They had said little, but she gained the impression they would have plenty to say to Owain when he recovered.

Kate's eyes roamed his face and love, compassion, confusion and desire fought for dominance inside her. By the light of the candle his skin looked the colour of parchment and there were hollows beneath his cheekbones. He had a couple days' growth of beard, and his dark hair curled untidily about his ears and on his forehead. She placed the candlestick on a chair and gently smoothed a strand of hair from his eyelid. Then, unable to resist, she allowed the tips of her fingers to trace the outline of his lips. They twitched and she would have withdrawn her hand, but it was suddenly grasped by the wrist. Her pulse fluttered like the wings of a captive moth as he opened his eyes and pulled her.

She fell across him. He winced and immediately she pushed herself up and off the bed. 'This will not do, Master ap Rowan.'

'It definitely needs some thought,' he croaked.

'I should leave and fetch one of your brothers or Mistress Carver to sit with you now,' she said with a hint of breathlessness.

His head moved on the pillow. 'Please, don't leave me, Kate,' he pleaded huskily. 'I need you.'

She was aware of a responding need, so strong that she felt faint. How she wanted him! Yet since catching sight of him in that devilish mask, she'd had to ask herself why he had not spoken up when she had told him about the devilish figure who had saved her life. She went over to where she had placed a pitcher of honeyed elderflower water containing a few drops of poppy juice. She poured some of the liquid into a cup and, kneeling on the bed, held it to his lips. 'A drink first, I think,' she murmured.

He did not argue, but drank down the contents of the

cup in three swallows before sinking back against the pillows. 'That's better,' he said in his normal voice. 'My throat was as dry as sand.'

'More?'

'Later. Tell me, Kate, what is it that disturbs you?'

'You dressed up as Ol' Nick.'

He sighed. 'I should have told you earlier, but I truly believed the less you knew the safer it was for you.'

'But why dress up at all as the devil?'

'I could not risk Sir Roger recognising me whilst I searched for evidence that would prove him to be my brother's murderer—he and his followers showed such a great interest in the devil that I thought it would be a great jape to trick them.'

Kate smiled faintly. 'Even so…why didn't you recognise me in Spain if you rescued me?'

'I couldn't always see clearly through the mask… and you forget it was some time since I'd seen you or your mistress.'

She accepted his excuses. 'So what next? You believe you have found your murderer in the Comte?'

'I believe, once they became lovers, Gwendolyn played her part, too.'

She was thoughtful a moment. 'What do you think the Comte will do now she is dead and he has no money to pay his mercenaries?'

Owain rubbed his unshaven jaw. 'He did not love her…or the child being a girl would not have mattered. Now the money…if he has any sense he will forget it and make his escape to France.'

'So we might never see him again,' said Kate with a happy sigh.

She made to rise from the bed, but Owain stayed her with a hand. 'Don't go, Kate. Lie beside me and share your warmth with me.'

'You feel cold?' she said, placing the back of her hand against his forehead. 'Nay! You've no fever.'

He protested, 'But I could take a fever if I'm not kept warm. Have pity, sweetest Kate. I'm a wounded man and have not the strength for seduction.' She hesitated and he added hastily, 'Just for a short while let us hold each other.'

Still she hesitated and then, with a heavily beating heart, stretched herself out beside him. Placing an arm across his bare chest, she rested her cheek against his un-injured shoulder. He brought her even closer against him and kissed her hair. For a while neither of them moved, but relaxed against each other, finding comfort and se-curity in just being held close by the person they desired most in the whole world. Such stillness could not last.

For Owain, it was the awareness of soft flesh that yielded beneath the fabric of her gown as his fingers gently stroked the rounded curve of a breast. Kate's breath caught in her throat and she lifted her head and looked in his face. 'You mustn't,' she whispered.

'Mustn't I?' He smiled and bringing his head close to hers, kissed her. His mouth moved over hers in such a beguiling way that she could not but respond, return-ing his kiss fervently. Her lips parted beneath his, al-lowing entry for his tongue to taste the sweetness of her mouth: honey and elderflower. Her hand pressed against his chest and her fingers explored the black hair on his chest, toying with the jet black curls before wrap-ping one around a finger. Their lips parted and he began to press kisses down the beautiful line of her throat, filling her with a delicious lethargy and she was hard put to think sensibly. 'If anyone was to enter now they would consider my behaviour most unladylike.' Her voice was husky with emotion.

'Lock the door.'

'Wouldn't that make them suspect we—we were behaving in a manner that didn't…bear scrutiny?'

He nibbled her ear. 'The servants believe us betrothed. Surely my having missed death by inches means they will understand our need to comfort each other?'

Kate knew she should argue with him but, instead, she locked the door. Returning to the bed, she snuggled against him with a deep satisfying sigh. His hand kneaded one of her breasts and her breath quickened as he caressed a nipple through the fabric of her gown with fingers that proved more sensitive than she could have ever imagined. He shifted her higher against him so that her skirts were dragged up and he stroked her thigh. 'You mustn't,' she whispered.

'Mustn't again? You don't like it?'

'You should not ask me such questions.'

He smiled and began to unfasten the ties on her gown and kirtle to bare her breasts. He licked a nipple before taking it into his mouth. She gasped with pleasure as ripples of sensation spread throughout her body. She became aware of his manhood against her stomach. 'I should have wed you when Davy took his Joan,' rasped Owain, his eyes smouldering with desire as he gazed into Kate's dazed face.

'We could plight our troth here and now,' gasped Kate.

'You would do that?'

'Aye! I, Kate Fletcher...or should I say Stanley?' Her breathing quickened as he caressed her. 'Whichever, both of me take thee, Owain ap Rowan, for my husband. I vow to be true in the name of the Father, Son and Holy Ghost.' Her voice deepened with emotion as he placed a hand between her thighs and she experienced an urge so strong that the source of her femininity throbbed and she moaned with longing.

'I, Owain ap Rowan, take thee, Kate Fletcher Stanley, for my wife. I promise to cherish and be true to you, in the name of the Father, Son and Holy Ghost.' His fingers searched, probed and pleasured her and waves of ecstasy spread inside her. Having prepared her, he turned her on her side and entered her. She gasped. He hesitated. 'Again!' she urged, pushing against him. Ignoring the agony in his shoulder, he obeyed her, moaning with pleasure as his seed filled her.

Only afterwards, when Kate unlocked the door and inspected his shoulder, did she upbraid herself. Blood had seeped through the bandaging. 'I should never have allowed you to tempt me,' she scolded, putting down the candlestick and unwinding the soiled bindings.

Owain laughed weakly. 'I tempted you?'

'It is true.' Her lips twitched and she blushed. 'And do not shake so much with laugher or you will have the wound bleeding even more. I will tend it and this time I will smear more goose grass salve on the wound. Then you must behave yourself and rest.'

He did not argue, but did as she said, his loving glance taking in every aspect of her face, the tiny lines of concentration on her forehead and the lips, rosy with his kisses, pressed together as if she was feeling his pain. 'I will behave and rest if you will come back to bed,' he said.

She did not look up from her task but said gruffly, 'You will tell everyone that we have taken each other for man and wife?'

He raised an eyebrow. 'You expect me to deny it?'

She met his stare. 'No. But perhaps it would be wiser if we kept it quiet for now.'

He thrust out his jaw and the candlelight caught the flash of anger in his eyes. 'You would have me treat you like your father did your mother? No, Kate. We might not have exchanged our vows in the presence of a priest, but I intend to keep mine.'

She was deeply moved. 'But what of Sir Thomas? If he were to hear from someone else that we have exchanged vows of marriage without his permission, then he could be angry and hold back my father's inheritance and his help in our gaining Merebury. Let us keep quiet and face him together. When you tell him that you have solved the mystery of Sir Roger's death, then you tell him what we have done.'

Owain was silent for so long that Kate thought he was not going to let her have her way. Then he nodded, 'But I tell you, Kate, I will not go quietly if he were to attempt to separate us. I would fight for you.'

She cupped his face between her hands. 'I want no talk of fighting. I would want to die if you were killed.'

His features softened and, taking one of her hands, he pressed it to his lips. 'Let there be no talk of dying.

We will worry about Sir Thomas and what he will say and do when the need arises. For now let us make the most of the time we have together.'

Chapter Fourteen

'A messenger has come at last,' called Kate, pausing in the stable entrance.

'From Sir Thomas?' asked Owain, straightening from inspecting the mare who had cast a shoe. Over a month had passed since he had been wounded.

'He wears the Stanley livery and says he has come from Knowsley.' She could not quite suppress her nervous excitement.

Owain allowed no emotion to show on his face as he asked Diccon to take the horse to the smithy. The youth nodded and led it away, winking at Kate as she moved aside to allow him to pass. Owain wiped his hands on a piece of rag before placing an arm about her shoulders. 'I thought to hear from Sir Thomas before this, but it seems our affairs are of small matter in his scheme of things,' he said, adopting a cheerful note.

Kate fell in with his mood and smiled. Soon it would be Christmas and she prayed that, by then, Sir Thomas would have set his seal of approval on their match. They crossed the stable yard and hurried past the herb and vegetable gardens and entered the hall. They found the messenger, steam coming from his garments as he warmed himself by the fire, eating bread and cheese and drinking from a cup of mulled wine. He sprang to his feet when he saw them and inclined his head towards his host.

'You have a message for me,' said Owain.

'Aye, Master ap Rowan. Your presence and that of the Lady is required at Knowsley on the morrow.' The man reached inside his doublet. 'I have it written here in his secretary's hand.'

Owain raised an eyebrow and took the scroll from him. 'Your master is well?'

'Aye!' The man's eyelids blinked rapidly as he gazed at him.

'Good.' Owain smiled warmly. 'Tell him we will be there. Finish your repast, best you be on your way before darkness falls.'

The man looked dismayed. 'You have no written message for me?'

Owain shook his head. 'My word is enough.'

He took Kate's arm and strolled with her out of the hall. She made to speak, but he placed his finger to his lips and shook his head. He took her to the parlour and there broke open the seal on the folded parchment and spread it flat on the table. He read the letter silently until its end and then an exclamation escaped him.

'What is it? What does it say?' demanded Kate, resting her hands on the table and looking across it at him.

He read aloud, 'A complaint has been lodged against you concerning your enquiries into the death of Sir

Roger Miles. Your enquiries are prejudiced by your betrothal to Mistress Kate Fletcher.'

Kate gasped and he looked up at her with a faint smile. 'It does not end there. I'm also accused of having stolen two chests of money and of plotting with the Lady Catherine and the Fletcher family to kill Sir Roger in revenge for my brother's death. We must answer these charges forthwith the day after next at Lathom, taking the chest with us.'

Kate's face was ashen. 'We must not go. We will be imprisoned and even…' She stopped as he shook his head slowly. The colour returned to her cheeks. 'It is a fake. Whoever wrote this does not know I am a Stanley.'

Owain's blue eyes hardened. 'I expected a counter-attack for what happened at the Devil's Graveyard before now but, when a week—two weeks passed, I started to believe that without coin to pay mercenaries to do his bidding the Comte really had departed for France.'

'This letter is intended to lead us into a trap.'

'An ambush on the road.' Owain picked up the letter and folded it before placing it inside his surcote. 'He must think I'm a fool to believe I would take you or the chest with me. The road between Chester and Birkenhead is too well frequented to make an ambush easy, so his plan must be to surprise me nearer Lathom.' He eased his shoulders back. 'It is time to finish this. I will leave tomorrow and take the ferry to Liverpool. I have friends there. Sir Thomas could be on his way north and, having heard this, the Comte decided to take action before he arrives. Perhaps he has guessed that he has become my prime suspect for Sir Roger's murder.'

'You will not go alone,' said Kate, frowning. 'Your

shoulder has not long healed. The Fletcher family will ride with you.'

Owain frowned. 'That is not sensible.'

'It makes more sense than your plan to go alone,' she retorted, beginning to pace the floor. 'Better still...why don't we all go today? We could leave within a couple of hours.'

He shook his head and when he spoke his tone was steely. 'I will listen to no more of this, Kate. I will not put your life in danger. You will stay here. If it makes you happy, I will taken Diccon and a couple of men with me. There is not much for them to do until the new year.'

She shook her head stubbornly. 'I will not stay behind to fret myself into flinders over what might be happening to you and Diccon. If you leave me behind I will follow you...unless you intend locking me in my bedchamber?'

Owain continued to stare at her and then suddenly his expression changed and he held out a hand. 'So be it. I will leave my brothers in charge here so we will not be parted just yet.'

She took his hand and he drew her into his arms and kissed her deep and long. Immediately she responded and within seconds he had unfastened the bodice of her gown and had buried his head between her breasts. His hand slid up her skirts and she unlaced his breeches, praying no one would come in. She doubted there would be opportunity for lovemaking during the next few days and she could not help remembering last night when he had come to her. They had tried a new position because his shoulder was so much better and ended up collapsing with laughter in a tangle of arms and legs. After Gwendolyn's death, Owain suggested that

Beth might move into his stepmother's chamber and
share the care of Anna with Agnes. Beth had fixed him
with a knowing look, but agreed. Since that time,
Owain had been a regular visitor to Kate's bed and now
she gasped with pleasure as he entered her and quickly
caught his rhythm. The risk they took acted as a stim-
ulant and they came together almost immediately. Soon
she was fastening her bodice. 'That is going to have to
last until…'

'The next time,' said Owain, smiling.

The journey to Birkenhead passed without incident.
Occasionally Beth commented on the passing scene
and made reference to their flight from Merebury. At
Owain's request, Kate had not discussed the contents
of the letter with her mother, but Diccon knew what it
said. When they reached the Mersey, Owain paid the
toll for the ferryboat to the monk at Birkenhead Priory
and waited its arrival from Liverpool.

Kate gazed across the water towards the cluster of
buildings on the other side. The tower owned by the
Stanleys and the castle that spoke of the other great
power in that place, the Molyneuxs, could clearly be
seen. In the shadow of these two edifices lived those
who made their livelihood from the sea. Several wind-
mills showed starkly against the sky on top of the hills
that rose behind the small port. To the south lay a vast
heath of common land crossed by several paths, one
of which led to Sir Thomas's manor of Knowsley;
Lathom and Merebury lay to the north. As the returning ferry boat neared the jetty, Kate was apprehensive.
Suddenly she wanted to return to the comfort and

safety of Rowan Manor, but there was no going back. They had to go forward to meet their fate.

To his amazement, the first person Owain set eyes on as they landed in Liverpool was Nat Milburn. He was standing on the quayside in conversation with a mariner. Owain wasted no time strolling over to his friend and hailing him.

Nat started. 'What do folk say? Think of the devil and he's sure to appear. You were on my mind and here you are.'

Owain could not help grinning. 'Why was I on your mind?'

'I was talking to Sir Thomas Stanley only this morning and your name cropped up.'

Owain's grin slowly faded. 'He's here in Liverpool?'

Nat gazed at him severely. 'If you'll just listen. I mentioned seeing you in France with your betrothed, Lady Catherine, and he said that it could not have been her because she was dead. I told him that he must be mistaken, that I'd seen her in your company in France. He said the Lady was definitely dead as you'd sent him word to that effect and that the person I'd met was his cousin, Katherine Stanley.' He scratched his head. 'Now I might be approaching my fortieth birthday, Owain, but I'm not going deaf. I'd swear on Holy Scripture that you said the lady was Lady Catherine Miles. I remember I recognised her.'

Owain wondered what Sir Thomas had made of that word *betrothed*. 'I misled you. I'll explain later. Tell me…where is Sir Thomas now?'

'Set out for Lathom this morning. There's a dispute concerning salvage rights in a ship that ran aground on a sandbank, which requires his presence. Told me that if I were to visit you then I was to give you a message from him.'

'And what was that message?'

'That you were to attend him forthwith. Something about another will belonging to Lady Catherine turning up.'

Owain scowled. 'Who has produced this will? And did he want me to bring the Lady?'

'The prior at Burscough Priory has the will.' Nat screwed up his face. 'Can't remember what else Sir Thomas said about the Lady. Someone interrupted us, but he did mention something about the twelve days of Christmas.' He added in a disgruntled voice, 'So why did you fool me into believing that his cousin was Lady Catherine Miles…and how was it I knew her face?'

Owain said shortly, 'Later, I'll explain later. It'll soon be dark and the lady and her mother are weary and I need to find somewhere for us to shelter for the night.' He indicated Kate and Beth with a gloved hand.

Nat looked in their direction and immediately said, 'You remember my aunt who lives at Old Moore Hall? She will happily provide hospitality. Although your men will have to stay at the local hostelry.'

Owain smiled and thanked him. 'I always knew I could rely on you to come to my aid, Nat.'

Nat brushed his thanks aside and said gruffly. 'Just remembered Sir Thomas mentioned your father's death. Sorry to hear of it.'

Owain's expression sobered. 'It was a grief to me. I would have liked to have made my peace with him, but it was too late.'

'How has your stepmother taken it?'

Owain grimaced. 'She's dead, but leaves a daughter.'

Nat sighed. 'Died in childbirth, I suppose. Sad, very sad.'

Owain did not correct his supposition, but instead said, 'Tell me what brings you to Liverpool?'

'Family trouble,' said the older man, rolling his eyes. 'Sickness at home and so the children have been sent here to my aunt. My sister is remarrying at Candlemass. Now she and my aunt insist that I must take another wife.' Nat rasped a fingernail along his unshaven chin. 'My aunt suggested that I ask a spinster of her acquaintance. So having met the woman and believing her one of good sense, I did what they suggested…only to have my proposal thrown back in my face,' he said indignantly. 'She said she didn't want a husband who was always carousing on the continent. I tell you, that knocked the wind right out of my sails.'

Owain chuckled. 'You'll have to find a woman who'll be more than willing to have you stay at home with her.'

Nat said gloomy, 'Show me one.'

Owain smiled. 'Let me introduce you to Mistress Beth Fletcher.'

'Master Milburn,' said Beth in a voice that was just a breath of sound. 'I don't know if you remember our first meeting here in Liverpool ten, twelve years ago?' There was a blush on her cheeks.

Nat stared at her as if seeing a ghost and then he blinked and grasped her hand. 'Aye! But I thought you were dead.'

Kate glanced at Owain, who winked and took Merlin's reins from her before turning to his men and speaking to them in a low voice. Kate could scarcely believe what appeared to be happening between her mother and Master Milburn. 'I have told Owain that you all may stay at my aunt's home,' he was saying. 'I'm sure she will make you welcome.'

'That is kind of her and you,' said Beth.

Nat beamed down her. 'She'll enjoy your company.' He offered her his arm and she took it and headed up-hill towards the castle.

The others followed. 'You might be interested to know, Kate, if you don't already, that Nat's relatives in Liverpool own a mill, a kiln and a lime pit, as well as being involved in shipping,' whispered Owain. 'And Nat, himself, is heir to land in Yorkshire. His family own great flocks of sheep and they export woollen cloth.'

Kate cast him a smiling glance. 'You consider that news is of interest to me?'

'I know he's looking for a wife,' he said softly.

'You are suggesting that Mother and Master Milburn could make a match of it? They've only just met each other again after…you heard her…ten, twelve years.'

'But they're obviously taken with each other. Falling in love can happen at any time and in an instant.' His eyes held hers and a delicious shiver rippled through her as she saw he wanted her.

'You have great experience of love?' she murmured, attempting to look demure.

'Of a surety! It means, of course, giving all of oneself.'

'Surely that is the only way to truly love a person,' she responded, meeting his burning gaze and feeling a singing in her spirit.

'If only we were alone, I would kiss you in such a way you would not want me to stop,' he whispered.

'We must walk on or Diccon will hear you,' she murmured, wishing she had allowed him to tell everyone that they had plighted their troth.

Dusk was falling by the time they reached Old Moore Hall. They passed through a pair of iron gates into a courtyard. Nat directed Owain and Diccon to the stables.

Kate gazed at the house, which was partly covered by climbing ivy. The building was two storeys high and built of sandstone like many in this part of England. Its ground-floor windows overlooked the courtyard and to the front of the house lay a lawn and empty flowerbeds, protected from winds that swept in from the Irish Sea by a high wall. The front door was opened to them by a serving man, whom Nat sent to inform his aunt that she had guests.

Kate and her mother glanced about the old hall, noticing that the fireplace was in the centre. Smoke from the log fire wended its way lazily through the rafters to a hole in the roof. Towards the rear of the hall was a double staircase that led to a gallery on the first floor. An elderly woman suddenly appeared at the top of the stairs.

Nat called up to her and she descended with a rustle of skirts. Her face had the colour and texture of a weathered apple and her grey hair was covered by a hood, tied beneath her chin. She was followed by several dogs and a girl. The old woman's eyes were speculative as they alighted on Kate. 'It came as a great surprise to me when Nat told me that Sir Thomas had a cousin whom I have never met,' she said in a high-pitched voice. 'But you have a look of the Stanleys.'

'It seems your cousin wants the relationship known, Kate,' said Owain.

'And why shouldn't he?' said Mistress Moore, beaming at the pair of them. 'Welcome to my home. I hope you enjoy your stay with me.'

They thanked her but, before Kate could introduce her mother, Nat Milburn stepped forward and did so. 'Aunt, this is Mistress Beth Fletcher. She is not a stranger to Liverpool. In truth, we recognised each other when we were introduced. Please make a friend of her for my sake.' There was such warmth in Nat's voice that his aunt looked at him sharply before shaking Beth's hand.

'I'm pleased to have you here. I wager my nephew did not tell you that his three children are staying here, too? The lads are twins and imps of Satan. Fortunately I've managed to get them into school, so they won't bother you much. The girl, Cicely, has seen ten summers and is a great help to me.' She ushered them over to the fire. 'Please make yourselves comfortable. No doubt you're hungry.'

They murmured agreement. Beth smiled at Nat's daughter and whispered something to her. Kate removed her gloves and held her hands to the fire, listening to Mistress Moore order a serving man to mull wine. Already another man had been dispatched to the kitchen for meat, cheese and bread.

In no time at all they were seated by the fire, warming their hands on cups of mulled wine, fragrant with nutmeg and slices of fruit. The old woman settled herself in a great carved armchair, its hardness softened by a cushion. Nat's daughter sat on a footstool at his feet, darting glances every now and again at Diccon.

Kate was amused. It was obvious that her brother had found someone to admire him and he was kind enough to treat her gently. It boded well for family relations if all went well over the next few days. At least for the moment they were safe. It wasn't fit for man or beast to be outside. The wind howled round the eaves and the faint roar of waves pounding the shore could be heard despite the thickness of the sandstone walls. She smiled at Owain sitting across from her and regretted that he would not be sharing her bed that night.

After they had eaten their fill and drunk more mulled wine, Mrs Moore gave Cicely the task of showing Kate and Beth to a bedchamber on the ground floor. It was not very large and had only a couple of wooden pegs on the wall to hang their cloaks but a fire had been lit in a brazier, taking the chill from the room.

'I hope you'll be comfortable here and not have to leave too soon,' said Cicely, who had her father's fair hair and freckled face.

Kate considered some of the places she had slept in during the past year and assured her that everything was fine. Clad in her shift, Kate slid between the cold sheets with a sigh.

'Why do you sigh, Kate?' asked Beth.

Kate knew she could not tell her the truth, so instead said, 'I was thinking that Master Milburn seems to have taken a fancy to you. What are your feelings towards him?'

Beth said sleepily, 'I like him very well and I am thinking that his daughter is of an age when she needs a mother.'

'Owain tells me that Master Milburn is looking for a wife.'

'Then he need look no further,' said Beth with a chuckle.

Kate smiled, hoping that Master Milburn would not delay in pressing his suit. Both were past the bloom of youth and had no time to waste. Also it meant that her mother would need not concern herself about what the Stanleys might think if she married Master Milburn and went to live in Yorkshire. Of course, Kate would miss her, but her mother's happiness was what mattered. Still, she was perhaps thinking too far ahead. They had yet to face Sir Thomas. She turned onto her side and closed her eyes, hugging part of the pillow against her cheek and pretended it was Owain's broad chest.

'Wake up, Kate! Master ap Rowan and Diccon are leaving,' cried Beth.

Leaving? With her eyes still shut, Kate sat up and flung back the covers and slid out of bed. The wooden floor was cold. As she straightened up, she felt suddenly nauseous and had to force down the bile that rose in her throat. She sank onto the bed and took several deep breaths before repeating her question and asking for her clothes.

'To Lathom and then to Merebury. Here, daughter. I'll help you to dress…and do open your eyes. The wind has blown all the clouds away and it's a lovely day.'

'But they did not say they were going to Lathom to-day…and it's freezing!' said Kate, shivering as her mother enveloped her in her red kirtle.

'Diccon is impatient to see what changes might have been made at Merebury and Master ap Rowan will not allow him to go alone. Perhaps he, too, wants to see how the land lies and what people are saying about us.'

Kate gasped. 'You should have woken me sooner.'

'You were deep in sleep and looked so happy I didn't like disturbing you. But then I thought you'd be angry if you didn't have the chance to wave them off and wish them God speed.' Beth thrust her daughter's arms into her green woollen gown, the neck of which Kate had recently embroidered with leaves of yellow thread. She put on her shoes and, with her hair loose about her shoulders, hurried out of the bedchamber and along a stone flagged passage and into the hall.

Owain was just about to leave when Kate called his name. He turned and she ran across the hall, her hair like a golden cloud about her pale face. He seized both her hands and for a moment neither of them spoke. Then she said crossly, 'You would have gone without saying farewell.'

'I knew you'd want to come and I thought you'd still be tired after yesterday's journey.' His eyes were concerned as he gazed down at her. 'I will be back before you have chance to miss me. Make the most of your time here to rest and decide what to wear when you meet Sir Thomas.'

'You will be on your guard?'

'Of course.'

Her brows puckered and her blue-green eyes were thoughtful. 'You are not keeping another secret from me, are you, Owain?'

He smiled faintly. 'If I was, then it would only be because I value your safety. Now kiss me and I will see you on the morrow.'

She wished she knew what he meant and still felt vexed with him. Even so she stood on tiptoe and pressed her lips against his, regardless of those watching. He returned her kiss and held her close before releasing her so abruptly that she had to reach out and cling to the doorpost to stop herself from falling. She looked up at her brother and thought she saw a suppressed excitement in his eyes. Then they were gone.

'So that's how the land lies,' said Mistress Moore. 'The sooner Master ap Rowan has Sir Thomas's permission to marry you, mistress, the better, I say.'

Kate was tempted to say that they were already wed, but decided she had kept her mouth shut this long, what did a few more days matter.

After breaking her fast, Kate wanted to talk to her mother about the gown she was to wear when they met Sir Thomas, but she could not find Beth in the house and soon discovered Master Milburn was nowhere to be found either. When they did reappear, it was obvious they had eyes only for each other and whilst Kate did not begrudge them their delight in having discovered love in the autumn of their days, she would have enjoyed her mother's company. She could not wait for that day to be over so as to be reunited with Owain once more.

The next day Kate woke to find the bedchamber empty. She rose and felt that same nausea she had experienced yesterday, but this time she was unable to control the sickness and barely had time to drag out the chamber pot and vomit into it. Afterwards she lay on the bed, feeling a little better and with the realisation dawning on her that the reason for her sickness could be that she was with child. Her monthly courses were late. If that was so, then she had a surprise up her sleeve when she and Owain met with Sir Thomas. She could not wait to tell her secret to her husband.

Chapter Fifteen

After a late breakfast Kate kept Mistress Moore and Cicely company whilst she waited impatiently for the return of Owain and Diccon. But noon came and still they had not arrived. Her mother and Nat told her not to fret, saying that Owain could have been delayed at Lathom. He encouraged her to go for a walk with Cicely. Kate took up his suggestion and wrapping up warmly, she and the girl walked along the waterfront, watching the ferry plying its way across the river to the priory on the other side. There were other ships and small boats to watch and Kate could not help remembering shipboard life with Owain. She prayed that he and Diccon would be at the hall when she returned.

But they weren't and still Master Milburn and her mother seemed not to be concerned, saying that a horse could have thrown a shoe and delayed them. That evening Kate attempted to keep her anxiety at bay by teaching Cicely how to play chess, but it was soon obvious that the girl was more interested in Diccon, asking Kate whether he was betrothed yet or not.

* * *

The next day Kate rose early, leaving her mother sleeping. She managed to reach the privy before being sick. An hour later, she felt better but ate little, still concerned about Owain and Diccon.

Later that morning, Mistress Moore's son arrived from his manor at Bankhall to the north of Liverpool. He had news of the dispute over the salvage rights, saying that Sir Thomas had settled the matter.

Nat asked him if he had heard anything of Owain ap Rowan. 'Aye! He was in disagreement with the local prior at Burscough over the will of Lady Catherine. Rumour has it she died on pilgrimage and left all her property to her companion, a Mistress Kate Fletcher. Apparently there are two wills and the abbot says that the one Master ap Rowan gave to Sir Thomas Stanley must be a forgery and that the Lady promised her property to his priory so prayers could be said in perpetuity for her soul.'

Kate, who had been listening in anger to the conversation between the two men, sprang to her feet. 'That's not true! If she had meant to leave money to the church, it would have been the one at Merebury.'

Master Moore looked at her in surprise. 'It's said that the prior had the will from the hand of the rector of Walton church.'

'Who is a Molyneux! You must know as well as I do that they and the Stanleys are always trying to score off each other,' snapped Kate. 'He has betrayed Lady Catherine's wishes. Perhaps because she confided in him that I was a Stanley.'

'These are only rumours and no doubt Sir Thomas

will see that justice is done now he has finished with the other matter,' said Nat, soothingly.

Master Moore agreed and, placing a hand on his kinsman's shoulder, said, 'Now I need to talk business with you, Nat.'

Kate left them to it but she was not satisfied.

A grim-faced Owain swept out of the judgement hall. When it came to money and possessions there were those in the church who would deny truth. He and the lawyer had been arguing his and Kate's case all yesterday and most of today in the church court. The Bishop had ruled that no decision could be made on Kate's claim to Merebury until Sir Thomas produced the will he had sent to him or the King regained his wits. In the meantime, perhaps, she should be brought before the court to answer the rumours that had been rife in the area since she and her family had disappeared with the Lady Catherine after Sir Roger Miles's mysterious death. This was what Owain had feared and he knew he had to speak to Sir Thomas immediately. As for Diccon, he had his orders to keep well out of sight. Besides, he had another task to perform.

Unfortunately, when Owain arrived at Lathom, it was to be informed that Sir Thomas had received a message that required his instant departure. It occurred to Owain that the message might not be genuine. Worried about Kate's safety, he decided to return to Liverpool. He hurried to the stables but, no sooner had he stepped inside the building, than he felt a blow to the back of his head. He staggered and his hand went to his sword, but, before he could use it, he was hit again and slumped to the ground.

Kate could stay in bed no longer. She'd had such a nightmare that she had woken in terror in the wee small hours and been unable to get back to sleep. With the dawn she decided she must do something. Yesterday had dragged by as she had waited for Owain's return, but he had not come. She feared for his safety and would not wait any longer. Especially when she had such good news to tell him.

Suddenly the dogs began to bark and Kate's heart lifted. Perhaps Owain and Diccon had returned at last and her nightmare had been just a result of her over-wrought state. She hurried to the window to see two monks inside the courtyard. Their horses were in a lather and she could see blood where one had spurred the poor animal. That rider was a tall man and of stocky build and bellowed for a stable boy. He pushed back his hood and she could see his profile clearly and recognised him as one of the monks from Burscough Priory. Her heart began to beat with heavy strokes, setting her a-tremble. Had they come for her?

Suddenly Kate heard Mrs Moore's voice and realised she must have come out of the house. Kate heard her name mentioned and was filled with trepidation. The next moment the old woman invited the monks into the house.

Kate delayed no longer, but dressed swiftly, fighting against the now familiar nausea. She tied up her hair in a linen veil and then pulled on a hat and fastened her cloak before easing her hands into soft leather gloves. Beth murmured in her sleep and Kate hesitated. Should she delay and wake her mother? She was certain that Master Milburn would see that no harm came to her. She decided she could delay no longer. She would make for Merebury and hope to find Owain and Diccon there.

Having made her decision, Kate climbed out of the window. Hugging the wall of the building she made her way to the stables, glad that the day was dry, cold and crisp. The stable lad looked at her in surprise and asked was there aught he could do for her.

She shook her head and saddled up the only decent horse left in the stable. She told him that she was off to Knowsley to speak to her kinsman and led the horse to the mounting block. Her heart was thumping in her chest. She heard her name being called as she mounted. Without delay she dug her heels into the horse's flanks and urged it towards the gateway. She was aware of a sense of urgency and could only hope that nothing evil had befallen Owain and Diccon.

It was past noon by the time Kate passed through the forest of Ince Blundell, and she had covered half the distance to Merebury. Clear skies had given way to clouds that had swiftly blanketed out the sun. She thought that before the day was out, it would be snow. She was hungry and thirsty, but dared not stop. That sense of urgency was still with her and she knew that she must put more miles behind her before she dared consider resting and seeking succour.

Owain attempted to ease the agonising cramp in his calf, but he was bound with leather straps by his hands and his feet in a space smaller than that of the average-size coffin. He was unable to stretch out fully. When he had first gained consciousness it was with a splitting headache, and the Comte's voice had been coming at him from a distance, demanding to know where the chest of money was that Richard Fletcher had stolen and hidden. Owain did not remember giving him an answer, but had drifted in and out of consciousness. There had been one terrifying moment, on waking, when he had wondered whether he had revealed Kate's whereabouts because there had been no voice demanding answers from him. Now he was fully awake and it was pitch dark. Perhaps the Comte had finished with him and buried him alive. Then as the minutes ticked by and he could still breathe, Owain realised that what lay beneath him was stone. Perhaps he was in a sarcophagus, and, knowing it would be impossible for him to kick off the lid, he almost despaired. Then by dint of searching with his fingertips and tongue he discovered that there were gaps between the stones and he could smell vegetation. Which meant two things: he was not going to suffocate, but that air was icy cold, so, unless he could get out of his prison soon, he would freeze to death.

He spent the next hour struggling against his bonds and trying to figure out where he could be. He could only pray that Diccon was still free and Kate was safe in Liverpool. He did not want to believe that he could have betrayed her to the Comte whilst half-conscious. His eyes had now become accustomed to his surroundings and it seemed to him that it was lighter. In truth, it was a strange white light coming through the cracks, but it revealed to him that he was lying between what looked to be large chunks of limestone.

He was reminded of an *allée couverte* built by the Celts in Brittany. Taking note of the way his prison was constructed, he decided that most likely the stone over-head could be moved. Immediately he set about trying to shift it; no mean task in such a cramped space, but at least he would get warm in the attempt and he just might succeed. He also decided to shout for help every now and then, in the hope of attracting the attention of a shepherd or Diccon.

The first flakes of snow began to fall as Kate reached the outskirts of the market town of Ormskirk, but she knew that she dared not stop if she was to reach Mere-bury before nightfall. Skirting the town, she rode on. She felt exhausted and the horse was tiring and could only plod along now. She came to a crossroads and took the left fork. Already the snow was beginning to blanket the fields and woods. It altered the familiar outline of the land and she knew that, if she wandered off the path in the dying light of day, she could lose her life.

Suddenly she thought she saw a light. It disappeared only to reappear. The hairs stood up on the back of her neck. Perhaps it was a will'o'the wisp. Then she real-ised the light came from a lantern on a stick and was being carried by a dark hooded figure. Now where could he be going at this time of day?

Kate slid from the horse, only to collapse in the snow as her legs gave way. For a moment she lay there, her whole body aching with exhaustion. She did not want to move, but knew she had to for Owain and their

child's sake. Forcing herself to her feet, she took hold
of the reins and stumbled forward, needing to get her
limbs moving. She was determined to see where the
hooded figure was going, sensing he was up to no good.

Her feet sank into the snow, but at least she made no
sound as she moved stealthily in the wake of the lantern bearer. Within moments she realised he was heading in the direction of the limestone quarry that lay in
the vicinity of the place where Richard Fletcher had
fallen to his death. Only for an instant did she question
the wisdom of her actions in following him. Even so,
she continued to dog his footsteps. Snowflakes clung
to her eyelashes and she had to keep wiping them away.
Then, praise be, the snow began to ease off and suddenly it stopped altogether. With the remaining light in
the sky reflecting on the snowy ground, it was enough
for her to see where she was going. Cautiously she
rounded a rocky outcrop only to be seized and whirled
round. The lantern was held aloft and its light shone on
her face, almost blinding her.

'*Mam'selle* Fletcher,' said the Comte, staring down
at her in astonishment. 'Eet must be sorcery which
brings you here.'

As Kate looked up into that hawk-like profile, she
fought down her fear. Her instincts had been right when
she had followed him, but she did not underestimate the
danger to herself. She must keep calm. 'I have no truck
with the devil. I answer to a higher power. M'sieur le
Comte, you should fear for your soul this night.'

His face twisted in an ugly scowl. 'You would
threaten me, *mam'selle*?' he sneered, and bringing up

his hand, he would have hit her if she had not lashed out at him with both hands.

Thrown off balance, he staggered back and dropped the lantern in the snow. She lunged for the stick and seized it at the same time as he did. They struggled for it, Kate's desperation making her strength almost equal to his, but eventually he managed to wrench it from her hands. As he lifted it to whack her with it, she ducked and caught him in the midriff with her head. He gasped, but dropped the stick and put both his arms round her.

Suddenly there was a roar of fury and the next moment he was being dragged away from her. Breathing heavily, Kate drew back and through the twilight managed to make out the shape of two men struggling, both obviously intent on gaining the upper hand. She picked up the stick from which the lantern had fallen and its light extinguished. Her pulse beat rapidly as she realised that the Comte's assailant seemed intent on bashing the Frenchman's head on the ground so it would crack like an egg. Her spirits soared because there could be only one man so determined to destroy their enemy. 'Owain, you're alive!' she cried.

'No thanks to him,' he responded in a grim voice, staggering back. 'He ambushed me and knocked me out, brought me here and no doubt would have left me to freeze to death once he realised for certain I could not tell him where the missing chest of money was hidden.'

Kate peered at Owain through the gathering darkness. His face was filthy and strips of leather dangled loosely from his wrists and ankles. She drew in a breath with a hiss, but before she could speak, a voice called from the top of the crag. 'I think you've killed him, Owain.' She recognised her brother's voice.

Owain nodded and pulled the remains of the bonds from his wrists and ankles. Then he reached out a hand to Kate. She took it and instantly noticed where the skin was broken and bleeding and pressed kisses on the raw wounds. 'My poor love,' she murmured.

Diccon said, 'I'm glad I decided to revisit the place where Father died and make a proper search of the quarry for the chest I was convinced he had hidden somewhere round here. Otherwise I would not have heard Owain's calls for help.'

'Praise the Trinity that you did,' said Kate.

'And did you find it, Diccon?' asked Owain.

Diccon grinned. 'Aye, I did.'

Owain smiled. 'Good. We'll hand it over to Sir Thomas for the King. I'm sure we will be rewarded and it should help gain us a few favours too.'

Diccon said, 'I certainly hope so. I need all the help I can get to make my fortune.'

'So how do we say the Comte died?' asked Kate, clinging tightly to Owain. She was beginning to feel light-headed.

'We tell the truth,' he said. 'He's a black-hearted villain. I believe Sir Thomas will say the world is well rid of him…and his death will save all the cost and bother of putting him on trial for Sir Roger's murder.'

'So it is over. Our enemies are vanquished and we are safe,' whispered Kate. Suddenly she swayed against Owain. He looked down and caught her as she fell.

* * *

Kate woke the following morning to find herself in the largest bed she had ever slept in. She was not alone. Sitting up abruptly, she gazed down at Owain's dark curly head, where it nestled on a lace-trimmed pillow, twin to hers. For a moment she could not remember how they came to be there, but then the purity of the light, shining through the window, caused the events of yesterday to come flooding back. She remembered Owain taking her up before him on one of the horses that Diccon had fetched. She had thought they would go to Merebury, only to be told that the house was in no fit state to welcome visitors. Instead Owain had brought her to Lathom House. Here they had found a welcome as any traveller lost in a storm would have done.

The Lady of the manor had come forward, fussing over them like a mother hen. She had ordered bedchambers to be made ready and ushered them over to the fireplace, where a huge log threw out an enormous amount of heat. Already the hall was decorated with holly and ivy for Christmastide and the smell of roasting meat had been so mouthwatering that Kate thought she might faint again with hunger. Supper was being served and they were led straight to table, where a serving boy brought a bowl for them to wash their hands.

Owain had fussed over her as much as Sir Thomas's Lady, and Kate had been astonished when he had introduced her as Mistress ap Rowan, my wife. Diccon had rolled his eyes at her, and she had taken him aside and told him that they had plighted their troth secretly.

Afterwards the Lady had apologised for her husband's absence, saying that he had been called to Knowsley unexpectedly, but hopefully he would return on the morrow. Later it had come as a great surprise to Kate to be shown to this sumptuous bedchamber. Despite her good intentions to tell Owain everything that had happened since he had left Liverpool, she had fallen into a deep sleep as soon as she lay down.

Now she reached out and touched Owain's unshaven cheek with the back of her hand. He stirred and turned onto his back. His eyes opened and he gazed up at her sleepily. The next moment he shot up in bed and his blue gaze took in the bedchamber with its hangings of scarlet velvet and gold embroidery. There was a great oak armoire and a chest carved with the Stanley emblem of the eagle and child. Her eyes followed his with pleasure and wonder, washing over an oak writing table, two cushioned chairs with what appeared to be clean clothing on them, a washstand with an enamel bowl and thick woven linen drying cloths patterned with lozenges. Most welcome of all was the fire burning in a brazier.

She waited for him to speak but instead he lay down again, and reaching out, brought her against him. 'Now tell me how you came to find me? I know it was not by magic.'

So she told him all that had happened since he had left her in Liverpool. 'You took a great risk making the journey alone, but obviously God was with you.' He brushed his lips against hers as gentle as thistledown before kissing her again more deeply. She clung to him, enjoying the feel of his firm body against hers, debating whether she should tell him about the baby now or later. It could be that he would decide they should not make love and in that case…

Before she could make a decision, there was a knock at the door. 'Master ap Rowan, Sir Thomas has returned and wishes to see you and your Lady immediately.'

Owain groaned. He buried his face against her neck a moment before lifting his head and saying, 'Tell him we will be with him in an instant.' He climbed out of bed and dressed quickly. Kate stared at him, but did not speak. 'Come on, Kate, move!' he ordered.

Slowly she got out of bed, hoping that for once she would not feel nauseous, but, almost as soon as she stood up, she retched. Putting a hand to her mouth, she said in a muffled voice, 'You must go without me.'

Owain looked at her with concern. 'What is wrong with you, my love?'

'A baby,' she gasped, shooing him away with one hand.

He looked stunned. 'A baby?'

She nodded. 'Go!'

His face lit up and he picked up the bowl. 'Nay! We will face Sir Thomas together. For the moment he will have to wait.'

Owain held the bowl for her and, once she had finished being sick, wiped her face tenderly with a damp cloth. He helped her to dress in the green linen kirtle and saffron silk gown left for her use. Then he combed her hair and assisted her in fastening on her wimple. She slipped her feet into the soft leather slippers and then, hand in hand, they hurried from the bedchamber.

Sir Thomas stood in the hall with his back to the fire, drinking from a silver goblet. As soon as they entered the hall, he signalled to those present to leave them. Only after they had departed did he beckon Owain and Kate forward. He was richly clad in a doublet of blue velvet beneath a full-length sleeveless green cotehardie trimmed with fur. On his head he wore a basin-shaped hat with a rolled brim. He looked older than Kate had believed him to be. She bobbed a brief curtsy and then dared to look him straight in the eye. 'So you are my kinwoman Kate,' he said.

'So I have been told, Sir Thomas.'

He lowered his head and brought his face close to hers so that his wine-scented breath filled her nostrils. 'You have a look of your father. He requested that I find you a suitable husband.' He straightened and stared at Owain. 'What have you got to say for yourself?'

'Do not blame Owain,' said Kate, deciding not only to take the initiative, but also that boldness was called for, too. 'Like my father I dared to choose whom I would love and wed. I believe that he would be pleased with my choice.'

'Do you indeed!' Sir Thomas frowned.

She tilted her chin. 'I am, after all, a Stanley—do they not go after what they want? I want this man.' Kate ran a hand down Owain's arm. 'I would not be standing here if it were not for him. He has saved my life!' she said stoutly.

Sir Thomas cleared his throat. 'You're bold-faced, I give you that, Kate.'

'Is that not a Stanley trait, Sir Thomas?' said Owain, deciding it was time he took part in their defence. 'Surely Kate needs a husband just as bold. One who wants her to stand by his side and fight for what is theirs.'

Sir Thomas said, 'You talk of Merebury. Yesterday I was sent on a wild goose chase—I deem it was so that I could not speak on your behalf in the matter. I will send for the bishop and speak to him concerning the two wills. I will tell him of Friar Stephen's devil-worshipping ways, a man of his own order, and also of the other matter of which you wrote to me. No doubt he will be greatly shocked.'

'Does that mean Merebury will come to me as Lady Catherine intended?' asked Kate, her eyes glowing.

'That depends on what the King has to say and if Owain has fulfilled the task he was appointed,' said Sir Thomas, gazing at him intently.

Owain said gravely, 'I have written down all my findings, including what happened in the cave of the Devil's Graveyard. I am happy to inform you that only yesterday another chest of money was discovered but a few miles from here. No doubt its contents belong to the King. Also Sir Roger's murderer is dead.' Briefly Owain told him what had taken place last evening.

Sir Thomas's eyes widened and a guffaw broke from him. He slapped Owain on the back. 'It is good. I cannot wait to hear your version of the Devil's Graveyard. I also have good news. When I left London, the King was much improved. Hopefully he will soon be himself again. When that day comes then I am sure he will see that you are suitably rewarded.'

'My thanks to you, Sir Thomas,' said Owain, inclining his dark head. 'The wife of my heart has also told me this day that she is with child. A double cause for celebration.'

Sir Thomas's eyebrows almost disappeared beneath

the brim of his hat. 'You have wasted no time, Owain. I agree with Kate—my cousin would have approved of you, and I give you both my blessing.'

Kate whooped with delight and, turning to her kinsman, she stood on tiptoe and kissed his cheek. 'Thank you, Sir Thomas.'

He placed an arm about both of them. 'You will stay at Lathom for the twelve days of Christmas. And, Owain, I look forward to the day when you set up your stables at Merebury. Now go.' He dismissed them.

Kate and Owain almost ran out of the hall; as soon as they were alone, he pulled her into his arms and gazed down into her happy face. 'So, my Lady Kate, there is no escaping me now.'

'It would do me no good to try because you hold my heart,' she replied.

'And you mine.'

'Ours is indeed a love match,' she murmured.

He nodded and taking her chin between his fingers, said, 'Kiss me, Kate.'

She wasted no time in obeying him.

* * * * *

With over 11 million copies of her books in print, the novels of award-winning author Brenda Joyce brings 1902 New York to life, through her compelling amateur sleuth, Francesca Cahill.

Read on for an exclusive excerpt from Brenda Joyce's sensational new novel. Deadly Kisses will be available from June 16th, only from M&B.

Deadly Kisses

by

Brenda Joyce

"Miss?" Her personal maid, Betty, appeared at the far end of the corridor. In her hand was an envelope.

Francesca was surprised to see her. "Betty, why didn' you go to bed? I told you, I do not mind." She saw n reason for Betty to wait up for her. Other young ladie might be incapable of getting out of their gowns, but sh could manage quite easily and hardly needed a servan to help.

Betty, who was Francesca's own age, smiled at he "Oh, miss, it is so hard to get those buttons opened b yourself! And it's my work to take care of you. Beside this come for you, and the cabbie who brought it said was urgent, miss, terribly so."

As it was almost midnight, Francesca was intrigue She took the small envelope, noting its premier qualit It was addressed to her at her Fifth Avenue home, b bore no sender's name. "A cabdriver brought this?"

"Yes, miss."

Francesca unsealed the envelope and pulled out a small parchment. The note was brief and handwritten.

Francesca, I am in desperate need. Please come to Daisy's.
Rose.

Francesca leaned forward eagerly in the hansom cab she had hired. Stealing out of the house at the midnight hour had been easily accomplished, with her father still in the library and her mother upstairs and presumably in bed. The doorman, Robert, had pretended not to see her escape—but then, she gave him a weekly gratuity to ensure that he look the other way at such times.

After leaving the house, she had walked to the prestigious Metropolitan Club, but a block south of the Cahill home. There, she had merely waited for a gentleman to arrive at the club. Traffic was light, as it was a Monday night, but this was New York City, and eventually a hansom had paused before the club's imposing entrance to discharge his fare. Not wanting to be recognized, Francesca had bowed her head as a gentleman walked past her, but she knew he stared, as genuine ladies did not travel about the city at such an hour alone.

Francesca clung to the safety strap, straining to glimpse Daisy Jones's residence as her cab rumbled toward it. She simply could not imagine what Rose could want.

Daisy Jones was Hart's ex-mistress, and one of the most beautiful women Francesca had ever seen. When they first met, she had also been one of the city's most expensive and sought-after prostitutes. Francesca had been on a case at the time, working closely with Calder's half brother, Rick Bragg, the city's police commissioner. In fact, at that time she barely knew Hart— and had thought she was in love with Rick.

Francesca had not been surprised when she had learned of the liaison between them. She understood why Hart would want to keep such a woman. In fact she and Daisy had become rather friendly during that investigation—but any friendship had vanished when Hart had asked Francesca to marry him. Jilted, Daisy had not been pleased.

The large Georgian mansion appeared in her view. Daisy continued to reside in the house Hart had bought for her, as part of a six-month commitment he had promised her and was honoring. Francesca thought, but was not sure, that Rose was now living there, too. Rose was Daisy's dearest friend—and she had been her lover, before Daisy had left her for Hart.

The hansom had stopped. Francesca reached for her purse, noting that the entire house was dark, except for the outside light and two upstairs windows. Alarm bells went off in her mind. Even at such a late hour, a few lights should remain on inside on the ground floor.

Francesca paid the driver, thanking him, and stepped down to the curb. She paused to stare closely at the square brick house as he pulled away. There was no sign of movement, but then, at this hour that was not unusual. Uncertain of what to expect, she pushed open the iron gate and started up the brick path leading to the house. The gardens in front were lush and well tended and Francesca cautiously scanned them. Her nerves were on end, she realized, and she almost expected someone to jump out at her from behind a shrub or bush.

Just as she was about to silently reassure herself, she noticed that the front door was open.

Francesca halted, fully alert now. Suddenly, she thought about her mad dash from home. She had not bothered to go upstairs to retrieve her gun, a candle or any of the other useful items she habitually kept in her purse. She made a mental note to never leave home without her pistol again.

Francesca glanced inside the house. The front hall was cast in black shadow. She slowly pushed the front door open fully, the hairs on her nape prickling, and stepped in

She had a very bad feeling, oh yes. Where was Daisy? Where was Rose? Where were the servants? Francesca moved quietly to the wall, groping for the side table she knew was there. Pressing against it, she strained to listen.

Had a mouse crept across the floor, she would have heard it, for the house was so achingly silent. She desperately wanted to turn on a gas lamp, but she restrained herself. Francesca waited another moment for her eyes to adjust to the darkness and then she crept forward.

A dining room was ahead and to her right. Francesca opened the doors, wincing as the hinges groaned, but the large room was dark and vacant. She did not bother to shut the doors but quickly crossed the hall, glancing nervously at the wide, sweeping staircase as she passed. The closest door was to the smaller of two adjoining salons. Francesca pushed it open. As she had thought, that room also appeared to be empty.

She paused, swept back to another time when she had stood in that room, her ear pressed to the door that adjoined the larger salon, spying upon Hart and Daisy. She had barely known Calder, but even then his appeal had been powerful and seductive; even then, she had been drawn to him as a moth to a flame. That day, she had been audacious enough to watch Hart make love to his mistress. Such an intrusion on their privacy was shameful, and Francesca knew it. Still, she had been incapable of stopping herself.

She shook the recollection off. That had been months ago, before she had ever been in Hart's arms, before Hart had cast Daisy aside—before she and Daisy had become enemies and rivals.

None of that mattered. If Daisy or Rose were in trouble, Francesca intended to help. She left the salon the way she had come in. The moment she stepped back into the hall, she heard a deep, choking sound.

She was not alone.

Francesca froze. She stared at the wide staircase facing her, straining to hear. The guttural noise came again, and this time, she felt certain it was a woman.

The noise had not come from upstairs, but beyond the staircase, somewhere in the back of the house. Francesca wished she had a weapon.

Throwing all caution to the wind, Francesca rushed past the staircase. "Daisy? Rose?"

And now she saw a flickering light, as if cast by a candle, coming from a small room just ahead. The door was widely open and she quickly discerned that it was a study, with a vacant desk, a sofa and chair. Francesca rushed to the threshold and cried out.

Rose was sitting on the floor, hunched over a woman whose platinum hair could only belong to Daisy. Rose was moaning, the sounds deep and low and filled with grief.

Surely Daisy was only hurt! Francesca ran forward and saw that Rose held her friend in her arms. Daisy was in a pale satin supper gown, covered with brilliantly, shockingly red blood. Francesca dropped to her knees and finally saw Daisy's beautiful face—and her wide, blue, sightless eyes.

Daisy was dead.

FREE!
2 Books
and a surprise gift!

We would like to take this opportunity to thank you for reading this Mills & Boon® book by offering you the chance to take TWO more specially selected titles from the Historical Romance™ series absolutely FREE! We're also making this offer to introduce you to the benefits of the Reader Service™—

- ★ **FREE home delivery**
- ★ **FREE gifts and competitions**
- ★ **FREE monthly Newsletter**
- ★ **Exclusive Reader Service offers**
- ★ **Books available before they're in the shops**

Accepting these FREE books and gift places you under no obligation to buy you may cancel at any time, even after receiving your free shipment. Simply complete your details below and return the entire page to the address below You don't even need a stamp!

YES! Please send me 2 free Historical Romance books and a surprise gift. understand that unless you hear from me, I will receive 4 superb new titles every month for just £3.69 each, postage and packing free. I am under no obligation to purchase any books and may cancel my subscription at any time. The free books and gift will be mine to keep in any case.

H6ZE

Ms/Mrs/Miss/Mr ....Initials................................

BLOCK CAPITALS PLEAS

Surname ....

Address ....

....Postcode ....

Send this whole page to:
UK: FREEPOST CN8I, Croydon, CR9 3WZ

Offer valid in UK only and is not available to current Reader service subscribers to this series. Overseas and Eire please wri for details. We reserve the right to refuse an application and applicants must be aged 18 years or over. Only one applicatic per household. Terms and prices subject to change without notice. Offer expires 30th September 2006. As a result of th application, you may receive offers from Harlequin Mills & Boon and other carefully selected companies. If you would prefer not to share in this opportunity please write to The Data Manager, PO Box 676, Richmond, TW9 IWU.

Mills & Boon® is a registered trademark owned by Harlequin Mills & Boon Limited.
Historical Romance™ is being used as a trademark. The Reader Service™ is being used as a trademark.